THE FACE

THE FACE

GARRY BUSHELL

JOHN BLAKE

Published by John Blake Publishing Ltd,
3 Bramber Court, 2 Bramber Road,
London W14 9PB, England

First Published in Paperback in Great Britain 2001

ISBN 1 903402 07 7

British Library Cataloguing-in-Production Data:
A catalogue record for this book is available
from the British Library.

Typeset by Mac Style, Scarborough, N. Yorkshire

Printed and Bound in Great Britain by
Creative Print and Design (Wales),
Ebbw Vale, Gwent.

3 5 7 9 10 8 6 4 2

Papers used by John Blake Publishing Limited are
natural, recyclable products made from wood
grown in sustainable forests. The manufacturing
processes conform to the environmental regulations
of the country of origin

With much love, the author dedicates *The Face* to Bernie Wager.

Sunday People editor Neil Wallis - he had sod all to do with the book but he buys a decent lunch. He would also like to acknowledge the help and inspiration of the original Bushwhacker – you know who you are – without whose friendship and encouragement this book would not exist. Special thanks also go to Michael Fournaris.

Long acknowledgements lists are usually just a cheap ploy to up book sales. The author hates them, and so do: Tania, Julie, Danny, Robert, Jenna, Terry and Pat, Vic and Mandy, Mick and Helen Pugh, Lol Pryor, Paul and Sue, Garry and Julie Johnson, Jim and Sharon, Scotch John, Tommy in Wales, Joanna Burns, Garry and Leah Hodges, Jimmy Jones, Kara, Colin Blood, Colin and Kathryn, Dave Lee, Kelvin MacKenzie, Richard Desmond, Dale, Tony Clayman, Dougie the Gold, Frankie Boy, Panny and Gil, Peakey, Henri Brandman, everyone at the Circus Tavern, Andy Russell and Longshanks, Jim Davidson and CAFC.

CONTENTS

"Society is built on lies, mate. And you've just hit on the biggest. All men are equal? Where? It's utter bollocks. The basic truth of human life is that all men aren't equal. Tom is stronger than Dick who is cleverer than Harry. Life is about winners and losers, the élite and the also-rans. And if you're born at the arse end of society like we were, all that matters is if you're hard enough and smart enough, you have to become part of the élite. Kick, claw or cheat your way in. It don't matter how. Otherwise you'll just be ground into the dust with all the other monkeys."

Johnny Too, September 2000

CHAPTER ONE

THE VAN

There are days when every part of England seems to be curling up at the edges. Stuck in mid-morning traffic made ten times worse by speed bumps, artificially narrowed roads and lashings of late summer rain, Harry Tyler would normally have been ranting aloud about town planning "minges" by now, not to mention poxy women drivers who were forever SLOWING DOWN for fellow shoppers, parkers, cyclists, pedestrians, pensioners and all the other pond life who had nothing better to do all day but HOLD HIM UP! TOSSERS! But today Harry was cool. He barely noticed the slow screech of the new wiper blades against his windscreen as the rain eased to a drizzle. He didn't even take a second glance at Croydon's new "shining pearl", the tramlines installed to – whoopeedoo! – celebrate the millennium. Having a big trade on was better than Prozac. It perked him up and concentrated the mind. Harry steered his dark blue G-reg Granada 2.0L smoothly into a lay-by, got out and walked to a telephone box – why do we still call the ugly little grey slab of aluminium a box? Needless to say the handset had been ripped off. Bollocks. In his day the thing to do with a phone box was shag in it, not fuck it.

He stepped over the diluted remains of last night's pavement vomit. South London had always been a pisshole and Croydon had gone the same way. East London had the edge and the certainty, that aggressive "oo-wants-it?" sense of moral and physical superiority. When did Charlton or QPR or Tottenham or any other London club fire the imagination like the Hammers? Sure South London had Millwall – MUGS! – and West London had the boys from The Shed constantly battling for the silver medal, but everybody knew that *bona fide* real bastards were home and away with West Ham. The East End! That's where the real wide boys came from, the real gangsters, the real *earners*. PROPER people.

Harry Aaron Tyler was born in Colchester, Essex, in 1958, but the family had moved to Romford when he was five. His mum and dad's marriage had lasted eight more years. He was a working-class boy, educated at grammar school where even the teachers took the piss out of his "fink-and-fort it" council house accent. Youthful naïveté had prevented him seeing what a right old slapper his mother had been. Not that he had ever believed his fireman father had been the bastard Mum said he was. Immaterial now. Who gave a toss? He had his own kid, little three-year-old Courtney Rose, the product of his second marriage.

The Granada nudged back into the traffic. Tied up in his own thoughts, Harry didn't notice the burly man on the powerful motorbike peer into his car as it glided past or the woman in the car behind which had a baby-seat but no baby. He was early.

The mobile phone on the passenger seat rang. It was a sensible ring, not one of those aggravating loony-tunes that pasty-looking office prats in cheap off-the-peg whistles always go for.

Harry answered. "Yeah?" he grunted.

"Harry?"

"Yeah."

"It's Sonny."

"Really? It's bin pissing down 'ere."

"What?"

"Yes, don't panic. I'm running on time. I'll be 45 minutes."

"Yeah, it's Sonny."

"I know. I've just been to a box but the poxy thing's smashed. I'll be there."

"Yeah."

"Oh, and, Sonny, I've got something to tell ya."

"What?"

"I'm shagging yer granny."

Silence. "Me granny's dead."

"Yeah," Harry paused for a beat. "I know."

"You bastard."

"Yeah, laters."

Harry noted the time. It was 12.15 pm. He tossed the phone back on the seat and reached for a Wrigley's Extra sugar-free gum. The early morning wake-up breakfast of double sausage, double bacon, egg, chips, beans and two slices was lying heavy on his guts. The beans were a recent addition to satisfy the nagging concern at the back of his mind that he ought to have a bit of fibre in his diet. All them poncey, tanned-at-our-expense telly quacks must have got to him. He even had one day a week off from the sauce now. He just had a habit of forgetting which day it was ...

As Harry drove into the near-empty pub fore-court he noticed the green Mercedes van parked in full view of the pub windows. He drove slowly across and circled it. The front right-hand tyre was flat. He pulled up about eight car lengths from it and gathered his thoughts. It was 12.25 pm. He picked up his mobile and strolled into the pub. What a shit-hole. The main bar was deserted. It was typical of public houses built on 1950s council estates: dark wood everywhere, dull brasses hanging limply, utterly devoid of class. A dead fruit machine stood next to a wall dotted with cheap mirrors: Coca Cola, Newcastle Brown Ale, Becks Bier. Central heating pipes ran up the corners of the bar. It was more Jim Bowen than Laurence Llewellyn, thought Harry. The ceiling was low and stained by the smoke of a million fags. Carpets, which had once been pink and patterned, were now frayed, shabby, and sticky with God knows what human ooze. The only sign of life was the small foot-high stage at the far end where Harry imagined the strippers performed on a Friday night. They weren't even bright enough to have lap-dancers. There were only two punters, old boys playing crib.

Debbie Hodges watched the stranger saunter in and liked what she saw. The bloke was mid-thirties, she thought; about six-foot-one and powerfully built. His dark-brown hair was closely cropped in a vain attempt to disguise premature balding and he had the start of a beer belly but she'd never minded a veranda over the toy shop. Everything about him, the way he walked, the way he held himself, said this was a fella who could handle himself. Nicely dressed too. Blue Ben Sherman shirt, black YSL jeans, black Kangol boots. Smart.

He got closer. Debbie noticed the twinkling blue eyes. She caught a whiff of his L'Eau D'Issey and felt herself tremor.

"Yes, luv?" she said, pushing the latest copy of OK! magazine to one side.

Harry had a good look at the over-painted peroxide blonde behind the bar. Her eyes said, "Come to bed," the face said, "After ten pints." She croaked when she spoke, in a voice that had been coarsened by 40 fags a day for 25 years. She was about 38, 39 with eye-lashes like tarantulas and no less than twelve gold chains around her neck. There were a pair of gold boxing gloves on the end of the longest one which dangled inside the crevice of an enormous cleavage. Knock-out knockers, he thought – love the Tom. It might be gold but it ain't cold. But the Doris? No. He wouldn't be going the distance in her ring.

"Pint of lager," Harry grunted.

"Foster's or Oranjeboom?"

"No, I said lager, luv. Got any Stella?"

"No, just Foster's or ..."

"Foster's is fine, angel."

Debbie poured the pint. Harry noticed she was wearing white slacks cropped halfway up her calf. The look had been fashionable with teenage girls the previous summer. Mutton dressed as lamb foetus, Harry mused.

"That's £2.20," she said.

"What, do I get shares in the pub as well?"

"No, you've just bought it outright, darling," Debbie laughed. "And very welcome you are, a big strong lad like you. We've got a menu if you want food."

Harry glanced at the sandwiches behind her. Watercress! Who the fuck *likes* watercress? There was a board above them covered in chalked specials: meat pie and chips, pastie and chips, prawn curry and chips, lasagne and chips. Even, God help them, *coq au vin*, which didn't seem to come with chips although you could probably get them as a side order.

Harry was Old School on the subject of pub grub. The only food he wanted to see behind a bar were crisps, pork scratchings, ham rolls, and cheese rolls with a layer of raw onion. Pub meals were to be frowned on, along with boozers that sold coffee and men who paid for their drinks with loose change from little *purses*. MUGS!

"See anyfing you fancy?" Debbie asked coquettishly.

"You cooking?"

"Yeah."

"I'll give it a miss."

"Saucy bastard."

"Nothing like polite service, is there?"

"No, and this is nothing like it. Give us a shout if you need anything." She winked.

It certainly won't be a bunk up, Harry thought. Aloud he said, "OK, ta. I'll be back in a minute. I'm gonna shift me jamjar."

"It's all right out there," Debbie said.

"Yeah, but I don't wanna get blocked in by the one o'clock rush."

She gave him a funny look. "Are you from round here?"

Harry pointed at his left wrist. "Yeah, look. Can't you see where I tried to slash it?" He sipped his beer. It was flatter than the tyre on the van outside. "Oi, luv," he said, pushing his luck. "Give that the kiss of life while I'm out, will ya?"

He walked back to the Granada, checking out the car park and surrounding area. A bloke on a powerful motorbike was sailing past the more northerly of two entrances. A woman in a car with a baby-seat but no baby was parked up outside a papershop fifty yards down.

Harry got in the car and drove out on to the street, parking outside facing north, towards God's country. He picked up that morning's copy of the *Newham Recorder*, put his mobile in his jacket pocket then walked back into the boozer. There was a new pint waiting for him on the bar.

Debbie returned. "Sorry," she said, hitting him with a maximum force smile. "I've swapped that for a good 'un."

"What's that? Another tenner?"

"You'd get me for that," she leered.

"I meant ten sovs, not ten pee."

"You really are a cheeky bastard," she laughed. "I like you."

Harry's mobile rang. He turned away from the bar and looked at his watch. It was 1.05 pm.

"Yeah?" he said.

"You about?" It was Sonny.

"Yeah. Where we said."

"Be two minutes. Where's yer motor?"

"How long you gonna be?"

"Two minutes."

"Yeah," said Harry, ending the call.

Eight minutes later Sonny bowled in. He was tall and thin, about six-foot-three, with hair cropped back to the bone. Sonny was black, Nigerian-looking, and dressed casually but well in designer gear. He appeared to have most of the missing gold from the Brinks-Mat robbery around his neck and wrists. The link bracelet on his right arm alone must have been worth £1,000, wholesale.

Harry liked him. They had the same sense of humour. Probably came from playing the same games of buying and selling nicked gear. Behind him waddled George, a short, dumpy man who was perpetually out of breath and wore shirts so bright they nearly scorched your retinas. George was lighter skinned. He probably had a grandad in the West Indies. His mobile was almost lost in his wide, podgy hand. Harry looked him up and down. Georgie boy liked his fried chicken all right. Compared to Sonny, George was a mug, a plum ripe for picking. Show him a monkey, his cock stands up and his brains fall out of his ears.

"Drink?" asked Harry.

"Guinness," said Sonny.

"Same," piped up George in a squeaky little voice that didn't match his body. He sounded like Elmer Fudd, thought Harry.

"Please, luv," Harry said. He laid a tenner on the bar and steered Sonny away, leaving George to collect the drinks and bring him his change. It was one of Harry's little tricks. Split up a double act. Not so much to divide and conquer, more a way of working out who was the gopher on the firm and who was the guv'nor. The guv'nor wouldn't wait for another man's change. Sometimes it was that easy.

Harry and Sonny sat down at a corner table, adorned with attractively chewed beermats.

"She has got blinding jugs," Sonny drooled.

"Yeah," said Harry, "and a face to keep 'em safe."

"Leave it out, H. She could be that one behind the bar in *EastEnders*."

"Yeah, Frank Butcher."

"You're wicked, man. You got the money?"

"Yeah."

"All of it?"

"The computers?"

"Nearby. Ten minutes."

"The money's about me. Five minutes."

"I don't see your motor outside."

"Nah. I left it at home. I borrowed one."

Sonny looked at him for a moment. "If you follow us down the road I'll show you the parcel. Got the full shit, printers, screens, everything."

"No, hold on," Harry said, a note of anger in his voice. "You said the trade was here. I ain't fucking going nowhere with 25 grand on me own."

George walked over with the beers and change on a tray. "No," Sonny was saying. "This was the meeting place to make sure we're not getting tucked up."

"What's wrong?" asked George.

Harry ignored him. "You told me we were trading here," he snapped. "I ain't going nowhere with all me dough on board."

"And I ain't bringing thousands of quids' worth of brand new half-inched computers up here," Sonny snarled.

Harry shook his head. "I ain't taking my money through some iffy council estate neither," he said. "So the ball's in your court, mate. I understood you was gonna fetch it here in a van, we trade and offski."

"Well, let's see the money," Sonny replied.

Harry leaned his face into the black man's. "Sonny," he said. "You know people I know, I know people you know. Do business this way first, next time you come to my slaughter with it. It ain't that I don't trust you but, well, let's just get the first trade out of the way and then we'll both be ... *happier* with each other.

"No, no, no," Sonny said. "I ain't doing it here."

Harry stood up. "This is bullshit," he said tersely. "This is your manor. How do I know I ain't gonna drive off the estate with your van and then get a pull from Mr Shitcunt Traffic Cop saying I've got a fucking brake light out?"

Sonny smiled. "Cos you'd come back and haunt me, that's why, innit? I ain't a wrong 'un, H."

"Neither am I," said Harry, sitting back at the table, "and if I thought you were I wouldn't fucking be here. But I think the Old Bill would stick one nice one up from Mr Dixon's or Curry's or PC wanking warehouse or wherever they got nicked from just to get 'em back."

"No," said Sonny. "The deal's off."

"Fine," Harry replied. "No harm done. Perhaps some other time." He held out his hand, shook with Sonny, got up again and walked. Harry was in the car park when he heard the pub door open behind him. It was George, shouting, "'Arry, 'Arry, come back!"

Harry stopped. George wheezed up alongside him. "Come back, we can sort it."

Harry shook his head. "No," he said. "This is all bollocks, mate."

Sonny joined them outside, all smiles. "OK, Harry," he said. "If you were trying to fuck us you wouldn't have gone. Let's go back in and work it out."

"OK," Harry said hesitantly, "but I ain't got all day. I've got to get the parcel over to the Mile End Road and people at the other end are waiting."

In the distance, a police siren rang out. Wheezy George looked nervous. "Is that the Filth?" he asked anxiously.

Harry smiled. "Well, it's going too fast to be a fucking ice cream van."

Sonny laughed and patted Harry's shoulder as

the siren faded. "Make yourself useful," he told George. "Go and get the van."

"Where's he off to?" asked Harry suspiciously.

"We came up in the motor," Sonny explained. "The van's about five minutes down the road." He turned and they walked back into the pub. "Sorry, man. We're both a bit jumpy. Thing is, H, I got off of shooting an Old Bill up in Wandsworth last year and I'm paranoid. It's on me all the time."

Harry smiled. "You wanna leave that Charlie alone, mate," he said.

"Not me, mate," Sonny protested. "Don't touch that stuff. Just the odd spliff, me. That shit fucks yer head up."

"It don't do yer schnozz too many favours, either, judging by Danniella Westbrook's 'ooter. Talk about paying through yer nose."

"What about the money, Harry?"

"Soon as I've viewed the parcel, you count it and we go our separate ways," Harry said decisively. "I'll be back with your van about eight o'clock tonight and pick me motor up."

"Sweet," said Sonny. "Me brother won't be long."

Harry laughed. "He's about as much your brother as I am," he said. "I mean, you and me could be twins compared to him and you."

Sonny laughed, too. "Don't we look like brothers, then?" he chuckled.

"Well," said Harry, "you've both got your mother's eyes."

"Where's your family out of, H?" Sonny asked.

"Brentwood mainly. You know Brentwood?"

—

"What, Essex, yeah?"

"Yeah. What about you two?"

"West London. Acton way."

"You're a long way from home."

"Yeah, Georgie's got a baby mother over here, place called Addington, not too far away. I was giving her sister one."

"Was or are?"

"No, I was. On and off. But her old man's out of the boob now and he's one fuckin' mean mother. He's wrapped up with the Brixton and Peckham boys."

Harry pursed his lips. "Bringing a lot of attention to 'emselves at the moment, all shooting each other. I thought that puff was supposed to make you all laid back and shit."

"Laid back?" Sonny snorted. "If he knew I was giving his old lady one, I'd be laid out, mate, in a casket at Francis Wosname, Francis Chappell's."

Harry's mobile rang. "Yeah?" he said, walking away from the table. "What? ... Yeah ... No, I'm in Basildon at the moment, seeing me sister. I'll be back about eight tonight ... Yeah ... later."

As he laid the phone on the table, Sonny's smile exploded into a chuckle. "Basildon!" he sniggered.

"Listen," said Harry. "I never tell anyone where I am. Well, unless they owe me money." He grinned. "D'you remember when the Derby was on a Wednesday?"

"Yeah."

"'Undred times better, wunnit? A proper event. Everyone skived off work for it. And the bollocks

"You like the horses?"

"No, do I bollocks! Just a good day out on the piss."

"I'll ring George, see where he is."

"No hurry. One thing, though ..."

"Yeah?"

"Well, you mentioned shooting Old Bill." Harry hesitated. "If there's any tools about, I ain't trading."

Sonny shook his head vigorously. "No," he said. "That's when I'm going out to party or work, man. There's some mad muvvas out there. I ain't got nothing about me, anyway."

"Same go for your brother?"

"There's no tools about," Sonny insisted.

A large white box van was pulling in outside. It parked in the far corner, away from prying eyes. George looked all about him before turning off the engine and calling Sonny on the mobile. "I'm in the car park."

"Right," said Sonny. "We're coming out. Undo the padlock."

Harry and Sonny left the pub together. Harry put his mobile in the inside pocket of his black combat jacket and carried the *Newham Recorder* in his right hand, rolled up like a cosh. They crossed to the van. George was at the back of the long vehicle. All three of them looked about, surveying far-off passers-by and pedestrians suspiciously. As Harry got to the rear, Sonny was slightly ahead of him, opening the doors. The entire length and breadth of the van was half full with cardboard boxes.

"There," beamed Sonny. "You gonna get the money?"

"Open a box," Harry commanded. Sonny pulled at the flaps of the nearest one. It contained a computer screen in pristine condition.

"What about them at the back?" asked Harry. "Open a few of them up."

Sonny and George clambered over the load to get to the end nearest the driver's compartment. They started opening them, box after box full of goodies.

"OK, I'll push the doors to and go and get the money," Harry said. The two men started to close up the boxes as the doors shut and the light faded.

As Harry crossed the car park, he tossed the newspaper into a rubbish bin. He was suddenly aware of the eight or nine cars moving towards the car park and other cars already parked, disgorging men and women out on the road. Baseball caps were going on, dark blue ones with black and white chequered bands. A powerful motorbike roared into the forecourt, followed by a woman in a car with a baby-seat but no baby – the police surveillance team. Harry knew the time had come. His heart started to pound. He began to jog then sped into a run. He fumbled for his keys. He didn't want to look back.

No sooner had he reached the Granada than the door was open and he was in. His pulse was racing. In the films this was where the engine doesn't start. The Granny drew breath. Harry steadied himself and pulled out on to the road, a road that lead to happiness, joy and civilisation. East London, la-la-la! Nothing in front. Nothing coming up fast behind. His pulse was still racing. He accelerated, but not enough to draw attention to himself, and that was it. He was gone. Away. Free.

The racing pulse gave way to uncontrollable laughter, then a burst of song:
"Hey ho, hey HO!
To Upton Park we GO!
With a bo'le an' a brick an' a walkin' stick,
Hey ho, hey ho, hey ho ..."
Back in the van, the brothers were getting bored. H had been five or six minutes now. Where was he? "C'mon," said Sonny. "Let's go and collect that nice big earner." George started giggling. Sonny chuckled too. 25K! It was like something out of the movies. By coincidence, they started laughing out loud about the same time as Harry did. As they pushed the doors open, Butch and Sundance got the real joke.
"ARMED POLICE! FREEZE!"
George's eyeballs bobbled. How many Old Bill had shouted that? The entire Mexican army was out there. Was it ten, eleven, twelve ... how many guns were pointing at them? And, Christ! Their dabs were all over thousands of pounds' worth of stolen gear. How do you bullshit your way out of that?
"ARMED POLICE! ARMED POLICE!"

The National Crime Squad moved in.

It was one thing getting nicked with your hands on the parcel in the back of a van hired on a nicked licence, but did that big lump of a copper really have to slam poor podgy George's head face down into a puddle?

Within seconds the plastic 'cuffs were on and the load was recovered. In the background, Sonny heard confirmation that "the third man" – Harry! – had got away after a manic chase through Addington.

"Good luck, H," thought Sonny. "Good luck, mate ..."

Ten minutes later, Harry pulled over into a lay-by and made a call on his mobile.

"Can you talk, guv?" he asked.

"Yes, I can," came the reply.

"Result?"

"Absolutely. We got both the mugs, sweet as. Give us a couple of hours then see me at Sutton nick. I'll sort your pocket book and expenses, OK? Nice job. Well done, Harry. I'll have a large one waiting."

CHAPTER TWO

HAVING IT LARGE

For centuries people have stood at the rear of the Mayflower public house in Rotherhithe and watched the Thames roll by. The sun, the water, the sense of history ... it's mesmerising. Close your eyes and you can almost hear the raucous banter of dockers and stevedores from times past when the river was king. "Living 'istory," Freddie the landlord calls his pub. "It dates back from when Millwall played in doublet and 'ose." He'll offer you a pint of Ann Boleyn bitter. "Very old and no 'ead," he'll say. And the first time you might even laugh.

Regular as clockwork, the tourist boats toddle down from Westminster Bridge on their way to Greenwich and the Dome. Even now, six months in to the new millennium, Freddie still claims it's the world's biggest wok, built to feed all the "Tiddlies" who live thereabouts. None of his jokes have tell-by dates.

Rotherhithe is a lot like the Thames; it keeps moving but nothing really changes. Historically, the cream of Britain's blaggers, the FACES, the aristocracy of the armed robbery fraternity, have come out of Rotherhithe. But these men aren't set in their ways like the old T&GWU dinosaurs who once ruled the docks. The faces adapted to the modern world – they packed away the sawn-offs and moved in to Es, whizz, puff and Charlie. Why get blown away by the Sweeney going across the pavement for ten grand's worth of stolen Tom when you can get some soppy gopher to serve up grams of cocaine (cut to shit with hay-fever tabs)? The profits were fifty times bigger – SWEET! – and there were no armed response units lurking about waiting to administer a swift injection of lead poisoning for your trouble.

Keeping in front of the game was all that mattered, whatever side of the law you were on. It was the key to survival for men like Johnny "Too Handsome" Baker, a powerfully built, for-real gangster who was looking out from the Mayflower's back patio, watching all the politely excited Japanese holidaymakers on their way to snap-snap-snap at Mandelson's folly.

From the corner of his left eye, he clocked a tourist taking shot after shot of him. Johnny realised at once that he was Filth, but didn't react. So fucking what? Just another pretty piccy for the Old Bill's album. He smiled archly at his unknown admirer. The day he graduated to proper satellite surveillance was the day he'd made it, he thought. Not that Johnny had any intention of being involved in anything vaguely nickable by this time next year. He had minor legitimate businesses in place and his eye on e-commerce. Johnny had got the internet bug after he had started ordering his CDs from Amazon, and his puff from the Dam. His first venture was an e-florist delivery service, BudsR-us.co.uk (he'd toyed briefly with stamen.busters) which was already enjoying a decent trade with two major West End record companies, Express newspapers, and ITN.

They called him "Too Handsome" because he was. His old auntie Em had said it first on Johnny's 14th birthday. "That boy is too 'andsome, 'e'll break a lot of 'earts," she'd said. She didn't seem too worried about the necks or legs. The lager might have puffed him out over the years – Johnny was 37 – but he still turned heads more often than Linda Blair in *The Exorcist*. He was six-foot-two with light brown hair and a barrel chest. His eyes were so blue they made the Med seem murky. He dressed well, it was a Paul Smith whistle today, and boy did he have the gift of the gab. When he turned on the charm, Johnny made Danny Baker (no relation) seem shy and retiring.

To his associates he was Johnny Too, or JT. To anyone else he was Mr Baker.

Respect due.

A heavy presence loomed up behind him. His older brother, Joey, a big sprawling bear of a man, appeared with two pints of lager in his large, sinewy hands. Rival villains called Joey "Two Planks" but never to his face. What he lacked in brains he more than made up for in raw aggression and brute strength. Joey was 40, but just as crazy now as when he was 16. He'd always been pretty fucked up in the head. His criminal record had begun, not unusually, with a series of house-breakings. The "presents" he used to leave in his victims' beds earned him his first visit to the trick cyclist after he was nicked. The shrink told him he would grow up a sexual deviant if he kept defecating in people's beds, which goes to prove psychiatry isn't always a con-trick. Early doors he was nicknamed Joey The Turd, but since he was 30 he had been known as Pyro Joe thanks to his unique way of disposing of a rival mini-cab firm – funny how so many car engines spontaneously combusted on August 9, 1980. And not a single complaint to the cops. Definitely a case for Mulder and Scully. When old man Colin Baker popped his clogs, Johnny Too took over the family business with Pyro Joe as his enforcer. The Baker empire included a backstreet casino, a thriving mini-cab firm, a bar in Marbella, an escort agency, various properties and three pubs, none of which were the Mayflower. The now-defunct cabaret club had been a long firm - a long time fraud.

Johnny had tried to excite his brother about Net activities just the once. It had been like trying to teach algebra to a garden gnome. In Cantonese. Joey was a different man – no frills, no foreign grub and definitely "no fuckin' compooters".

"He ain't here," Joey growled.

"I can see that, bruv."

"I'll go round, see his missus again, give her a fuckin' slap."

"No, he'll turn up. It ain't her fault, the skaggy slut."

Joey frowned. "She said this was where he was drinking."

Johnny put his arm round his brother's massive shoulder. "Joe, mate, chill. I ain't breaking me bollocks chasing that piece of shit for a few quid. He'll get it when he deems to pay up. Kick the fuck out of him then. It'll help his memory for next time." That seemed to cheer Joey up. Johnny drained his pint. "C'mon."

Constant police surveillance is a fact of life for top-quality villains like the Bakers. Johnny Too prided himself on being able to spot a wrong 'un. Most of the time he was right. As it happened, the BT engineers up to their eyes in spaghetti wire just down the road from the Mayflower were genuine. It was just unfortunate for them that they looked such a pair of hapless bastards.

"Feds?" said Joey.

"Maybe."

"Wait here."

"Leave it."

"Bollocks."

As John got to the V-reg Mercedes, Pyro Joe strolled over and crossed his arms, towering over the nearest engineer in his pit.

"All right, mate?" the BT man said, but just one look at this looming, wild-eyed bastard told him it wasn't.

Joey unzipped his suit trousers, produced a fat cock and urinated into the hole. "No, it fucking ain't," he snapped. "Take a picture of that for the collection." He zipped himself up and walked back, unabashed, to the gently purring Merc.

Lesley Gore focused her eyes on the bedside clock. 11.38 am. Fuck! Her head hurt. And oh, God, what had she done? Not Dougie! She'd only fucked Dougie! Dougie the fucking Dog. She curled herself up into a foetal ball but it didn't make the shame go away. It wasn't that he was married, or even that he was her boss's cousin, but he had to be the worst fuck she'd ever had – too small, too quick, too rough, no attempt at foreplay. And he was probably down the Ned blabbing about it already. What was that going to do for what little reputation she had left? Fuck! She was dying for a fag. Lesley sat up. It made her head ten times worse. Coffee. She needed coffee – strong, black and sweet. She pulled on her dressing gown and lit up an Embassy. Why Dougie? Why had she let him take her out, and take her in? Hadn't she decided after Tom McCann that she was never going to fuck another fella from the Ned? And what had it taken Dougie to pull her? Three lines of Charlie, a Chinese, and a litre of Bulgarian Chardonnay. Fuck it!

She stumbled up the corridor of her flat. The postman had been. Bills, junkmail. Didn't anyone send proper letters any more? Lesley looked in the hall mirror. Big mistake. Her blue eyes were blood-shot. And talk about the St Valentine's Day mascara. She poked out her pierced tongue at her own reflection. The tongue was off-colour but at least the stud still glistened. It had been the only one in her bed last night, that was for sure. She shivered. Fucking Dougie! It would be all over the Ned. How could she work there today? Bollocks. She'd get her mum to ring in for her, go back to bed and watch last night's *EastEnders*. Lesley smiled. Dan Sullivan, now he would be worth fucking.

Pyro Joe sat in the passenger seat, pulled on his seat belt, and opened the *Sun* at Page Three.

"Abby Essien," he said. "Smashing tits."

Johnny Too glanced over. "Know what I hate about Page Three now?" he asked. "They've done away with the funny captions. You don't just wanna see a picture, you wanna know what the bird does for a living, what she likes on telly. Y'know, 'Kelly from Leytonstone, 19, works in a fish shop', so you're thinking, Works in a fish shop, does she? I'd serve her up a portion."

"I could reach me vinegar with Abby," leered Joey.

"Where's she from?"

"Blackpool."

"There y'go, in my mind's eye I've already got her riding the Big One."

"Who was your all-time favourite Page Three girl, John?"

"Linda Lusardi! She had it all, the looks, the brains, a touch of class. She could have bin an English Teri Hatcher – who you know is my number one girl in the world."

"Oh yeah, Lois Lane."

"Who was yours?"

"Suzanne Mizzi," Pyro Joe said without hesitation. The big man thought for a moment. "Do you think Superman could ever have fucked Lois Lane, what with him being super and all?"

"You mean would the man of steel have a rod of iron?" Johnny Too laughed. "Maybe not. Might hurt an earth woman, what with all that superspeed. Think of the friction burns once he got going, and his super-spunk shooting out, prob'ly rip right through her belly."

Joe chortled. "'E might be blowing in her ear, get carried away with passion, and her head could end up in Gotham City."

"Their honeymoon night would be poxed. I mean, what would she wear? A see-through nightie? Why? The geezer's got x-ray vision."

"Superman didn't really do much shagging, did he? Wonder why? With all those powers he'd be beating the birds off with a stick."

"Maybe he was shy. Or maybe he really did come from Smallville."

The brothers chuckled. The lights ahead went red, and Johnny Too braked. As soon as the Mercedes stopped, the Kosovan refugees moved in with their squeegies.

"Here we go," Johnny muttered, adding loudly, "NO! Not today, mate."

He waved his hands to translate the sentiment into body language. The lead Kosovan, an unshaven man in his thirties gave him a gap-toothed grin and squirted detergent over the Merc's windscreen. Johnny was out of the car in a heart-beat, pushing the Kosovan away. "What part of fucking 'No' don't you understand, you mug?" he shouted. Pyro Joe got out of the car too, and growled at the other refugees who kept their distance. Johnny went on: "I do not want scumbags like you rotting my rubbers with your cheap fucking detergent, *capisshh?*"

The Kosovan lunged at his assailant. Johnny grabbed him in a neck-lock under his right arm and smashed him in the nose with his left fist. "Oh for Chrissakes," he said. "Now you're bleedin' on me whistle."

He let the Kosovan drop to the floor, put his right boot on his head and shouted at his companions. "Why don't you bunch of mongrels fuck off back to your own shithole country instead of poncing off of us? Asylum seekers! What the fuck are you seeking asylum from? Eh? EH? Fucking soap by the stench of yer. Newsflash! The war is fucking over, GO HOME!"

The man on the floor stirred. "Grnnkkkk" he murmured.

"Oh, excuse me, mate," said Johnny, "am I standing on your head?" He turned, putting his whole weight on his victim's cheek, then kicked him hard in the guts, got back in the car and drove off, straight through a red light.

The Ned Kelly in Rotherhithe is the flagship of the three pubs owned by the Baker clan. In itself, it's nothing special. It's got an ancient pool table; one for us, one for the taxman fruit machines; a cash pay-phone nicknamed the Hoover because of the way it sucks up your cash, and its very own rogues' gallery on the walls. There were pictures of Johnny Too with the stars – Billy Murray from *The Bill*, Barbara Windsor, Glen Murphy, Terry Marsh, Dennis Stratton formerly of Iron Maiden, and even one of the two Bakers with Lord Tebbit from a Dorchester function they had gate-crashed. Below them were pictures of "Gangsters United FC" as the Ned Kelly football team has been known unofficially since the late sixties, when old man Baker first bought the pub. Pyro Joe was notorious in his footballing days. It was said he'd have your legs quicker than polio.

Dougie "The Dog" Richards saw young Mickey Fenn looking at the photos and decided to lay it on thick. "Gangsters United," he said, shoving half a donut into his mouth. "We only got beat once last season, but seeing as the team 'oo beat us ain't got a pub no more, there's no worry about losing this season, know what I mean, Mickey?"

Fenn, who was just 17, was in awe of the older man. Dougie The Dog was only 25 but his reputation for violence was awesome. Not only was Dougie one of the ace faces at Millwall, he was also the Baker boys' cousin.

"Ain't, ain't that old Pete?" Mickey stuttered pointing at one of the older pictures.

"That senile fuckhead," snorted Rhino, Doug's shadow, a huge black man from Kennington who took his nickname from one of the TV Gladiators and called his cock his pugil stick.

"Leave it out, Rhine," Dougie protested. "Pete Miller was a real player in his day."

By which he meant Miller kicked higher than

anyone else on the pitch. Football? No, but see him go to work with a cosh, or his Frankie, now that's when he was a player ... Everyone in the Ned was either a face, a player, a wannabe or a woza (as in "he was a face"), just as everybody in South London knew that Johnny Baker was the Man. Christ, you didn't even use his name in conversation. If you were talking about Johnny and Joey, you just say the Brothers, pronounced "Bruvvas". The one pre-condition for drinking in the pub was to have a CRO, but nothing recent. Well, nothing recent if it was a conviction for shit-all, because a con for shit-all meant you weren't much of a villain.

"I hear he's a right little tear-away," said Dougie as Mickey sloped off. "A right 'andful."

"Little acorns," Rhino smiled.

"You've bin watching *The Long Good Friday* again."

"You fuck that Lesley last night, Doug?"

"What d'ya reckon? She ain't here for work cos she can't fuckin' walk!" He grabbed his crotch. "I gave her plenty."

"The Bruvs won't be happy."

"Don't worry," Doug said, pinching the black man's cheek. "I'll sweeten it."

The Ned had rules, one of them was don't piss off the bar staff, but that came low down on a list. Rule one concerned the goose that laid the Bakers' golden egg, cocaine. The only Charlie consumed in the pub had to come from a licensed vendor, one who was authorised by Johnny Too or Pyro Joe. Rule two was "pig in the trough", meaning you sell stolen parcels outside the pub for a modest profit or you trade inside and the big boys tell you how much you're selling it to them for (and you do). Then there was the pecking order rule, that's the easy one: in the Ned the monsters and the crazies come first, the lunatics second, the crooks and conmen come third and human beings trail in a distant fourth. But seeing as any unsuspecting mug punter who did chance upon the Ned would be greeted with a curt "We don't serve wankers in 'ere" by Ron "Slobberin' Ron" Sullivan, the cultural attaché for South London who doubled as bar manager, fourth place never really applied.

The pub and the police had an understanding. The cops understood that the Ned was full of the pride of South London thievery and "pharmaceutical distributors", and the pub regulars understood that the Filth could do fuck all about it. The two sides were like matter and anti-matter, kept from meeting explosively by the greasing of palms and force of habit. It was far easier for the boys in blue to nick the odd knobhead for possessing a gram of Chas a few miles down the road. That's how it had been for two years now.

It's how it would have stayed if Pyro Joe had listened to his brain, i.e. Johnny, and left "the skaggy slut" alone, but Joe had a bee in his bonnet about Sean Irvine. The bloke was a liberty-taker. He owed them 750 notes. Why couldn't Johnny see that made them look weak? If the word got round that the Brothers were going soft, North London would try and move in faster than Bill Clinton could whip out his dick on new intern day. No one could be seen to owe the Brothers.

Irvine had been a good screwsman in his day – you may have seen his handiwork on *Crimewatch* – but his cocaine addiction had messed up his head. Everybody knows that a £750 Charlie debt is best paid quick to people you owe, but likewise those who crave the sweet stuff develop a different set of priorities. Sean Irvine had made a monkey that morning from shifting snide Hackett jumpers and £500 would see him sorted for booze and Chas all weekend. Unfortunately, before he had a chance to spend it, Sean got a tug from Old Bill for a little bit of drumming. He was sitting in the boob at Maidstone police station when Joey Baker forced his way in to his flat, brutally slapped his wife Shirley to the floor and booted her hard in the belly. Sean had no idea he had just become the ex-father of his first son.

David and Tony O'Shea, Shirley's brothers, had been promising amateur middleweights in their day. David, the younger of the two, had fought professionally as "The Tasmanian Devil" for a few months until he realised crime paid better. The O'Sheas were semi-faces and regular drinkers in the Ned, well acquainted with the Brothers' reputation and aware of their lowly position in the pecking order. But hearing that your "skaggy slut" sister has been hurt and has lost her baby has a tendency to make even the smallest of big brothers feel a little put-out.

"Are you sure it was Joey?" David asked the sobbing Shirley for the third time.

"I couldn't mistake that ugly fucker, could I?"

"Was JT with him?" asked Tony.

"No, he was on his own."

"Where's Sean?" said David.

"Fuck knows. I never want to see that bastard again."

"We'll deal with that cowson later," said Tony. "Dave, we've got to speak to Johnny Too. That cunt has gone too far this time."

"Speak?" Dave snapped. "SPEAK? You're having a fucking laugh."

"David," Tony said sternly. "Do not do anything stupid. I can sort this. We do not need warfare with the Bakers. I will talk to Johnny. Nothing will bring the baby back, but we can get Joey reigned in and make sure Shirl is safe. If you wanna fight, hunt down that no good bastard, Sean, all right? Now, promise me you'll stay away from Pyro. All right?"

David O'Shea said nothing.

Slobberin' Ron Sullivan eyed Dougie The Dog suspiciously. He didn't like the fella. He was too flash, too mouthy and too quick with his fists. He ate like a pig, too. But Doug was family to his bosses, so Slobberin' Ron swallowed his contempt. Ron suspected Doug was the reason Lesley wasn't at work today, but it was midweek and the Ned wasn't busy ... only about 16 people in. Pyro Joe was sitting quietly at the bar sipping Red Bull and vodka and chopping out a fat line of cocaine when David "Tasmanian Devil" O'Shea crashed through the door, a two-foot lump of scaffolding pole in his hand, and charged right at him, bringing the tool smashing down towards Joey. The big man moved with impressive speed, twisting his torso so the pole just caught his right shoulder before whacking into the bar and sending up a pricey cloud of white powder. Pyro hit the floor and rolled. O'Shea didn't need to be told that having started this he'd have to go all the way. He lifted the pole quickly and slammed it down, catching Joe hard in the stomach. Sadly for O'Shea, Pyro Joe's paranoia levels, unusually high even by villains' standards, meant he had taken to wearing body armour some months earlier.

As O'Shea raised his tool to deliver the *coup de grâce* to Joey's head, he made the fatal error of pausing to say, "This is for my sis ..."

This was all the time Rhino needed. He shot over from the pool table like Jenson Button on a promise, his prize pool cue in his hand, and delivered the sort of whack English cricket fans can only dream of seeing to the back of O'Shea's swede. The Tasmanian Devil hit the floor. Half a second later Dougie The Dog was over his body smacking his skull repeatedly with a 330ml Budweiser bottle. As it shattered, O'Shea's head became a bloody mess of claret, beer and shards of broken brown glass.

"That's it, Doug," said Rhino. "He's sparko." Rhino laughed. "Fucking good night nurse." Dougie wasn't smiling, neither was Pyro Joe who had grabbed a handful of O'Shea's hair and dragged his unconscious body eight feet to the pool table. One-handed, Joey slung his attacker across it. Coolly he walked back for the scaffolding, and with his face a mask of hate he proceeded to smash each kneecap repeatedly. Slobberin' Ron stopped counting after the 23rd blow. His rage finally vented, Pyro grabbed O'Shea again by the hair and threw him out on to the street. Then he turned to one of the "c" category drinkers and barked, "Scrape that shit up off my pavement and drop him off at casualty." As an after-thought, Pyro picked up the length of pole, cued up the white ball and potted the black. He turned to the crowd of regulars and said, "How about that for a fucking trick shot?" They laughed and Pyro roared. He hadn't lost face. He *never* lost face. Dougie The Dog took his cousin's head in his hands and kissed it.

"Who luvs ya, baby?" he said. "C'mon, Joe, we're going up West. I feel like a party." Pyro grinned. He looked at his watch. It was 9.35 pm.

Exactly 43 minutes later the van and car rolled up outside the Ned, blue lights flashing and sirens wailing. Six of the Met's finest marched in. Slobberin' Ron was busy polishing glasses with a dirty tea towel. A couple of lads were throwing arrows at the dartboard. An older man sat on his own, absorbed in Lenny McLean's autobiography, *The Guv'nor*. No one was playing pool because the table had gone. Seeing the police, a little mob of half a dozen Millwall boys laughed into their lager. The boldest of them, Mickey

Fenn, clocked the Inspector and said, "Mine's a lager top, mate, if you're going to the bar." His mates laughed. Inspector Frank Turner did not.

"We got a call to a fight," he said to Slobberin' Ron.

"Spiteful bastards ringing up wasting police time," the guv'nor replied.

Turner glared at him. "There is blood on this carpet," he snapped.

"Yeah," said Ron. "Some bird come on all of a sudden. We had to send her 'ome cos the Tampax machine in the Ladies is fucked, know what I mean?"

The Millwall boys erupted. Slobberin' Ron rode the laughs. "Yeah, some little toe-rag poured water into it, ripped the dispenser clean off the wall," he said.

Turner raised his eyes to the ceiling. What is the fucking point? he thought. But out loud he said, "Where's John?"

"Mr Baker's out," Ron said.

"Joey?"

"Not been in all day, Inspector."

"So, no trouble?"

"I would be the first to call you if there were any, Inspector."

Turner nodded his head towards the door. The police filed out. Just a token show, same as always.

"Thank you cunt-stable," said Mickey Fenn as the door slammed shut.

"See ya, orifacer," piped up his acne-faced side-kick. "Eat shit and die, ya Filth."

Geraldine Bielfeld topped up her glass out of sheer boredom and stared at Tony Golding's stomach. They had been sleeping together for what, six months? And he must have put on at least a stone. Tony was dull and self-important, but a partner in the law firm of Edmonds-Sachs & Co where she worked as the senior partner's PA. On their second date he had bought her a £300 bracelet. Geraldine had slept with him that night. Now Tony was telling her that his wife was getting suspicious. "I told her not to be silly," he chuckled. "I said, 'Why would I want to leave two women sexually frustrated?'" Geraldine smiled, but Tony's "joke" wasn't that far from the truth. "Pony Tony", was her private nick-name for him. God, he was a lousy shag. Geraldine was 29, Tony Golding was 46. He had already told her he would never leave his wife, which was information Geraldine had been thoroughly relieved to hear although she had feigned hurt until he'd bought a Karen Miller designer suit. His generosity had long since evaporated, though. Look where he'd taken her now! A naff comedy club in Camden Town where some fat middle-class student type was on stage talking about her periods. How could she get out of this one?

The guy on the next table seemed as unimpressed with the comedienne as she was. "Fuck me, how long can that live out of water?" he'd said when she walked out and he had maintained a running commentary ever since. As Tony wobbled off to the gents, Geraldine heard the guy cruelly jibe, "A pig born that ugly would have demanded plastic surgery."

She laughed out loud, caught his eye and was mesmerised. What a hunk! He winked, and Geraldine actually felt herself blush. The woman he was with, an attractive but overly made-up blonde, noticed it too but didn't seem to mind. How was Geraldine to know she was a £500-a-night escort girl?

Tony returned but he was talking on the phone to another partner. Business, business, business. Geraldine excused herself and went to the bar. She took out a Peter Stuyvesand. A lighter appeared from nowhere. "Allow me." It was the funny guy.

"Shit this, innit?" he said.

Geraldine smiled. "I thought you were quite entertaining, though."

"Wanna move on somewhere, get a bite to eat mebbe?"

She looked into his face. The eyes were like a magnet. She had never seen eyes that blue. "Yes, I think I'd like that."

"Can you lose fatty?"

"No problem. What about your, uh, friend?"

"Who? Maddie? Don't mind 'er, she's me sister."

"Really? No, I don't think I want to know. Give me five minutes to feign a headache, and I'll meet you outside. He wants to see the headline act so he won't be a problem. I'm Geraldine. What do I call you?"

"Johnny, darling, Johnny Baker. They call me Johnny Too."

As soon as the police had pulled away from the Ned Kelly, Pyro Joe and Dougie The Dog burst back into the bar from upstairs and the whole place erupted into antique chants of " 'Arry Roberts is our friend, is our friend, is our friend. 'Arry Roberts is our friend – he kills COPPERS!"

Joey popped open two bottles of champagne and within minutes he was performing his party piece, knob out, lighted cigarette tucked under the foreskin. Slobberin' Ron bolted the door and dimmed the lights for a lock-in. This was going to be a late one. A few miles away, unaware of the excitement, Johnny Too's taxi arrived at its destination. Geraldine had wanted to go to Stringfellow's because she'd never been. She was surprised when the doorman not only recognised Johnny but treated him like visiting royalty. "I done a bit of business with Peter once," he shrugged, by way of explanation. "Back when the gaff was fashionable." There was a twinkle in his eye. Geraldine decided she didn't mind if that was the truth or not.

For his part, Johnny Too was quite taken by her. She was tall, about five-foot-eight, with shoulder-length black hair and magnificent breasts. She was posh, too, and a lot brighter than his usual bits of stray. Christ, she even got his jokes.

Geraldine sipped a glass of champagne. "After we've eaten, I'm going to take you up the back passage," Johnny said quietly. She almost choked on her drink. John grinned. "It's a little drinking club I know in Streatham," he said. "Very upmarket." Geraldine felt herself blush again and buried her head in the menu.

"See anything you want?" Johnny asked.

—

"Not on the menu ..." She couldn't believe she'd said that.

John laughed.

Geraldine made small talk to cover her embarrassment. "Funny how when you first look at a menu, you fancy everything," she said. "Starters, main, side dishes, cocktails, the lot. Then the starter comes and that fills you up on its own."

"There are defin't'ly two states of mind when it comes to restaurants," John said. "Pre-order and post-bill. Pre-order you want the works, but then the bill comes and wallop! Everyone has a steward's into it. 'Oo ordered the rum baba' and all that caper." He paused. "But you've got no worries with me, Geri darling. Order what you like. I had a right result last month, I got 10 grand from the big South London summer raffle draw."

"You won the raffle?"

"No, love, I organised it."

That twinkle again. Geraldine wanted to stroke his hand, but one of the bouncers came up and whispered something in John's ear. Johnny Too looked grim. "Tell him to keep on the other side of the club," he said angrily. "I don't want him coming over and shaking my hand, making small talk, chopping out Charlie or anything, all right? The bloke is a mug."

The bouncer nodded and walked off to an elderly well-coiffured man in an expensive suit who was gawping at a table dancer.

"Who ...?" Geraldine started to ask.

"Plastic gangster," Johnny Too spat. "The place is crawling with 'em. That fella once wrote a book about how he was a getaway driver for the Krays and I know full well he was the fucking tea-boy, excuse my French. You get it all the time, old geezers over the East End who reckon they used to run with the Krays. Yeah, right, maybe on school sports days but that's it. I don't have mugs like that wrapped around me." Then he smiled again. Geraldine looked at him. Johnny Baker was obviously a dangerous man to know.

"You know what, Johnny," she said. "I've lost my appetite. Would you walk me to Charing Cross station, please?"

He looked puzzled. "What did I do wrong?" he asked.

"Nothing," she said. "Yet ..."

They both smiled.

As they strolled down St Martin's Lane, Geraldine shivered. Johnny put an arm around her. God, she thought, he feels so strong.

"Where have you got to get to?" he asked.

"Bickley." She hesitated then said, "Would you like to come back for coffee?"

He stopped dead and turned her to face him. They kissed. He pulled her body into his. Geraldine felt him harden and knew that she had to have this man. Johnny Too hailed a taxi to take them the quarter of a mile to Charing Cross station. In the back, he slipped a hand down the inside of her stockinged legs and met no resistance. He thought his cock was going to burst out of his suit trousers. At Charing Cross he slung the driver a tenner. "You know what," he said as he helped her out. "I can't wait for Bickley." John glanced towards the Charing Cross Hotel. Geraldine nodded OK.

They were barely inside the hotel room when they were on each other, probing with tongues and fingers. Geraldine unzipped his fly, released his swollen cock and cupped it in her hands. It felt good, seven, maybe eight inches long with a nice girth.

"Well, you're certainly not Johnny *Two*," she laughed.

"It's short for Two-hander," Johnny said, slipping his right hand gently up the inside of her leg to rub her through her panties. They were already moist. He pulled her down and they fucked there and then on the floor.

It was inevitable that Detective Sergeant Gary Shaw would get to hear about the latest goings on in the Ned Kelly. Shaw was ex-Regional Crime Squad and even in this God-forsaken manor he had the odd informant who needed the occasional leg-up at court or wanted a few quid to invest at Catford Dogs. One of Shaw's oldest recruits was Tony O'Shea, elder brother of David and Shirley. Tony was in his early '40s and regarded himself as an ex-crook. His car-ringing days were behind him. All he got involved in now was buying and selling a bit of nicked gear, just to make life indoors a little easier. O'Shea had had a nice little earner in his day. Fords were his speciality. He could reduce a brand new stolen Granada to spares in under four hours. Even the smallest parts were then re-boxed and sold through his own spares shop at the front of O'Shea's Breakers Yard. That was the little racket that first attracted Gary Shaw's attention. Still, nothing lasts for ever.

Twenty-three hours after David O'Shea was out of intensive care, Tony sat opposite Shaw in the upper bar of the Tipperary pub, just a wig's throw from Lincoln's Inn. Shaw liked "The top of the Tip" for its privacy, but O'Shea was nervous. Villains get everywhere and what he was about to do broke every code that had never been written. O'Shea had never had a problem grassing kids who were nicking cars for him to Shaw, or letting slip where all the stolen car tax discs were being housed when the Ford operation hit the wall. He even showed Shaw how to lift a post office franking stamp off a nominal value postal order with wax paper and drop it back on the stolen disc. But this ... this was proper grassing. This was wrong. But then again it was *personal*.

"So get David to give evidence against Joey," Shaw was saying. "He's bang to rights on GBH and attempted murder by the sound of it."

"Yeah, but Joey can plead self-defence and Davey's gonna take a nick for starting it."

"But Joey did your sister."

"David won't do it. He'd be signing a death warrant for the whole fucking family if he did."

"So how do we tee Baker up?"

"Not your way, Mr Shaw. David's been told to wipe his mouth when he gets out of hospital. Being honest, I don't think the Bakers will let this go till they've wiped him out. I've had the visit. I've had the promises that it's finished. But you know it's bollocks and so do I. David's a dead man walking, if he ever walks again. Joey won't let it go. He can't. No one does what me brother did and goes back on the manor. But what do I do? I've got a missus, kids. What can I do, Mr Shaw? David's fucked the fucking lot of us."

"So set the Bakers up."

"Yeah and then the CPS can tell everyone at the trial who put the bit of work up, or they'll end up dropping the charges. Look, I know what's going on. I can't help that way – it's the same result."

"Can we hit the pub?"

"It's the only way," O'Shea said with certainty. "Every Monday afternoon, every Thursday and Friday ... you know what it's like. Why don't the uniform just raid it? There's always half a ton of poxy white powder everywhere, there's always parcels of nicked gear, half the people in there are on the wanted or they're proper tooled up."

"When's the best night?"

"It heaves on Fridays."

"Who's serving the gear?"

"The Taylor boys and Greg Saunders. They all hang around by the bog near the bar. There's that other little prick, what's 'is name? I dunno, but the main ones are Paul and Danny Taylor and Saunders. Saunders keeps it in a bag down his pants, the other two just pull it out of a jacket pocket."

Gary Shaw made a note of the names. "Leave it to me," he said.

CHAPTER THREE

STARK RAVING NORMAL

It was 3.37 am as Harry sped along the M11 and on to the A11 towards home. He'd had "a couple of light ales" – five bottles of Budweiser and three large JD and Cokes – with the operational team who had taken out Sonny and breathless George. He'd meant to knock it on the head after two Buds, but you know how it is. Harry smirked as he recalled DC Brennan describing the way George's face had drained of colour when he'd clocked that sea of pistols pointing at him. "Michael Jackson paid a plastic surgeon thousands to achieve that whitening effect," he'd said. "Harry Tyler could have done it for him for nothing."

The laughs had been followed by anxious glances. In today's brave new force, a good cop could get busted down the ranks or even fired for cracking a joke that could be construed as "racist" by any passing low-life/no-life *Guardian*-reading mug. One Met inspector had just been demoted to constable for a throw-away remark. Luckily, Detective Sergeant MacKay, the one West Indian officer in the squad, was generally considered "one of yer own" and had taken the remark in the spirit it had been intended.

Harry slowed down to 70 as he ejected the Blink 182 CD from his car stereo and replaced it with the latest Bloodhouse Gang offering. He was still buzzing from the success of the op. It had taken months of hard graft to pull off and before he got the chance to unwind, Harry had made his notes, been thoroughly debriefed, worked out his expenses, dumped the Granada and picked up a newish Cougar from the workshop. He'd been the man of the match in the bar though.

Harry had spent a good half hour chatting to Stacey, the woman detective sergeant from the surveillance team, the one with the baby-seat but no baby in her car. She was one of those Dorises you don't fancy at first but who, at times like now, when you're deadbeat, you start fantasising about. She was the sort of girl that you've really got to sack after the second or third shag … or maybe the fourth if she was a good bunk-up. He'd told her he had to go cos "one more drink and I'll be under the table." Stacey, laughing, had replied, "One more drink and I'd probably be under you." There was something about the glint in her eye that made Harry think she meant it. In his mind's eye, Stacey had cornered him in the bar, grabbed his balls and was whispering, "Anything you say will be held against me." Harry felt his best friend stir. He went to punch her number into the moby but thought better of it. He was only five minutes from home.

He clicked the CD on to the best number, "The

Ballad Of Chasey Lain", and sung along with his own words: "You've had a lot of dick, STACEY, but you ain't had mine." Harry laughed aloud. Fuck, he was tired. He swerved to avoid a splattered hedgehog and thought about breathless George again. The miserable mess of roadkill had had more chance than that gormless twat.

It was drizzling as Harry pulled up on his driveway. Ah, that wonderful English summer. The house was a sight. He rubbed his sore eyes and briefly studied his three-bedroom semi. That clump of grass was still growing out of the gutter. The outside needed to be painted again this year. The drainpipe had a leak.

The upstairs curtain twitched. Harry glimpsed his wife Kara. She didn't look too impressed. Bollocks, he thought. Why didn't I call to tell her I was coming home? It wasn't a lot to ask, one poxy phone call, but then Harry was selfish. He didn't mean to be. It was just … he got busy, OK? She didn't understand. You get so wrapped up in your work you can't ALLOW anything else to get in the way. If you lose focus it could cost you more than the case. It could cost your fucking LIFE! Fuck, now he was ready to ruck her and she hadn't said a word. He took a deep breath. Or was it that he just couldn't be bothered to ring any more? Don't go there. Just be Mr smiley-happy family man.

Who was he trying to kid? Harry just knew that when he surfaced for air later that day Kara would get aboard him about the house, about little Courtney Rose, about a holiday, about not ringing her. He scowled as he turned the key in the lock, but the door wouldn't open. The inner bolts were on. Of course they were. He rang the bell once. "Hang on, hang on!" Kara rushed to the door. "I was just moving Courtney back in her own bed. She was snuggled in with me."

"You should have left her, doll," Harry said, with a weak smile. "I'd have kipped in the spare room."

He held her close to him, close and tight, until Kara got uncomfortable and wriggled away. She put her face close to his. He expected her to tell him how much she loved him. Instead came the question that had become his wife's catchphrase. "Have you been drinking?" she said.

Harry didn't remember the rest of the conversation. He didn't even remember undressing and crashing into bed. But now he was there he couldn't shut his brain off. The harder he tried to sleep, the more his mind bombarded him with images from the day. He rolled on to his right shoulder and looked at the digital numbers on his Homer Simpson alarm clock. The bright green glow told him it was 4.45 am. Then 5.03 am. He saw 5.13 am and drifted off into sweet oblivion.

Harry came to at 12.37 pm. He was aware of Kara creeping across the room to the wardrobe. He glanced across at her. She had her back to him and was reaching up for something off the top shelf so that the short dress she was wearing rode up level with her white Tanga panties. She had fucking great pins. He wriggled his legs to let her know he was alive.

"Are you awake, Harry?" she whispered.

He gave it a thought. Was he ready to handle the world yet? He could certainly handle them legs.

"Yes, babe," he grunted. "I need a slash."

Great opening gambit, he thought. Move over, Casanova, there's a new stud in town. Harry swung out of bed and stumbled to the toilet on auto-pilot, then guided himself back towards the bed like a distressed Jumbo. Kara was undressing as he crash-landed. She had her back to him and was unhooking her bra. He turned his head to watch her turn around in all her naked glory and smiled weakly. Kara lifted the duvet and slipped alongside him, nestling into his body. Her left arm hugged his pot belly. He could feel her tight, firm breasts in his back. Her smell, that wonderful Kara fragrance, played around his nose till it twitched. He had a fleeting image of the cartoon kids in the old Bisto ads. Ah, rumpo, he thought to himself. Harry smiled and rolled over. Kara turned away, covering her breasts with her arms. Gently Harry slipped his right hand through her defences and cupped her left breast, then the right, softly squeezing the nipples before running his fingers over her stomach. Her skin felt good, like stroking satin. He nuzzled her long copper hair. Kara was 34, but had the body of a 20-year-old, firm in all the right places. Childbirth had not betrayed her.

"I'm afraid I'll have to caution you, madam," Harry said in clipped, Estuary cop-speak. "You have the right to remain gorgeous." She giggled. To his eager ears, the sound was like ambrosia being poured on rose petals.

His tiredness forgotten, Harry gyrated his already

hard cock against the cheeks of her arse. He parted her legs with his hands and left it lodged between the two ports of entry. Then his hand found her breasts again as he kissed the back of her neck. Gently, gently. His cock felt like cast iron. God, it had been a while. The kisses became a play bite, just to let her know it was mating time. But then Kara rolled over and took control, pushing Harry on his back and straddling him. Harry grabbed her hips and thrust his hardness against her. Kara retreated down his body and took him in her mouth. Oh yeah, that'll do, he thought, but after a minute or two she was coming back towards him, grabbing his cock with her hand and steering it into her. She was soaking wet already. Harry could have come there and then, but he grabbed the bed sheet and gripped it hard to slow himself down. He looked up at his wife's face. It was contorted with pleasure. She was already on Planet Kara – eyes shut, mouth open – and getting noisy. Fuck the neighbours. Again Harry felt a tingle in his loins. He gripped the sheet tighter and tried to think of anything but sex. He started to recite the 1998 West Ham team backwards in his mind, ending with the goalie. Always a sound delaying tactic, unless you're an Arsenal fan of course.

Kara was getting noisier. She was gripping his shoulders now and groaning in his face as her head exploded with delight. Harry held her close for about ten seconds before tapping her firmly on the back to let her know it was his turn. Kara lay next to him and spread her legs, but Harry told her to turn over. He wanted to take her from behind. She wasn't that keen on this position but she complied. He was in charge now. Harry thrust himself into her and started to pump forcefully. He was fully awake now and supercharged. He loved her tight, wet pussy. He loved being in control. He was near the point of no return in seconds. "Fuck me, fuck me!" Kara cried. Harry was lost in the rush that swept up his body and into his head. His brain was saying not yet but the wave was too strong to resist. He felt the detonation. God, there was a lot there. Kara felt it too. "Keep going," she said urgently. "Keep ..." He gripped her hips and kept on pounding into her. His cock was still hard. "YES!" she yelled. "YES!" They both collapsed, his body on top of hers. Harry lay there for a moment before rolling over. He could feel his cock deflating slowly, like one of Branson's air balloons. Kara hugged him tightly. "Any more where that came from?" she smiled.

Ten minutes later, Kara got up and walked towards the *en suite* bathroom. Harry looked approvingly at her firm breasts. "I'm running a bath," she said. "Shall I save you the water?"

"Please, darling."

She was in and out quickly then stood by the side of the bath obligingly drying herself legs apart as Harry soaked in the sweet herbal froth. He got a lazy lob on. Kara reached down and stroked his penis.

"That's it, darling," Harry said. "Take the law into your own hands."

"Is that all you ever think about? " Kara replied with a joke tut.

"No," he said, feigning hurt. "I sometimes think

about beer and murghi massala." She walked off and came back in her underwear to wash his hair. Harry tried to rub her nipples through her bra, but she gently nudged his hand away. Play time was over.

"Where's Courtney Rose?" Harry asked.

"Over Mum's. They've gone to Newmarket for the day."

"How are yer mum and dad?"

"Good. Dad's had a rough time of it with hay fever this year."

"I reckon he's on Charlie, the way he keeps sniffing. He's got the bugle for it."

"Don't talk like that, he wouldn't know what it was anyway. I hate it when you come home talking like a villain."

"Anybody ring?"

"What, from work you mean?"

"Yeah."

"No, and if they do I'll say you're out. Let's have a bit of time together without your job."

"Yeah. Of course." Pause. "Where's me moby?"

"On the kitchen table, where you left it. You going to look at that gate this afternoon?"

Fucking gate! He thought. You weren't thinking about gates an hour ago. "Yes, luv," Harry said meekly. Harry slung on some jogging pants, an old sweatshirt and his battered moccasins, then headed straight to the kitchen to put his mobile on charge. A plate of spaghetti on toast later and he was on the phone to work, as usual. Kara got upset and stormed into the garden. If her husband had seen her crying he hadn't let it disturb his conversation. Sometimes she felt the phone was some sort of evolutionary growth from his ear. Once, soon after they had married, Harry had actually stopped halfway through making love to her to take a call from work and then sauntered back to bed five minutes later expecting to carry on. "A case of 'coppers interruptus'," he'd called it, as if a cheap joke made it all OK.

After a couple of minutes, Kara came back in and said, "I'm off to Cambridge to do some shopping, do you want to come?" Harry shook his head and carried on talking. He blew her a kiss but it hit the wallpaper. Kara had already gone.

It was 6.30 pm when she finally got home to find Harry watching an episode of *The Sopranos* (the third in a row) on video. Kara had collected Courtney Rose from her parents, which pleased him no end. He'd hardly seen his daughter since her third birthday three months before. She was the image of her mum. Courtney's golden curls and cherubic face made her look like a refugee from a Pears soap advert. Kara loved to dress her in real girlie clothes. She wouldn't grow up a tomboy. No football boots would ever grace these dainty feet. Harry disapproved of women playing football. And boxing, smoking, wearing trousers, driving and drinking from pint glasses. He wasn't too convinced about them voting, come to that. According to him the only reason a woman put on a soccer strip was to get their old man's attention when the football season was on.

Harry played with Courtney until her 8 pm

bedtime. He even feigned interest in *The Tweenies*. Kara slipped out for a take-away curry. He'd asked for a vindaloo, but she bought him a rogan josh, saying, "I'm not having you stinking the house out tomorrow." It had pissed him off but he'd bitten his tongue and spiced it up with HP Chilli sauce when she wasn't looking. Two cans of supermarket lager and a large brandy later and Harry was ready for his bed. He slept well that night.

Unusually for Harry, he'd taken two days out of work. Kara was delighted. What she didn't know was his DCI had ordered him to clear some of the time-off he had built up. He hadn't actually wanted to take any leave whatsoever, but he played the situation to his advantage of course. Harry even left his mobile at home to keep Kara sweet and ensure another bunk-up later on. She had rustled up a picnic for them that he pronounced "pukka!" The sun had even come through for them, blazing away as if it were auditioning for a Cornflakes packet.

They headed for Mildenhall and found a spot on the heath. Harry took a bite on a turkey leg and watched a US transporter climb up into the picture-book sky. This he could suffer. After lunch – he called it dinner – they cuddled up on the grass, dad, mum and daughter. It was idyllic. And then Kara made her move.

"Harry, will you ever give up undercover work?"

"Not for a while, darling. Why?"

"We never see you any more."

Harry stiffened. "Don't spoil it!" he snapped. "Why do you have to fucking spoil things?"

"Because it's true. You're always away working. I never know where you are, what you're doing, when you're coming home. You've got a lovely daughter here. She needs her dad. I need her dad."

Harry's mental drawbridge shot up. Oblivious to the growing drama, little Courtney was playing feed the dolly a chicken wing. Kara, with right on her side, took Harry's silence as tacit agreement. "When are we going to get away like other families do?" she asked.

Here it comes, he thought, bang on cue.

"When are we going to have a decent holiday?"

Harry had spent much of his undercover work tripping around the nightspots of Amsterdam, Rotterdam, Madrid, Malaga, Geneva and Munich. Europe was his playground. Kara wasn't envious of it, but she hated them being apart. She regularly got a postcard from him, seldom a phone call. Harry was everywhere, but her life was going nowhere. She was trapped at home, an hour's drive from any of her childhood friends, never allowed to tell the few cronies she'd made from ante-natal classes about her husband's real job – they all thought he was on the oil rigs. There were days when she could have cheerfully screamed the house down. Kara had rehearsed this speech a hundred times, and yet now, as she opened her heart to her husband, she could sense he wasn't really listening. So she changed gear.

"Harry, do you care about us at all? Do you really want this? Me and Courtney Rose, are we part of your life?"

Harry rocked a little at this one. He knew he

loved Kara as much as he could ever love anyone. And he loved Courtney beyond question. What he couldn't grasp was how much the adrenalin-charged thrill of adventure, the dangerous highs of his demanding job were poisoning his mind. His marriage and his mental health was suffering because compared to THE JOB, nothing mattered. Nothing else came close. But how could he tell that to Kara when he wouldn't even face it himself?

Rather than row, Harry caved in. "OK, book somewhere. Let's go away, the three of us."

"When?"

"I dunno. Christmas. Book Christmas away."

"Where? Where can I book? I don't wanna book somewhere and you say it's off limits because of your work."

"I dunno, doll. You think about it and tell me where you fancy."

"Florida."

"Fine."

"I saw some great deals on Teletext for Orlando."

"Fine, great, yeah."

"TALK TO ME!"

"What do you mean?"

"'Fine, great, yeah'," she mimicked. "Don't you have any thoughts about it? If I'd said Timbuctoo you'd have said, 'Fine, great, yeah,' just to shut me up."

"Here we fucking go! I said yes, Florida, yes! What else do you want from me? I want to go there. We'll have a great time. Why do you have to start a row?"

"I'm not, I just want some discussion, that's all."

"For fuck's sake! YES! Florida's fucking brilliant. I can't wait for Christmas, let's go and watch some tosspot paedophile dressed up as a giant rat trying to get into Minnie Mouse's knickers."

Courtney Rose started to cry. Harry got off the blanket and marched off to the car. The picnic was over.

They drove home in silence. Courtney Rose was asleep in her baby-seat as soon as Harry had hit the first bend. They hadn't said a word for 13 miles.

"Are you going to talk to me?" Kara asked eventually.

"Why is it me not talking to you? You're not talking to me, either."

"You do it every time, try and make out it's my fault. That's the policeman in you. Why can't you just admit you're at fault for once?"

"What's my fault? You're the one who starts it and it's my fucking fault."

"Don't keep swearing."

"Bollocks."

"Don't ever swear in front of Courtney."

"She's fucking asleep."

"HARRY!"

He turned the CD on. Kara turned the volume down. Both knew their marriage was flawed, but was it doomed? Harry could see it all slipping away. He didn't want that. Not yet, at any rate. He pulled over into a lay-by. Kara looked at him apprehensively.

Harry glanced at Courtney, and made a grab for Kara's hand. "I'm sorry, luv. OK?" He leant over and kissed her gently on the lips. "I am so sorry." He cuddled her and she responded. "It's just my head," he said. "It's buzzing all the time. I don't mean to upset you. Book the holiday. I really fancy Florida. She'll love it, and when she's a bit older, we'll take her to Vegas. Book Florida. I'm sorry."

Kara started sobbing, then tried to talk through her tears.

"Shhh," said Harry. "Come on, girl. You know I love you."

He was adept at emotional manipulation. What wasn't clear, even to Harry, was if what he was saying was deception or the truth. Was he really sorry, or just keeping the peace? Did he want to save his second marriage, or could he really not give a toss? Perhaps it was just the ag of the divorce and the squabbling over property and maintenance he couldn't stomach.

"When we get home I'll ring work and take a couple more days off," he said. "I've got plenty to do indoors." Big house points being scored here, he thought. And a leg-over guaranteed.

Peace reigned on the domestic battlefield for the next two days. Harry spent time mowing the lawn and tending flower beds. Even the gutters got cleaned out. Harry was most of the way through a weed patch when Pete, his next door neighbour, stuck a cold beer over the fence. He was an amiable sort of guy, and one of the few locals who knew Harry was a "secret copper". Pete had retired from "the gas". Before that he'd been a frontline soldier and knew how many marbles made six. He never asked about Harry's work. They spent 40 minutes shooting the breeze – football, local gossip, the bloody yobs who were vandalising the local primary school. Everyday shit. Harry realised he hadn't thought about work all day.

Kara came out of the house with a trowel in her hand. She was wearing pink shorts and a tight-fitting pastel yellow T-shirt. "You two are like a couple of old women," she joked, and Harry smiled. He was at peace with himself.

That evening Harry fired up the barbeque and slung on some quarter-pounders and butterfly chicken breasts, half-cooked in the oven. He loved to cook outdoors, it was the only cooking he'd ever do. There was something primordial about it. Man the hunter preparing his kill. A million years BC, Fred Flintstone was doing this with mammoth steaks and spicey hot pteradactyl wings. Harry raised a large glass of red – a 1998 Fleurie – to his lips, winked at Kara and said, "What do you think the poor people are doing now?"

She had smoked half a joint in the shed and was feeling as mellow as her husband. She didn't even notice the mobile phone had slipped back out and was lying on the patio table behind the sea salt. It was exclusively a work phone. Kara didn't know the number. If she didn't know it she couldn't ring it and compromise an operation. Besides, as Harry had explained, it had caller display. He couldn't afford to have a target clock the number or by chance overhear a conversation that would put his safety in jeopardy. Harry regularly changed numbers anyway. Once a big op had been successfully concluded, the mobile would be off for a week or two and then sacked. Kara had been working on a cross channel ferry when she had first met Harry. She was a stewardess on the Felixstowe to Gothenburg line that crawled across the North Sea. The first time he set eyes on her, he knew he had to have her. She had smiled at him, green eyes sparkling, and he'd frozen. If he'd been in a cartoon his eyes and his heart would have been out on stalks. If the cartoon had been *Fritz The Cat*, his groin would have been out there too. Kara's reaction to Harry was similarly cathartic. It was almost like the guy had an aura about him.

She was a strange girl, bright but naïve at the same time. No one could accuse her of being worldly-wise. Kara came from Hadleigh, near Ipswich, originally. Her parents had moved across country to Dullingham which is a stone's throw from Newmarket and Cambridge. She'd had just three previous boyfriends.

Kara and Harry had been together for six years now, married for three of them. At first she had enjoyed hearing stories about his exciting work, until the demands of The Job had shunted her into a kind of slipstream of his life. Back then she'd been enthralled to hear how easily Harry gained the trust of big-time villains and how even the smartest suckered themselves when they saw money on the table. He described his job as "like hunting a tiger in the jungle armed only with a pointed stick ... but with a back-up team packing surface to air missiles." Kara knew he was a special kind of man, and tried

—
66

to make allowances for it. Harry was brilliant at his job, the best of the best. He believed in himself totally. His ability to lie fluently under pressure would impress a convention of door-to-door salesmen who had qualified as lawyers and were aiming at becoming MEPs. And he was tenacious. Like the Mounties, Harry Tyler always got his man.

Kara was dead proud of him, of course she was. She just believed that, in fairness to families, the force should put a sell-by date on undercover operatives. Most of the men in Harry's line of work ended up as serial divorcees. Kara questioned if anyone in authority really cared about the men's well-being. Maybe some of them did, a bit. But there were fabric softeners that cared more. As long as the bodies were getting put away, no one was ever going to say, "Move over, H, go enjoy some downtime with Kara and your kid." And there was no one she could really talk to about it. Oh, her mum, dad and sister knew vaguely what Harry did for a living but she was too much of a trained soldier to give much away. Harry had drummed the "loose lips cost ships" message into her from day one. It wasn't even as if there were other wives she could confide in. Friendships between families of undercover officers weren't forbidden, but they weren't encouraged. Besides, could she cope with being around more than one professional porky-pie merchant at a time?

Kara had met many undercover buyers, operators whom Harry rated as quality. They were all like him. Male, female, black, Chinese, Irish, Yank or Canadian, they were all Harrys. Some of them were very sweet, some OTT on two pints of lager, but they shared Harry's supreme confidence, his ability to flatter and box clever. "Bullshitters with cast iron bollocks", was how her husband had proudly described his profession. Not one of them had a home life to talk of.

In her heart of hearts Kara knew Harry could never go back to being a normal cop. How could he be setting up a gang of counterfeiters one week and trying to detect who nicked old Mother Wade's knickers off the line the next? The only thing he could do was leave the Force and get into some kind of private detective work. He was smart enough to run his own agency and when they got to Florida she resolved to plant the seeds in his mind. It was about time her husband made some serious money from his talents.

Harry didn't know it but his one true friend was his wife. She was the only one who would never betray him.

All his life Harry had kept people at arm's length. He had no friends at all from his schooldays. His job meant he couldn't socialise regularly with other cops and he was only on nodding acquaintance with the men he sat with at football. His drinking buddies in the village pub were just that, faces to have a laugh with and who swallowed his oil rig cover story whole.

After school, he'd found it hard to put down roots. He'd bummed around from one job to another, drifting from flat to bed-sit. Harry was working as an office clerk in Ilford, Essex, when he'd fallen for a legal-audio typist called Dawn, a year his junior, who had proved easily impressed when he acted the clown. A bright, attractive brunette from a working-class background, Dawn was shy and had had a sheltered life. She still lived locally with her parents and two younger sisters. Her father, Bob, was a retired cop, and when Harry asked for his daughter's hand in marriage, Bob suggested he get a job "with prospects" with the Essex police.

Harry had been neither pro nor anti police at the time. He vaguely considered the boys in blue to be the enemy of the working classes but had no time for the arseholes who glamorised the Kray twins and other two-bob thugs. His own father stirred the pot telling him how he wished he'd joined the police instead of the brigade. One morning on a whim Harry rang Directory Enquiries and got numbers for Metropolitan Police recruitment and Essex police. For no reason at all he rang Essex first and the forms were in the post. The summer of 1979 was a blur. He joined the police, married Dawn and got a flat in Braintree, all to a soundtrack of The Jam and Ian Dury. Harry was happy. Or at least he was until Dawn started playing away, and the great betrayal brought the whole house of cards crashing down around his ears. Thank fuck they hadn't had kids. It was the lowest point in Harry's life. He had briefly considered suicide but decided that, the way his luck was poxed, if he'd hanged himself the rope would have broken.

To escape the pain, Harry flung himself into his work. It was amazing how fast "Please come back, darling" turned into "Fuck her, the prat." Harry learned how to use a washing machine and that funny metal thing that straightens out the creases of your trousers. He never did master the oven.

Harry Tyler stayed in uniform for six years. He was a natural thief-taker and made the inevitable transition into the CID and then the Essex wing of the Regional Crime Squad. He loved the fringe benefits of coppering back then, the hard drinking, the easy access to strippers and Toms. Harry amassed snouts the way Jim Davidson collected speeding fines. He moved easily in the criminal underworld, and had the innate ability to persuade the best lying thief to give an honest confession.

His bosses soon noted his gift of the gab. Harry's patter was like a force of nature. Forget Parkinson, Harry Tyler could talk to anyone and get them to open up. It made him an obvious choice to go on an undercover officers' course in Bristol. He learned quickly. At first Harry was second fiddle to the experienced players, acting as their pretend gophers, but within months he was pushing himself forward. He wanted to be the main man, the guy the faces would show their parcels to, and when he got the chance he performed with breathtaking self-assurance. The ritual was always the same. Target the bad guys, gain their confidence, see their parcel, and then send in his gang – more undercover men – to collect the goods. And, as Cilla would say, surprise surprise, one of them turned out to be a lousy, no-good cop. Harry would be long out of the frame by now, of course. He always distanced himself before the trade fell down, so he would retain his integrity and "honour" among the thieves, most of whom were soon doing deals with the feds, sacrificing other faces in exchange for lesser sentences.

By the time he met Kara Cooper, Harry Tyler was acknowledged to be one of a dozen key players in England who were regarded as the masters of their art. He was a consummate professional. A true thespian. Police colleagues called him "The Bushwhacker."

CHAPTER FOUR

THE UNTOUCHABLES

Johnny Too couldn't remember the last time his cock had felt this sore. Five times he'd fucked it, six if you count the time he didn't come. Geri was worth seeing again. Dirty bitch. John smiled. He tucked into a fry-up in Mario's cafe in Covent Garden, sipped a cup of extra-strong espresso with four sugars and started reading that morning's *Sun* from the back page. He'd see what John Sadler had to say about Tottenham getting hammered 4–1 at home then bowl over to Mr Eddie's in Dean Street and get measured up for a new whistle. Sweet.

Gary Shaw felt good. For the first time in years he was actually excited about the job, despite, perhaps even because of the hurdles he had to negotiate. Shaw knew the Bakers were flagged targets of just about every big squad in London and the national boys as well. Hitting their drinker was problematic for a number of reasons, the main one being getting permission from the major players. They were supposed to be watching the Bakers round the clock, waiting for them to go "hands on" the big parcel. Hands on, bollocks. Shaw knew Johnny was too smart ever to go up front for any serious dealing. They had plenty of soldiers for that. Problem two was could the local uniform be told in advance what was about to happen? How many owed it to their snouts to tip 'em the wink and keep 'em out of the Ned on the day?

Shaw went to his boss the first thing Monday morning. He wasn't looking forward to it. Detective Chief Inspector Gordon Hitchcock was a nice enough bloke, it was just that ... well, he was end-of-century man personified. Hitchcock was one of that breed who had done so well under Major and Blair. He didn't believe in anything except management, order, and personal advancement, which meant toeing the PC line at all times, no matter how illogical or insane it might be. All his service, Hitchcock had been a good, honest uniform man, but not a crime fighter. Becoming a DCI had been a career move. He didn't want to be a detective but, like most modern policemen of rank, Hitchcock had viewed the move as a springboard to the Superintendent job he could ride out to retirement time. His experience of prosecuting publicans didn't stretch beyond catching a landlord serving a couple of regulars ten minutes after last shout. Much easier to roast Albert and Mary for provoking the police by being up past their bedtime than to take on a pub that Tony Soprano would have thought twice about frequenting.

To his credit, Hitchcock knew about the Ned, and the grief that the Baker firm had been giving the police for years. Now was the time not so much for revenge, he said, as justice. Shaw listened open-mouthed as that word tripped off the DCI's lips. He could almost hear the fanfare of trumpets and the heavenly chorus burst into song.

"Yes, sir," Shaw said. He couldn't bring himself to say "Yes, *guv'nor*" cos guv'nor was a term reserved for *real* CID men who warranted respect.

"Let's get hold of the Licensing Inspector and the late-turn relief Inspector for Friday," Hitchcock said in an Estuary drawl that positively screamed *Guardian* reader. "We can have a scrum down on Friday on how we're going to do it."

That was it. Gary Shaw's interest evaporated as each familiar catchphrase came into play. "Hit the ground running ... community consultation ... operational co-ordination ..." it just went on and on. The pub raid Shaw had envisaged to put away the worst gang of hardcore villains in London was turning into a promotional springboard before his very eyes.

"And you, DS Shaw," Hitchcock was saying, "you organise the interview teams for the prisoners. Remind me, we must have an outer cordon to deal with drink-drivers who might try to flee the scene."

Gary Shaw closed his eyes to keep his composure. Beam me up, Scotty, he thought.

Where better to celebrate your 21st birthday with all your mates and family than the Ned Kelly public house, Powder Mill Road, Rotherhithe, London, SE16? Cheap beer, plenty of puff and Charlie, loads of silly slappers ready to drop everything if you powdered their noses ... all that and you're just the lob of a brick away from the New Den, too. They even had a DJ in, Lucy Loud, to crank up the drum and bass till your eye-balls bulged out of their sockets and your chest physically vibrated. "It's Friday night!" she hollered. "And we are game on!"

Johnny Too was renowned for his generosity. Easy to be when you're spending other people's money.

"Johnny, you old bastard," said Trevor Richards as he ploughed through the throng. "Why you looking so happy? You diddled the VAT man again?"

"No, Unc," Johnny Too smiled. "Me inflatable girlfriend finally said yes."

He gave his uncle a cuddle. He was a lovely man – *diamond!* Trev had stood his ground when Millwall played West Ham, Arsenal, Spurs and the shitters from Chelsea, too. Johnny, Joe and Trev had been at Stamford Bridge the night Fashanu dumped Chelsea out of the FA Cup on their own turf. When it all kicked off outside, Trevor Richards had led from the front, jumping into eight Headhunters and showing them the business end of "Excalibur". That was his pride and joy, a customised iron cosh liberally adorned with rusty screws. How Joey admired his uncle's engineering skills. It was Trev who, back in the late 70s, had first come up with the idea of leaving calling cards which informed victims which particular firm had put them to sleep. "Congratulations," they said. "You have just met Millwall Away."

A meticulous master of detail, Trevor also planned and carried out armed heists on various security vans that deliberately invited robbery by their provocative habit of driving to the same banks and building societies at the same time every week. That, said Trev, meant they were just "gagging for a blagging".

Trevor loved his work and he loved his play, but nothing meant more to him than his youngest son, Steven. Whenever he had been banged up, photos of his sons, Steven and Dougie, had always been fixed up just above the Millwall team picture. He adored both boys, but Steven, who had been a sickly child after a prolonged bout of pneumatic fever, was his favourite. Neither Trevor nor anyone else in the Baker circle had any idea he was gay.

Young Steven was bright, IT literate and business minded. At 14 he had been organising raves. It was Steven who had hooked the smarter of his two uncles on the Net and its unsurpassed money-making potential. Johnny had given him the readies to set up his own website, www.ftroopaway.com. F-Troop were a fictional crew of Millwall ruckers who *World In Action* had been duped into "exposing" in the 1970s. The website was a heavily coded events page for up-and-coming hooligan fixtures. Steven had visions of headcases in the near future organising via pocket-sized computers – an intranet for nutters.

Like his pals, Steven had been born to be Millwall. The crowd attending his 21st could have probably filled the New Den, or that's how it looked to Steven. There must have been, what, 100 of them in the bar, plus the birds.

Mostly in their early and late 20s, they were arrogant, swaggering yobs, foul-mouthed but frighteningly articulate. Young hounds, Johnny Too called them with something akin to paternal pride. "Look at all me young 'ounds." The majority were white, but at least ten were black or mixed-race. Cockney blacks. Trevor had been NF through and through in the late 70s, but no one under 25 was in to race hate now, not in inner London at any rate. White powder, yes. White power? Forget it.

At 8.30 pm, Steven's pal, Billy French, told Lucy Loud to turn down the music. "Important announcement," he slurred. Like most of the young men present, French had an earring in his left ear. If his hair had been cropped any shorter, the Sioux would have claimed it as a scalp. "Very important announcement," he slurred again. Then he took the mike and began to sing:

"Fuck 'em all! Fuck 'em all!
United, West 'Am, Liverpool,
Cos we are the MILLWALL and we are the BEST!
We are the MILLWALL so FUCK all the REST!!!!"

The whole bar erupted in song. If Johnny Too could have smiled any wider the top half of his head would have fallen off. This was going to be a great night. It had already started memorably when a couple of clearly deranged students, one female, one half-male, had come in the pub and tried to sell copies of the *Socialist Worker*. Dougie The Dog had looked at the paper.

—

"You support the IRA," he'd said, stony-faced. "This is for Harry Shand!" – *The Long Good Friday* again! And he'd headbutted the greasy-haired man, knocking him out cold.

"Sorry, miss," the laughing Dougie said to the student's equally scruffy companion who screamed:

"Don't you miss me, you bastard."

"OK," said Dougie, and he decked her too. Classic. That anecdote had spread round the party like wildfire.

Tonight, everyone was happy. Certainly the Taylor boys, Saunders and a couple of other licensed dealers were sending out for more Charlie than they had sold in many a week. It was pukka "Club Class" cocaine too, cut straight off the block. No wonder there was what seemed like a two-mile tailback in the gents.

At 9.17 pm barmaid Lesley Gore had to ask Johnny to tell the lads to stay out of the ladies. Not because the delicate flowers wanted a piss in private, but because they couldn't get to the arse-level cisterns to toot their own gear. What a fucking night! The sounds were good, the gear was great, the River Ooze was flowing. Pint glasses were drained as soon as they were full. It was like the charlied-up clientele were out to drown themselves in one huge, gut-bloating cascade of fermented jolly juice. Johnny Too felt splendid, the King in his castle, surrounded by his troops, his 'ounds. "Staunch" to a man, every last one of them.

"Break out the bubbly, darlin'," he told his wife, Sandra. "I've gotta 'ave a lash. Me back teeth are floating."

"Ain't 'e charmin'?" Sandra laughed. But as soon as John was in the gents he was on the mobile phone to Geraldine telling her exactly how he was going to make missing the party up to her.

Sandra was bottle blonde, an ex-model, wannabe cabaret singer heavily adorned with weighty but tasteless jewellery. She had ebony eyes, large breasts and less than perfect skin, and she was pregnant again with their third child. She went to the fridge and brought back a jeroboam of Moet which Pyro Joe popped open with a have-summa-that Grand Prix winner's flourish to roars of approval from the older men gathered around him. Everyone was a face. Anyone who meant anything in South London was here tonight. If you were invited you turned up and put up with the "fuckin' racket".

You had to show respect, even if it meant just a glass or two of shampoo before it was off in the chariot up to a grown-ups club in the West End.

At 9.38 pm, Lucy Loud turned off the head-splitting drum and bass, and the Ned erupted in a raucous rendition of Happy Birthday – " 'Appeee birfdayyy, dear Steven, 'appy birfdayyy to you-ah."

The sense of event had lured the Bakers into dropping their guard. No sentries had been posted. No one had noticed the two unmarked removal vans pull up a street away, just behind the gas board van that had been parked up for a couple of hours. On other nights the van might have been spotted and given the once over but not tonight. Who would be mad enough to take on the Bakers when the whole firm was about them?

At 9.45 pm precisely, the rocket went up. The removal vans dropped their backs and disgorged 80 policemen. Four unmarked dog vans appeared from nowhere. Young PC Perry Jackson, 22 and keen, was the first to reach the Ned Kelly. His intention was to nick a Baker. Jackson booted open the doors and came to a dead stop. There was no way forward through the pilchard-packed punters. "What the fuck?" he said. As the shouting started, the music went off. Girls screamed and bottles started to fly in the direction of the uniforms. For each cop who entered five wraps of cocaine hit the floor and were ground under foot. Some of the flying bottles smashed windows, officers were trading punches with revellers, dogs barked, girls sobbed, voices raised in hatred, and then CRACKKKK! The unmistakable sound of a handgun discharging silenced everyone. A policeman went down. It was Perry Jackson. Almost immediately it seemed like everyone present was trying to get out through the pub doors at the same time. It was like a boil bursting, one of those tough ones that spurts out and whacks you in the eye.

Now police and thieves were fighting toe-to-toe in the street as well as the pub. Car windows went in. The air was thick with shouts and screams once more, only now they were mixed with car alarms and sirens, and the acrid stench of CS gas. Inside, Perry Jackson, who had been shot in the shoulder, was kicked more than once as his colleagues attempted to form a human barricade around him.

Gary Shaw looked on open-mouthed. The

street-fighting was in danger of becoming a full-scale riot. The Dixons in the nearby main-drag had just been ramraided. Aid was piling into Rotherhithe from all surrounding areas, but that meant opportunist thieves as well as the boys in blue. The Central London police reserve units were urgently pushing traffic out of their way.

In the midst of the fighting, Dougie The Dog was in his element. He always felt the same when it went off, like he wasn't really there, like he was caught up in a film and totally invulnerable. The sounds, sights and smells at the eye of the storm filled his senses to overload and he lashed out every which way. Maybe this was what they meant by Beserker Rage.

It took the police over an hour to quell the disturbance. As the Police Inspector handed Johnny Baker the drugs search warrant, Trevor's fist flew through what was left of the birthday crowd and laid him out cold. All the Baker clan were arrested. Prisoners were bussed to all nearby stations and hastily charged: assault on police, threatening behaviour, affray, criminal damage, possession of cannabis. "Everything," Johnny laughed later, "short of being drunk in charge of a birthday party."

DS Shaw stared into the Ned Kelly in total disbelief. The floor was awash with white powder, pills and lumps of cannabis. It looked like an explosion in a pharmacy, he thought. There must have been three grand's worth of illicit substances – whiz, Charlie, puff and Es – coating the carpet.

"Get everybody out," he barked finally. "Get me a photographer. Get a lab scientist. Get me a new job

..." Shaw couldn't have been more gutted. This was a major incident scene. A policeman had been shot, no gun had been recovered, half of Bolivia's national export was on the floor but only one of forty-eight prisoners had been found in possession of drugs, and that was a minor amount of Moroccan. Mission fucking accomplished.

Shaw edged out of the door. The rest of the revellers were being held outside. Shaw shouted to the uniformed officers in earshot who were still standing. "Get all their names and addresses, they've all got to be seen about the shooting."

DCI Hitchcock called over, "Shouldn't we arrest them all as suspects for shooting the PC?"

"Matter for you, sir," Gary Shaw said. "Matter for you."

Later that night, much later, Jane Shaw lay in bed with her husband and tried to calm him down. Gary had raged about Hitchcock for half an hour when he'd got in. He'd woken up the kids and drunk too much Scotch. It was, he assured her, "the biggest fucking cock-up in all my years in the force".

"The fucking papers say Old Bill are institutionally racist," he went on, "but believe me, darling, the only thing institutionalised in the Metropolitan Police is sheer fucking incompetence."

Jane massaged his back and purred sympathetically. When she finally dropped off, Gary ran the night's events through his head one more time. Years ago pub raids like that wouldn't have fucked up because all that shit on the floor would have ended up in someone's pockets. You wouldn't dare fit up a suspect now, with an army of bleeding heart barristers on hand to kick up a stink. But how wrong was it to bend the rules a little if it meant putting away the bad guys? In Shaw's early days as a Flying Squad detective, it was common practice to tap telephones illicitly, invent surveillance records, plant evidence, and make up verbal confessions. Not because detectives were lazy or they wanted to frame the innocent. On the contrary, The Sweeney did it to nail criminals they knew to be guilty. They did deals with guilty villains, too, to put bigger fish away. They turned a blind eye to others in return for information. That was the system. It was imperfect, and open to abuse, but largely it worked. The bad guys got captured, even if it was for the wrong job. As Shaw always said, he'd never put an innocent man in prison – and most villains accepted it. They wiped their mouths and took what was coming to them. But not now. Now to hear the liberals tell it, it was the cops who were the bad guys. The world was turned upside down and Gary Shaw was fucked if he wanted to go into work on Monday morning.

Detective Sgt Michael French took another look over his shoulder before he walked into the Blackheath & Newbridge Working Men's Club. It was 12 noon on Sunday, and no one was about. He signed in.

"Where's yer snooker room, mate?" he asked.

"One flight up," the man on the door with the hare lip replied.

French had only agreed to see the Bakers if the meet was "well off the plot ... I mean," he'd said, "right now you've got a hundred pairs of eyes watching the Ned round the clock."

Johnny Too and Pyro Joey had made the journey out to SE3 separately. Joey drove himself out to the M25 and back into London on the A20. Johnny took a mini-cab to Waterloo, cut across to Waterloo East, jumped on a train down to New Cross and took a black taxi from there, watching his back the whole way. It would have taken Batman to keep up with him, but it was Fatman he was going to see. They were the only people playing snooker when French arrived.

"Michael," Johnny Too smiled. "Delighted to see you. Drink?"

French nodded. Joey poured him a large malt. French grabbed the glass in his podgy fingers and downed it in one.

"I was gonna say meet at the Dome," Johnny said, grinning. "We'd be the only fuckers there."

The smile vanished abruptly from his face. He leaned close into the detective. "Now," he said sharply. "What the fuck was all that about?"

"Johnny, my life, it was as big a shock to me as it was to you."

Pyro Joe scowled.

"Are you seriously telling me you didn't even hear a whisper?" Johnny said.

"Not a dicky bird, John." French felt perspiration form on his temples.

Johnny Too turned to his brother. "Perhaps we're not paying him enough to keep his ears clean and keen." He turned back to French, picking up a pool cue and smacking it against his open palm.

"How much wages have you had off the firm this year?"

"More than enough, John," French said.

"And how much of my cocaine has gone up that big fat Filth bugle of yourn?"

"Johnny, I swear, there wasn't a word about the raid up front," French protested. "No one in the nick knew about it until the last minute."

"And phones don't work?"

"It was impossible for me to put a call in."

Pyro Joe snapped the pool cue in two. "It just ain't fucking good enough, Michael."

"So what happens next?" growled Joey. "Are your mob gonna wanna know again?"

"No way," French answered quickly. "I mean, the top brass are shitting themselves now. Word is someone senior is gonna have to take early retirement over this one and the smart money is on Hitchcock. Believe me, you ain't gonna have no more ag in the immediate future. Oh, they're watching ya, but no one is gonna move against you unless they can get you hands on, bang to rights and you, of course, are too smart."

"Well said, Michael," Johnny Too smiled. "Y'know, I can almost believe you. You're like fucking Prozac in human form. Give him another sherbet, Joe. Let's have a toast, to bent Old Bill. God love 'em cos no other fucker does. C'mon, Michael, drink. Fill yer fucking helmet, son."

Gordon Hitchcock felt nervous, like he were a school-boy being sent to the headmaster. How was the Chief Super going to be? Monday morning "prayers" with the uniform Chief Superintendent was a three books down the back of the trousers job. He knew that everyone above and below him in rank wanted him to cop it big time over the raid that that Sunday's *Observer* had dubbed "the policing fiasco of the decade". This morning's *Guardian* was calling for his suspension pending a full inquiry. Yet Chief Superintendent Neil Walker played it cool. The last thing he wanted was for Hitchcock to go sick and sue the force for causing him stress.

The meeting, involving six senior officers, began amicably. Hitchcock gave his version of events, details of prisoners, charges, cautions, complaints and an update on the shot officer (the last item on the list). The team of detectives called in to go door-to-door to seek witnesses had turned up just one positive lead, he said. Sadly, Mrs Savage at 46 Powder Mill Road was a certifiable nutter who believed *The X-Files* was a documentary. This surprised no-one. But Hitchcock did get a laugh when he announced that her tip, that Elvis was still alive and living his life disguised as the Ugandan woman next door, had been passed on to Special Branch for closer investigation.

Every partygoer had been seen, but sadly there was no trace of Mr Liam Gallagher, Miss Sheila Blige, Mr R Poon, or a dozen of the other volunteered names. Naturally, the genuine revellers had all been in the toilets when the raid occurred (but not taking drugs, of course).

When the dead wood vacated the room, the real meeting began.

"Well, Gordon," Neil Walker said. "Where do we go from here? Other than being dragged through the civil courts, that is."

Walker came from Birmingham and had a voice like a Brummie Eeyore. He spoke slowly. Every elongated syllable seemed heavy with resignation. Hitchcock shifted uneasily in his seat.

"I just don't know, sir," he said. "DS Shaw has suggested we might look at a U/C operation."

"U/C ..." Walker pondered aloud.

"Yes, sir. An infiltration by an undercover officer to try and get some sort of damning evidence against the Bakers and hopefully identify who shot young PC Jackson."

"Did DS Shaw have any other ideas?"

"The only other thing he came up with was Brazilian death squads."

"Let's stick to the sensible options."

"Right, sir. Death squads it is then."

Both men laughed.

"This undercover option, what are your views, Gordon?" Walker asked. "Won't the Bakers be expecting something?"

"On the contrary, sir. I suspect they'll be looking

to the usual breath tests and car stops, but one thing's for certain – they think they're untouchable now."

Walker stood up. "Feasibility study, Gordon. Get me a feasibility study."

"I'm on it now, sir."

The local press had a field day, of course. "The Riot Of Rotherhithe" they'd called it, with the sub-head: "Wrong Arm Of The Law". They couldn't match the *Socialist Worker's* "Police Riot!" splash for partisan reporting, but their pages were awash with quotes from salt of the earth Rotherhithe folk. Gary Shaw marvelled at the selective nature of their observational prowess.

"Fucking amazing," he said to Jane. "No-one ever witnesses any crime on this patch, not once, but when a police raid goes pear shaped, the world and his sister all see a copper putting the boot in, and three drug dealers giving one policeman a good hiding in self-defence ...

"Everyone – reporters, politicians, social workers, vicars – is on the side of the scumbags. It's like the world's turned upside down."

Jane kissed him on the nose. "Were you serious when you talked about taking early retirement the other night?" she asked. Gary Shaw said nothing.

It would be no great slur on the reputation of solicitors Bondman, Gable & Goode to say that Maurice

Bondman was as bent as they come. He didn't see himself like that, of course. To hear Maurice talk at dinner parties, he was some kind of Equalizer, a low-rent Michael Mansfield, taking up arms for the poor and the oppressed. Right now his biggest client was sipping tea in his Old Kent Road office and reeling off an appalling litany of police oppression. "I mean," Johnny Too was saying, "in my game I expect ag from the Old Bill, but they have gone right over the top this time, Morrie mate. This ain't yer normal New Labour militia having a pop at the struggling entrepreneur, this lot have really tried to mug me off. They've assaulted me, abused my civil rights, damaged me property, scattered half a ton of drugs from the police store all over me carpet. Even my MP is up in arms."

"Yes," Bondman nodded, running his fingers through what was left of his hair. "It's a terrible business. Tell me, Johnny, how many of your black clientele did they unlawfully stop outside the public house?"

"Oh, they really had it in for the black ones." Johnny winked. "Why, one of the lads, poor old Rhino, was called a black cunt and everything. Bastard cop sprayed CS gas right in his boat."

"Terrible business," Bondman said. "This is a very serious matter, I'd be surprised if heads don't roll. And clearly a considerable sum of compensation is in order." Maurice allowed himself a smile.

Johnny Too chucked his solicitor a wrap of cocaine and laughed. "I think the expression is trebles all round, my son."

DS Shaw and DCI Hitchcock arrived forty minutes early for the 11 am meeting in the conference room at New Scotland Yard, so they decided to grab a latte in one of the new, fashionable, little coffee houses in the Broadway underground station. It was just under four weeks since the disastrous raid on the Ned Kelly. Hitchcock opened a pack of brown sugar, poured it and began to stir his drink.

"I'll outline the project, Gary," he said. "You just come in at the appropriate time to fill in any gaps and answer questions."

"Sir."

Over the last month, Shaw had seen a stronger side to Hitchcock. He grudgingly admired the way the senior officer had batted off the local Labour MP and had managed to keep the positive aspects of policing Rotherhithe in the public eye. Hitchcock had also parried questions as to why the police hadn't tried to revoke the Ned Kelly's licence through the local magistrates court. "Better," he'd said, "to know exactly where Rommel and his Panzers are." Besides, he'd reasoned, pushing the Bakers over the border into another patch wouldn't have dealt with the problem, but merely edged it into darker shadows. Ah, the power of self-preservation.

The two men drank up and crossed the road to New Scotland Yard. Shaw pointed at the famous rotating sign on the pavement. "Did you ever see that sketch," he said. "I think it was on *Monty Python*. They had a pipe from that sign going underground and then up into the Commissioner's office where he was sitting at his desk pedalling away to keep it moving."

"That was coffee you were drinking, was it?"

Gary Shaw shrugged. He never felt quite at ease in the Big House. To him, it was the place senior officers went to hide from real police work ... the place where Inspectors who had screwed up on Division got promoted to become Chief Inspector of A3 paper, paper clips and staples, if only to hide the embarrassment. So why the fuck wasn't Hitchcock the Assistant Commissioner?

Once, he reflected, this building had been staffed with real coppers, real hard men. Now it was a job for academics educated to the point of stupidity. Gary Shaw detested the new Politically Correct officer caste. They couldn't catch a thief to save their arses, but somehow they emerged as the leaders of men. Well, men, women, homosexuals, bi-sexuals, tri-sexuals, transsexuals, transvestites, and every muddy shade of ethnic minority going. PC was a cancer which as far as Gary Shaw could see was eating the Force away from its insides. It had already taken the heart and was about to engulf the soul. Years ago there had been a bar called The Tank in this building. Now it was a fucking gym! Things can only get better all right. No more could hard-working officers discuss serious crime issues in their own time over a pint in the most private of private clubs. Far better, apparently, that they wandered 300 yards up the Broadway and confer in public bars ...

Hitchcock came to an abrupt stop. They were outside the conference room. Detective Chief Inspector Leonard Kent from the Covert Operations department was there to greet them. He was accompanied by DI Edward "Rottweiler" Richardson. Shaw's spirits lifted. He and Richardson had been regional officers together 15 years earlier. The guy was all policeman, 110 per cent on the square. Richardson had earned his nickname. He didn't know how to let go. Once he had his teeth into a case, he wasn't happy until both legs and an arm were off. Gary Shaw clasped the Rottweiler's hand with both of his. "Eddie, good to see ya." Perhaps this place wasn't entirely staffed with poncified fairies after all.

Detective Sgt Michael Boyce was already seated and waiting in the conference room. Nicknamed Bond, Boyce was from the Technical Support Unit and renowned for his espionage skills. It was said he could stick a miniature camera up a fly's arse and give you a better reception quality than Channel 5.

Everyone present was aware of the Bakers, but Hitchcock gave them a full run down of the major players. Johnny Baker got special attention. "He is one cocky little incubus, gentlemen," said Hitchcock gravely, "with aspirations to go big time." He produced surveillance pictures of Johnny dining at The Ivy with Geraldine and a couple of well-known, woolly-brained soap stars who enjoyed the company of villains. "Baker cannot be underestimated. Certainly he is a thug, but he is also intelligent. He has a bit of form for thieving and ABH but nothing recent. Behind his jolly hardcase act, Baker is a shrewd and cunning criminal entrepreneur. He has investment portfolios, legitimate business plans. If we don't capture him soon, Baker may become so far removed from crime as to be as untouchable as he already believes himself to be. He has two weaknesses, his arrogance and his brother." Hitchcock placed a picture of Joey on the table.

"Joey Baker is 100 per cent evil," he said. "You can't rehabilitate a scumbag like Joey any more than you could rehabilitate a cockroach. He has a record as long as your arm for violence and armed robbery. His preferred weapon is a Stanley knife. He jokes that he performed his own Caesarean with it. Joey never goes out without his "squirter", a nasal spray full of ammonia. He calls it Easy Stop."

Hitchcock reeled off a list of Joey's convictions and a further set of crimes with which he was suspected of being involved. He produced a picture of a man whose face appeared to be covered in miniature railway lines.

"David Long, a small-time con artist," Hitchcock said. "We know Joey Baker did this to him, but Long would never testify against him. These are his main accomplices." He removed pictures of Dougie The Dog and Rhino from his folder. "Douglas Richards is a violent psychopath, who has been heavily involved with football disturbances since his teens and was the brains behind the M25 raves. John Irvine, known as Rhino, is a more serious villain. He began life as a doorman and plays on his blackness. Irvine swallows a live goldfish every time he is about to go into battle. He says it gives him 'two souls' and the strength of ten men. He is reputed to have skinned a small-time Scouse villain called Terence Whicker alive. Whicker has indeed vanished but his body has never been recovered. Richards is married to a black girl, former pickpocket Antonia Hodge, whose brother Oggy is on the fringes of The Firm. Oggy connects the Bakers to the Brixton boys."

Hitchcock gave his assembled colleagues "the SP" on the rest of the hardcore Baker henchmen then opened the meeting for discussion. It was generally agreed it would take real cunning to put them away. Shaw couldn't help but be impressed by the level of questions put to him by DCI Kent. He wanted to know everything – what kind of people drank in the Ned Kelly, what were their ages, what cars did they drive, had any got legitimate jobs, did they have regular meeting places away from the pub, a café or a second-hand car plot? Was there anywhere that could be bugged where they think they are safe to talk? The only area skimmed over was details of police operations against the Baker firm to date. Every decent cop in London was fully aware of that particular catalogue of failure, involving the police and Customs & Excise.

The use of informants was kicked into touch when Kent revealed that two previous informant-led operations had been a disaster. One had resulted in the informant going "missing in action", the second had given Joey the opportunity to play Doctors and Nurses with a poor sod who thought he was helping the community by letting the local plod use his bedroom as an OP on Joey's front door. It had taken two weeks for all the body parts to wash up.

Gary Shaw appreciated Kent's energy and his thoroughness, but what next?

"So what direction do you see this going, guv?" he said.

Kent took a deep breath. "There is no question that the Bakers have got to go and a major operation has got to be mounted," he said. "I've been in touch with one of the National Crime Squad teams who have been working alongside the Church on this."

"Church?" said Hitchcock.

"Customs and Excise, C of E," Shaw explained.

"Sorry, Gordon," Kent said. "Bloody police speak. Work up here for five years and you don't even realise you're doing it."

"So how do you see this going forward, Len?" Hitchcock asked.

"Well, clearly you wouldn't have the back-up and resources to service a U/C officer," Kent replied. "And the commitment would have to be twenty-four hours a day. Then we have the problem of local officers knowing what's going on and, of course, that might compromise any covert operation. As I perceive it, any sting or long-term infiltration would have to be serviced by an operational team. I know the National Squad want another go and I think if we tie this in with what they've got going then we should get to a successful conclusion quicker."

Hitchcock looked surprised. "And us," he said. "Have we got any input?"

"Only from the intelligence-gathering side," Kent replied. "The National Crime Squad DI will keep you abreast of developments but not specifically of the details of the operation. Clearly, Gordon, your people will need to link in, but servicing any covert technical equipment and the U/C side of things are best left to them. If I've got your backing on it, Gordon, then I'll put it all into place."

"Yes, yes, of course," Hitchcock said. "DS Shaw can act as your point of contact for any running around."

Over the course of the next week, meetings took place with all interested players. The NCS and the Church sat at the same table and made some effort to try and be honest with each other over who knew what. Slowly, a plan came together that was simple, but clever. But it would need someone with balls to go in and shape it up. This was the hardest part – selecting the right U/C operative. Man or woman? Geordie, or carrot cruncher, or maybe some flash, good-looking, tough-talking Essex boy? Whatever, the infiltration would have to be done through someone the Bakers trusted. They needed a patsy, someone dumb enough to walk a cowboy into the teepee long enough to catch Johnny and Joey hands on and bring the entire Baker empire crashing down around their ears.

Gary Shaw was ordered to unearth Rotherhithe's answer to Homer Simpson, while the top brass decided on the right U/C man. When they did, he was briefed, a convincing background was agreed, and an almost water-tight history put in place.

CHAPTER FIVE

ONE MONKEY BASTARD

Outside the front door, a milk bottle rattled on the walkway. Harry Tyler shot out of bed like the five dog at Wimbledon, grabbed his Louisville Slugger baseball bat and erupted on to the third-floor landing looking as mean as any man in Kenneth Williams *Carry On* boxer shorts ever reasonably could. Half a minute later he was back in the flat.

"Did you get him?" said a voice from Harry's bed.

"No," Harry replied. "That's the third day that little Kosovan fucker has had my milk. Where's the Old Bill when you need 'em?"

"Yeah, you want the Filth wrapped round yer, 'Arry, don'tcha, with a front room full of moody trainers." The voice, lacerated by 16 years of dedicated 40-a-day trachea-trashing nicotine abuse, belonged to Elaine Geggus, Harry's new and currently nude next door neighbour on the run-down Turpin estate in Stratford, East London.

"They're no fucking use anyway," he replied.

"They'd hand him over to a social worker, who'd get a report from a shrink saying he had developed anti-social tendencies as a result of his traumatic child-hood, and the courts would give him a free holiday to fucking Barbados courtesy of me and you. Well, maybe not me and you but all the law-abiding, hard-working mugs who pay their taxes, when we all know he's a two-bob toe-rag who needs to learn you don't nick off yer own."

Harry paused for breath. "Why can't he get on the bus out to Epping and nick off the posh fuckers out there?"

Elaine sat up to light up her first fag of the morning. The duvet fell off her revealing a pair of heavy breasts adorned with stretch marks. Her nipples were huge and pierced, genuinely like the "blind cobbler's thumbs" to which stag comics always referred, Harry thought. She looked like a less stylish Annie Lennox … if you could imagine the sainted Eurythmics singer with "Satan's Slaves" tattooed on her biceps and a swallow in flight with a scroll bearing the name "Dougal" on her backside. Still, in a bad light, if you squinted …

Harry had moved in three weeks before and had taken four days to get ex-biker girl Elaine into his bed. Dougal, it turned out, was her deceased pit-bull. Elaine explained he had been her only true friend since her old man pissed off with her sister. Harry realised he was deep in Jerry Springer territory, hob-nobbing – make that hobgoblin knobbing – with the underclass and loving every minute. Once you got past her ingrained all-men-are-bastards defences,

Elaine was a good kid, with a decent sense of humour. She drank vodka and Red Bull, loved Iron Maiden as much as she did her three kids, and above all she really enjoyed shagging.

Harry stepped out of his boxers and got back into bed. Elaine stubbed her fag out and sunk under the duvet to nosh amicably on his morning glory. Her hand moved under the pillow and back again. Harry heard a buzz like a muffled road drill outside, then realised it was coming from down below. Elaine did love her toys and the thought that all biker girls love other girls – a lingering Mod prejudice – had never left his mind for a second ...

Two orgasms later Elaine lit up again.

"You want me to fix you some breakfast, babe?" she asked.

"No," replied Harry, ever the gentleman. "You fuck off next door and get them kids ready to bunk off school."

He pulled £20 from a wad of notes on the bedside cabinet and laid it between her breasts. "Sort yerself out some puff and get the clan some Teletubby-flavoured pop tarts or whatever kids eat these days. I'll get something out."

Elaine kissed him. "You're a lovely man, H."

"Tell me something I don't know."

She pulled on a tight black jumper, black mini-skirt and black sandals, put the kettle on for him and left. It was 7.57 am.

Thanks to Elaine, half of Clegg House believed Harry Tyler was making a reasonable living as a third-division tealeaf. Everything about his flat, the vast array of door locks, the alarm, the DVD player, said he was a small-time villain who'd had a few nice touches. The sparse furnishings confirmed his divorcee cover story. He never worked regular hours but always told her he had "things to do, people to see". It was particularly true today. Today he was making First Contact.

Shortly after noon, Harry Tyler sauntered into the Sir Sidney Smith, one of three South London pubs owned by the Bakers. It was just off the Old Kent Road, a ten-minute stroll away from the New Den, or one minute fifty seconds in a squad car. Combat-ready, Harry had the *Sporting Life* in his hand, his mobile and £350 in cash in his pockets.

Propped up against the bar was ex-face Peter Miller, 56 years old and a confirmed lush. If you wanted moody tenners or a snide tax disc for the motor, Miller could always supply, for the customary drink on top, of course. His breath could sterilise scalpels but Miller was still trusted by the Baker firm. For all his faults, Miller had never grassed. He'd never dealt with the Filth, except once when he'd sent a probationer PC two miles out of his way to the local nick – a story he's only told twice. This week. If he was caught holding, he took the rap, did his bird, came out and cracked on. He was your authentic South London good old boy, a likeable prat.

For Harry, hooking Miller was about as hard as signing a TV contract is for Carol Vorderman. He was over his shoulder as soon as Harry sat beside him studying form. A bit of chat about the nags and football, buy him a drink, let him see the wad, refuse to let him buy you one back, well, you had a nice win at the weekend … within half an hour, Miller was putty in his hands. Harry had four Buds and bowed out. He could find his prey any time he wanted and now they were mates for as long as he needed him.

Harry was back in the Sid three days out of the next four, claiming to have business in the area. By the end of the week, Miller wanted to super-glue himself to his generous new pal. The guy was skint – "borracic, H, some cunt knocked me" – so Harry offered him a "bulls-eye" to come and watch over him during a trade in his Stratford local. He jumped at the chance. The next day, Miller sat in the Trojan watching Harry do a deal at an adjoining table over a copy of the *Daily Sport*. The deal done, Miller followed the three black men out of the pub, watched them climb into a BMW and glide away. He wrote the car's plate number down on his comic and went back in to collect his £50.

The first seeds of doubt appeared in Miller's mind about ten minutes into the journey home. "If that's your local, H, why get me involved?" he said. "Why not one of yer mates?"

"The spades are all local too," Harry explained. "I needed someone they didn't know to clock the car."

Reassured, Miller heard a business opportunity knocking. "Do you want the number checked?"

"Yeah. Know someone?"

"Possible. What's it worth?"

"A drink."

"A nice drink?"

"For the right info."

"I'll ask."

"Whatever. I think they're OK, but first-time trade, you know."

"Big parcel?"

"Don't be so fucking nosey."

"No, no. It's just I know people who'll take a lorry-load of whatever."

"I'll bear that in mind. It was red wine by the way."

"I could get that shifted."

Harry looked over at him and appeared pensive. "Tell you what," he said eventually. "How good are them snide cockles and scores you said are about?"

"Yeah, OK. They pass in a busy boozer when the barmaid's hands are a bit wet, but I've had better."

"Sort me out half a dozen of each and I'll see how they move down this end."

"No problem, Harry."

Over the next few days, Peter Miller became a regular at the Trojan. He soon realised that Harry was a respected local face. He clocked all the hounds in the boozer pull Harry into corners to discuss deals. He saw how the barmaids flirted with him. He watched how popular he was with the regulars. He lost count of the number of times he left the pub muttering into his mobile. The black economy of London E15 appeared to rely on Harry Tyler waking up in the morning.

On day five, Miller was trusted with the biggest secret of all. He was allowed in to Harry's flat where

Elaine made him pie and chips. Peter Miller felt honoured. This he knew was a friendship that would last for ever.

Johnny Baker's fuck-off Mercedes was winding its way over Tower Bridge when he took a call from Geraldine. She was so upset she could hardly speak. Thirteen minutes later he met her in The Soho House. Her face was flushed, her eyes swollen from crying. Gently Johnny coaxed the story out of her. Between sobs, she told him how her ex-lover Golding had called her into his office and closed the door behind them. He'd been drinking. He'd grabbed at her breasts and forced his tongue down her throat. When she pushed him away her ex lost it. He'd slapped her face, called her a slut and a prick teaser and told her he was going to have her sacked. Johnny Too never heard the rest of what she'd said. The red mist had already descended.

It was 8.30 pm when the Merc glided past Golding's splendid detached home in Finchley, North London. Geraldine pointed the house out. There was a W-reg Lexus on the drive, next to a series eight BMW. Johnny got out of the car.

"Be careful," Geraldine said. Then wondered why. She wasn't concerned with Johnny's physical well-being, Golding was a tub of lard who got breathless popping the cork out of a bottle of Dom Perignon. But what had she started? Somehow she didn't think Baker would be telling Golding he'd been a naughty boy, but having lit the blue touch-paper now all she could do was sit back and wait for the firework display.

Johnny Too told his driver, Tony Boniface, to pull across the drive. Geraldine had the front door in full view through the blacked-out back windows.

Johnny walked up the drive and rang the bell. As Golding answered the door, a waft of soothing mid-brow classical music filled the air.

Golding studied the man before him suspiciously. He was well-dressed, but looked brutal. "Yes?" he said.

Johnny half-smiled. "What music is that?" he asked.

"I'm sorry?"

"What music are you playing? Who's it by?"

"What the hell has that got to do with you? Who are you and why are you disturbing our supper? What the hell do you want?"

Johnny Too grabbed Golding's tie and dragged him out of the front door, nutting him square in the face. Golding's broken nose went East and West as the claret gushed. Now Johnny was shouting. "I said what fucking music is that, you snivelling cunt?" Golding clutched his nose and shook like a shell-shocked war casualty.

"It's called 'Montagues And Capulets'," he stuttered. "It's by Prokofiev. P-p-please don't hurt me. Do you want money? Let me get my wallet. Just d-d-don't hurt me."

By Johnny Baker standards, Golding wasn't hurt. By the standards of reasonable men, he was battered to a pulp. When Johnny Too finally left him unconscious on the tarmac drive, a bloody mass of blubber, he looked like a whale that had been dropped 100 feet, face down on to jagged rocks. Johnny Too smirked. "Fucking nice music, geezer," he said. He strolled back towards the car. Geraldine saw him remove a hefty knuckle-duster from the fingers of his right hand. She felt strange. Half of her was horrified by the terrible violence she had just witnessed, but the other half was strangely excited, and just a little turned on. Confused she started to sob. Johnny opened the car door and his expression changed from psychopathic to concerned lover.

"Don't cry, baby," he whispered, holding her tight. "Don't cry. He won't ever hurt you again."

"But my job," she said.

"You just quit, darling. You work for me now. You are officially Johnny Baker's PA."

"Oh, Johnny," she said, kissing him. "I love you so much."

Johnny Too smiled. Then looked down at his suit trousers and scowled. "Who told that cunt he could bleed on my strides?" he said.

He had Boniface drop them off at the Tower Hotel where Johnny helped Geraldine get over the trauma of the day by introducing her to the delights of sucking cocaine off his cock in between giving her one in as many positions as he could manage.

The following lunchtime, Harry Tyler stood alone in the surprisingly busy Ned Kelly while Peter Miller did the rounds of his mates. It was the first time he had brought Harry here and now Miller was making like a bumble bee, buzzing from flower to flower telling everyone about his new pal. Harry was trying to study Templegate, but kept getting distracted by the vision of peroxide perfection that was Lesley Gore, rushed off her feet and cursing Slobberin' Ron for taking half an hour in the khazi. Harry rang Directory Enquiries, got the number for the Ned and rang it.

"Yeah, Ned Kelly," a harassed Lesley answered.

"Can you hear me, luv?" said Harry.

"Just about, it's chaos in 'ere. 'Oo is it?"

"One of your customers, turn left and I'm the one waving."

"Why are you ringing?" said Lesley turning.

"I was just worried I was in a no-service area ..."

"You cheeky sod ... what can I get you?"

"Aroused, I reckon, but I'll settle for a Bud."

Lesley hung up and took him a cold bottle from the back of the fridge.

"And one for you?"

"I'll have a gin and slim with you, please, darling. Thanks."

As soon as Harry took out a note, Peter Miller was by his side.

"And the usual for Pete, please."

Lesley pulled him a pint of Murphy's, gave Harry his change and was off serving on the other side of the bar, giving the handsome stranger a discreet glance. There was something about him she liked, the twinkle in his eye, the rough diamond patter, the whiff of decent after-shave.

Harry downed his Bud and told Miller he had to leave.

"But you've only just got 'ere," Peter protested.

"Business calls, Pete. Deals to do over my side. Laters, mate."

"Yeah, laters."

As Harry left, Lesley Gore gave Peter a pull. "Who was that guy?" she asked.

"'Arry?" said Peter. "Don't worry about him, luv. He's as sound as a pound."

"Yeah?" replied Lesley. "Nice arse, too."

Harry Tyler drove his latest toy, an S-reg Golf, through the Rotherhithe tunnel, turning left towards Wapping. He pulled up at the first phone box and made his call.

"Hello, boss, it's H."

On the other end of the line Detective Chief Inspector Lenny Kent brusquely said, "About time," then joked, "Spent all the Commissioner's money yet?"

"Only the bits that fold. Listen, guv, I'm in. I've just left Miller in the Ned doing my references for me. He told me he'll be picking up the moody scores and tenners tomorrow."

"Good work. The operational team want a meet tonight. I'll get a DI to ring you in the next hour on your mobile. I want all deals on tape and as much smudged up as possible. Where are you now?"

"Limehouse."

"Can you make your way over to Brentwood for the meet?"

"Yes, guv. I'll be an hour, hour and a half."

The meeting went ahead and the Bushwhacker was game on. From now on, all of his moves, all of his deals and all of his new chums would be filmed by DCI Susan Long's team. DI Ryan Suckling would be his night and day contact and DCI Lenny Kent would sign the expenses. A new plague was about to descend on South East London, a plague called Justice. Only the righteous need have no fear.

Over the next seven days, with Peter Miller's unwitting help, every lowlife in SE1 was doing business deals in Harry's car, or in Harry's box van, or in a bugged-up room (but never at Harry's flat). Concealed cameras whirled silently, tapes turned. Every snide note, every knocked-off computer and every ounce of stolen Tom was recorded while the back-up team "housed" every thief and made due note of the future exhibits. Each day brought Harry an inch closer to the Bakers.

Gary McCourt, a long-standing friend of Miller's, had put several small amounts of counterfeit currency in Harry's direction, and was now so confident of his contact that he, along with Miller, was even offering up small parcels of fake designer clothes and moody notes to punters in the Trojan.

Harry had to give them a pull. "Knock it on the head, lads," he'd warned. "Christ! You're treading on serious toes over here."

Miller was contrite. "Sorry, H," he'd said almost tearfully, although that might have been the gin. He'd shaken Harry's hand and hugged him. "Here's my 'and, here's my heart," he said. "It won't happen again, mate. My life."

That night Harry made contact with DI Suckling who told him that the Church – the Customs & Excise – had seized a substantial quantity of wines and spirits from a Brummie blade-runner. The lorry driver had been captured with 20 foot of tax-avoided booze, when his ticket said "office equipment".

"This could be the bait you need to raise the stakes," Suckling observed.

"Isn't it just," Harry replied. "This is too big for Miller and McCourt."

"So approach Johnny Baker."

"Not yet, Ryan. Let the mountain come to Mohammad. I'll dangle the hooch under Slobberin' Ron's greedy schnozz."

"You know what you're doing."

"Too right I do."

It was late Thursday morning at the Ned Kelly, just ahead of the rush. Harry Tyler perched himself on a stool near where Lesley Gore was serving, and flashed her a smile. "When you're ready, luv," he said.

She smiled back. "Be right with you, handsome."

Doreen the cleaner was just leaving. "'Ere," she said. "Did you see that *Big Bruvva* last night?"

"I would rather poke me eye out with a lit fag," Slobberin' Ron sneered.

"No, it's brilliant," said Lesley. "They've gotta chuck that Nasty Nick out soon."

"Why do you want him out?" asked Harry.

"Cos he's one devious shit," Lesley replied.

"But ain't that why it's good telly?" said Harry. "I mean, I've only caught it once or twice, and to be honest I couldn't give a shit if I never saw it again. But if you throw out all the bastards and eccentrics what are you going to be left with? It's a soap, and soaps need villains."

"Yeah, I s'pose …"

"I like that Caroline," said Doreen.

"No!" exclaimed Lesley.

"What old Medusa chops?" said Ron. "Leave it out, Dor."

"I feel sorry for her," Doreen said defensively. "She said she needed to be 'eld last night."

Slobberin' Ron laughed. "I'd hold her all right, under bath water for about three hours."

"You're a pig, Ron Sullivan," said Doreen, walking out.

Harry grinned. "Pork scratching, Ron?"

Slobberin' Ron furrowed his brow. "Wouldn't that be cannibalism?"

The two men laughed.

"You're wicked to her, Ron."

"Never mind," he replied. "Worse things happen at sea."

Harry leaned over the bar and gripped Ron's forearm. "Listen, Ron," he said. "Can I have a quick word while it's quiet?"

Lesley moved down the bar.

"Fire away, son," said Ron.

"You be interested in a case of Johnny Walker at three sovs a bottle?"

Ron looked at him blankly.

"Pukka Johnny Walker," Harry went on. "The real deal, nothing snide … I can get me hands on plenty."

"Whoa!" said Ron. "You're knocking on an open door, H. How much you got?"

"Lorry-load."

"Three quid a bottle? That's a done deal, my son."

"Nice one."

"How soon can you deliver?"

"Three hours?"

"The money will be waiting. We'll break one open to taste?"

"Goes without saying."

The two men shook.

"Oi, Les," Harry shouted. "I'm holding folding. Fancy helping me celebrate tonight?"

"What have you got in mind?"

"Knife and fork, somewhere nice?"

"OK, as long as it's not an Indian."

"Would I insult my favourite girl by taking her to the local curry khazi? I was thinking of this Chinese I know, off the manor."

"I can be ready by eight."

"Make it 'alf seven and I'll throw in a bottle of Asti."

"You know how to spoil a girl."

"As it happens, darling, I do."

Harry winked and left. Slobberin' Ron watched him go and said, "That is one diamond geezer."

"Yeah," said Lesley. "But I ain't gonna sleep with him tonight."

"Course you ain't."

Home for Johnny Too was a three-bedroom detached Victorian house in Bermondsey. He'd got up late and stuck on a *Sopranos* video while Sandra rustled him up an HP The Full Monty tinned meal on three toast.

She brought it in to him on a tray with a mug of sweet tea. Johnny was going through the morning post. He was pouring over a letter from an estate agent as she came in.

"Look at this place, Sands," Johnny said excitedly. "Electric gates, swimming pool, a jacuzzi, two acres of grounds, a sauna, a five-a-side fuckin' football pitch. It's a gaff of a gaff."

"Where's that?"

"Chislehurst, just past the Bull."

"I've told you, Johnny Baker, I am not moving to Chislehurst."

"But look at this place, treacle. It's a dream house."

"But it's not local, John."

"It's half an hour away."

"More like an hour and a half in the rush hour."

"Come on, doll. People like us deserve somewhere decent. Nice people live out there, bank managers, businessmen. What has Bermondsey and Rotherhithe got that Chislehurst hasn't? 'Cept for a dawn chorus of fuckin' car alarms going off."

"It's got my friends, it's got my mum."

"'It's got my mum'," he mimicked. "This place has got a granny annex, we can take the old cunt with us."

"Don't you talk about my mother like that. I am not moving to fucking Kent."

"Well, fuck you, Sandra. Fuck you fucking sideways."

He flung the tray up in the air. The tea went over the floor, the Full Monty splattered the settee.

"Johnny!"

"Fuck you."

He stormed upstairs and got dressed.

"Where you going?"

"Out."

"Where?"

"Business."

"You said you were spending the day with me and the kids."

"Yeah, well maybe there ain't nothing here I want to spend time with, all right?"

"JOHNNY!"

The front door slammed. Right on cue, the kids started to scream.

An hour and a half later, Johnny Too was studying the property details again, although now he was flat on his back in Geraldine's bed with her at his side basking in a post-coital glow.

"That is a lovely house, John," she said.

"Isn't it just?"

"Can you afford it?"

"Don't insult me, darling. I've just put an offer in. One and a half mill."

Geraldine smiled. "A bloke like you should have a place that reflects how well he's done for himself."

"That's exactly right."

"I mean, you've made a success of yourself. Why not enjoy the proceeds? I'm not saying there's anything wrong with the people you grew up with, but you must feel sometimes they're holding you back."

"I'll say."

She kissed him lightly on the forehead. "You're a working-class hero, Johnny."

"Working is stronging it a bit, darlin'."

"You know what I mean." She reached down and grabbed his cock. "How's Mr Happy?"

"Oh," he said, pushing her on her back. "He's perking up."

Harry Tyler and Lesley Gore had just finished their meal at Good Friends Chinese restaurant in Sidcup, Kent.

"You want blandy, Harry?" asked Tin the manager.

"Just a small one, Tinny. What do you want, Les?"

"Can I have an Irish coffee?"

"Yes, one Ilish coffee." Tin barked out an order in Cantonese. "Mind if I join you?"

"Normally I would love your company, Tinny," said Harry. "But I'm doing a bit of business tonight." He winked broadly and held Lesley's hand.

"No worries," said Tin, giggling. "You need to talk about oil ligs, I know."

"Harry," said Lesley. "You should have let him sit down, he's just bought us a drink."

"Oh, he's all right. Tin knows the score. We go back a long way."

"What was all that about oil rigs?"

"It's what he thinks I do."

"You piss-taker."

"Did I tell you his full name is Tin Hung?" he asked. "I know his brother Well."

Harry paused for the joke to sink in. Lesley laughed and whacked his shoulder.

"You," she said. "I like it 'ere. Good value, innit? All you can eat for £13.95."

Harry lent forward and whispered in her ear, "Well I hope you've left your knickers off cos I'm Hank Marvin."

Lesley nearly choked on her wine. "You cheeky fucker," she said.

"Yeah, but you like me don'tcha?"

Lesley smiled and said nothing. She'd had a great evening. He was so different from the normal blokes she went out with. He made her laugh and treated her with something close to respect. Harry Tyler liked her, too, because she had a sense of humour and laughed at his jokes. Harry had lavished all his charm on her, partly because having a girlfriend in the Ned Kelly gave him a reason to be so far off his manor so often, and partly because he was a dirty bastard who loved shagging. Lesley on the other hand was flattered by his attention, impressed by his car and his cavalier approach to spending. He didn't know or seem to care about her history and always had a nice few quid about him. It was inevitable that they would end up in bed together that night.

It was only after they had made love, in the missionary position, on her settee that Harry even gave a thought to Kara and Courtney-Rose. He didn't feel guilty but it did cross his mind that he should put a call in. The idea didn't linger long. His wife understood, she always did. Kara knew that when he was deep undercover that was when it was her duty not to worry, or care, pester him with the problems of bringing up a kid and running a home. The money was always in the joint account, calls came regularly from an unknown DI reassuring her that "Harry is fine, he sends his love, he'll ring when it's safe …"

He wondered whether Kara suspected that when he was deep undercover he was also deep under Lesley's or Elaine's or Marina's covers. And if she did, did she care? Did she deserve to be cheated on like this? The truth was no-one deserved it.

"Penny for 'em," said Lesley.

"Sorry, doll, I was miles away."

"Want to come to bed?"

"I would like that very much."

They lay together naked, squashed together in her single bed. Harry massaged her lower back tenderly. They kissed, then touched, stroked and licked. Harry moved to mount her. She stopped him. "Not like that again," said Lesley. "That's boring. Take me from behind this time."

"Oh, OK," said Harry, slightly surprised.

They made love four more times that night in as many positions.

It was 10.30 am when Harry got back to his own flat. Cocksure, and cock sore, he was feeling pleased with himself as he slipped the key into the lock, only to hear a husky woman's voice say, "Hello, stranger!" with just a soupçon of suspicion. Uhoh, thought Harry. 'Er next door.

"I waited up for you," said Elaine. "I thought you were coming home last night."

"Oh, sorry, doll, had a bit of business then I got webbed up in a poker game. You know how it is."

"As long as you've not got yourself another woman, cos this pussy needs feeding."

"Don't be daft. How could I sleep with anyone else after you? I'm not sixteen any more."

"Good, cos pussy is hungry, and I mean she's starving."

Elaine walked from her front door to his. She was wearing a dressing gown that she let slip open. She had nothing on underneath. Pushing Harry through his front door, Elaine kissed his neck and rubbed his cock. Somehow it responded.

Here we go again, thought Harry, when his mobile rang. Peter Miller's number flashed.

"Yo, Pete."

"All right, H, just giving you a quick ring to see if you remembered about the lunchtime strippers down the Ned today? They got three brand new girls."

"You're joking. Is he hurt bad?"

"Eh?"

"Don't worry about it, I'll be right there."

Harry hung up and looked grimly at Elaine.

"Sorry, darling, My mate's in a spot of bother."

"Can't it wait?"

"No, this is serious ag. I've gotta fly. Make it up to you tonight?"

"You better."

He kissed her, and squeezed her right breast. "You know I will." Harry flicked her piercing.

"I got clamped in Soho yesterday," he said.

"Did yer?"

"Yeah, thirty-five quid a nipple."

"You daft sod."

Harry grinned and walked back down to his car.

Harry Tyler could hardly make himself heard above the throng. He had never seen the Ned Kelly so packed. The UB40 boys were in spending a week's thieving money and talking about how Millwall would "defn'ly" reach the play-offs this year, and how in four years they'd be in the Champions' League, and how Charlton were sure to be relegated again, just like last time. Harry managed to wave to Lesley as he finally reached Peter Miller at the bar. Unusually, Miller insisted on getting a round in from a cheerful black barmaid called Sonia.

"What was all that about?" Pete asked.

"What?"

"On the phone."

"Oh, that ..." Harry tapped his nose. "Woman trouble."

"Not ..." Pete nodded in Lesley's direction.

"Nah, the other one, but keep it schtum."

Pete gave him a one-of-the-boys slap. "You dirty dog."

Harry noticed Miller's eyes were unusually bleary. "You all right, Pete? You look like you just tried to take yer contact lenses out ten minutes after you already had done."

"No, just had a late one playing cards. I'm well flush."

Harry looked around discreetly. The queue to the Taylor brothers' travelling pharmacy counter was as long as the line in the bogs snorting their wares. Over in the corner, the Baker boys were ruling the roost. They had a little firm of "real people" wrapped round them. Heavy-looking fuckers.

"So what's the coup?" Harry asked eventually.

"I told you, three new birds, all highly recommended," Peter shouted. "Wanna get nearer the action?"

Harry nodded and Miller led him towards the small stage. As they moved, Harry noticed four faces roll in, well dressed and well happy. They looked like they'd had a touch, a big touch. They made straight for the Bakers. Pyro Joey was off his stool first, throwing open his huge bear arms to greet them. Big smiles, big hugs. Now Johnny Too was on his feet, shaking hands and laughing. Harry hoped the covert camera outside was getting all this. It was like roll-call day for villains.

The doors flew open again and in strolled Stevie Adams and his five brothers. These were a South London family, no relation to the North London crime clan.

"Steve Adams," Miller whispered hoarsely. "Brother Derek got out the boob this morning. This is gonna be one fuck of a Friday."

The middle brother, Peter, went straight over to Greg Saunders and put down two £50 notes for two grams of Charlie. The atmosphere in the pub was more like a Saturday night in Ibiza than a lunchtime in South London. DJ Sal cranked up the music. His name was Salih, but everyone called him Sal or Sally. As he was a raving iron, Sally suited him best. He was deep in conversation with Steve Baker. "Those two boys must really love this drum and bass shit," observed Peter.

Harry noted the obsessive way Steve was tidying his hair in the wall mirror. Uncle Joey had "sorted" his £30 hairstyle by way of a friendly greeting and he didn't look too happy about it.

A big lump in a dinner jacket walked on to the stage and motioned for Sal to turn down the music so he could introduce the girls.

"Look," shouted Gary McCourt. "They've sent their cunt out first."

The big man flushed, but didn't answer back. He knew where he was.

"Can you hear me at the back?" he said hesitantly.

"Yes," shouted Johnny Too. "But I don't mind changing places with someone who can't."

The whole bar roared at that one, even the wannabe compere. A standard heckler-squashing one-liner shot through his mind, but he decided against using it. These blokes wouldn't be up for a battle of wits. Say the wrong thing and they'd just stab you.

"Thank you, gentlemen," he said, finally. "Let's hear it for the ladies."

All three women came out of the small dressing room and on to the stage. Their routine was to dance one number together, clothed, and then take turns for the serious stripping. Whoever wasn't performing would go through the crowd with a pint pot collecting notes and coins. If the audience were generous and there was no sniff of a police presence, they would usually pick a man out, lead him on stage, undress him and felate him. For exceptionally good audiences they would close the show with a three-way mutual masturbation play let, using mini vibrators and girl-on-girl urination. Today would go down in Ned Kelly folklore as Pissing Sister Friday.

As the first stripper, Antonella, got to work, the second, a black beauty from Ghana who called herself Princess Monique, was working her way round the crowd with her pint pot. Most of the punters seemed to be slipping in 30p and some lip, but over by the Bakers notes were already coming out.

Dougie The Dog was in his element. Chomping on a meat pie, he slung 50p in Monique's pot and leered, "I'll make it a quid when I've seen your gash, bet you've got a cunning stunt to show us." The words came out with tasteful pieces of half-eaten pie. Somehow Monique kept her smile in place and moved on.

Antonella performed mechanically. She looked like she was daydreaming about doing her ironing, thought Harry. As she finished, Sally was on the mike asking for a big round of applause for "AN-TON-E-LLA". The crowd erupted. The stripper smiled for the first time that day. Dougie stood forward and shouted "Who hit you between the legs with an axe?"

When she glared at him, he said, "Nah, you're all right, luv. You don't sweat much for a pig." Then Doug collapsed in hysterics.

Dark-haired Miranda followed Antonella on to the stage. Dancing to Shabba's "Mr Loverman", she performed a neat, sexually charged routine which culminated with her lying on her back with her legs akimbo, her panties stretched between her two big toes until disaster struck, the elastic went and the pink lace pants shot through the air and landed in Peter Miller's face. Miller, who had moved as close to the real faces as he could, picked them up off the floor and sniffed them to huge cheers all round. "Take 'em home and have a shuffle with 'em," shouted Gary McCourt. But Dougie The Dog had other ideas. He grabbed them to wear over his head, then noticed the small skid-mark at the rear. "Fucking hell," said Dougie. "She's shit herself. She must have heard about the size of my dick."

This had Johnny Too, Pyro Joe and their company crying into their beer. Dougie took a sniff, pulled a face and threw them back on to the stage. Unperturbed, Miranda slipped them back on and came out with her jug. Harry Tyler immediately shot off towards the gents.

"Don't worry, you tight sod," shouted Johnny Too. "We'll put in for you."

As Miranda reached the Bakers, she held out her pint glass and smiled. With precision timing, Harry appeared alongside her and said, "Here y'go, darling, something for yer pot." He reached into his jacket and produced a toilet roll which he squeezed up and wedged in the glass. The Baker clan erupted, Derek Adams looked like he was going to piss himself with laughter. Even Miranda smiled. The only person who didn't look impressed was Dougie The Dog.

Harry walked back over to Peter Miller who gave him a round of applause. The lovely Princess Monique was dancing now, and Antonella was doing the rounds with her jug. "I'll give you a miss," she said to Harry. "I only use Charmin Ultra." And everyone laughed again.

Monique leapt off the stage topless and strolled through the crowd with a predatory look, searching for someone to join her on stage. These Millwall boys would have taken on the Turkish army after three pints, but the sight of one little stripper clutching a bottle of baby oil had turned the Lions into mice. They didn't know Johnny Too had already "wedged her on" – he'd paid her to seek out Derek Adams, straight from prison, who hadn't had a shag for six months.

The crowd loved it. Derek's strides were already round his ankles as all three girls grabbed at his genitals. Within minutes his oily white body was horizontal on stage as all three women straddled him. He must have stayed erect for all of 33 seconds.

By the end of the afternoon, Miller had invited

Harry on to the periphery of the Baker crowd. Easy does it, Harry thought. Nice and slow.

Pyro Joey was on explosive form. "Oi, Gal," he shouted to Gary McCourt. "Is that right you tipped the black tart a snide score for a gobble."

"No, Joe, no," McCourt replied. "It was two snide tenners."

The men boozed and bantered for an hour or two more, then there was talk of going "up West", maybe to the Met bar. Harry, who had been drinking quietly, told Miller he was off home, but as he drained his pint Johnny Too gave him a tug.

"Where you from, Harry?"

"Other side, mate. Stratford."

"Who are the faces down there?"

"Who I know?" Harry replied cautiously. "Dave Turner, Vinnie Riordan, Micky Shaw, Ozzer O."

"How's Ozzer?"

"Banged up. He caught two with Eric Randall. You know 'em?"

"Yeah, course I do. That Turner's a cunt."

"I only know him through business."

"Beer?"

"No, ta, I'm making a bid. That Princess Monique put me bang in the mood for a bunk-up."

"All right, mate. Laters."

"Cheers."

"Oh, and Harry."

"Yeah?"

"Nice move with the bog roll."

Harry winked and made his way to the bar. Dougie The Dog watched him call Lesley over, say his goodbyes and kiss her cheek. Then he saw him catch Peter Miller's eye and nod towards the door.

Outside the pub, Miller looked worried. "I saw Johnny had a word. You OK?"

"Yeah. Is he on my case or something?"

"Nah, you know how it is, just being cautious. Slobberin' Ron told him he got the Scotch from you and he was asking who you were. I got a pull last night."

"So why didn't you mark my fucking card, then?"

"Calm down, H. No worries. Johnny likes a percentage of everything. He asked about you cos he can see pound notes around you, y'know the way psychics can see auras. You're ducking and diving. You're one of us ..."

Miller's voice trailed off as Dougie The Dog emerged from the pub and stood alongside them.

Peter nodded at him and finished his sentence. "Johnny said he liked the cut of yer jib."

"Yeah?" said Dougie with a snarl. "Well, I don't know who the fuck you are."

"He's all right, Doug," protested Miller. "He's with me."

"I was talking to the organ grinder, not the fucking monkey," snapped Doug. "Who are yer, Harry?"

"Nobody special," Harry said calmly. "I'm just a trader."

"Yeah, well, what are you doing sniffing round Lesley? Are you aboard it?"

"Leave her out of this," replied Harry. There was

iron in his voice now. Gary McCourt, who had followed them out, went back into the pub.

"Or what, ya mug?" said Doug. His hand moved to his right trouser pocket, producing something. What? Harry saw the flash of a switch-blade. Here we go, he thought.

Gary McCourt burst back through the doors with Slobberin' Ron.

"What's goin'on?" said Ron.

"I just don't know who this fuckin' geezer is," retorted Dougie.

"He's as good as gold," said Ron, positioning himself between the Dog and Tyler.

"Who's referencing him besides pisspot Pete?"

"I am," answered Ron. "He's a friend of *ours*." He emphasised the last word deliberately.

"And I am," said McCourt.

"And by the looks of things this afternoon so is your Uncle Johnny," Miller added.

"Yeah, well," said Doug. "We'll see."

And he backed into the pub, jabbed the air with his finger as he pointed at Harry Tyler sing-shouting, "Who are ya? Who are ya? Who are ya?"

Harry shook his head. "Thanks, guys," he said. "Is he always like that?"

"It's just the Charlie talking," said McCourt.

"Take no fucking notice," Slobberin' Ron chimed in. "That is one monkey bastard. And the tragedy is, Johnny Too don't know it."

CHAPTER SIX

THREE MONKEY
BASTARDS

Steven Richards looked out of the window of his flat on the fourth floor of the Oxo building, admiring the feisty grey splendour of the Thames in the hot August sun. A gaff this splendid ought to cost a grand a month, but Steven paid just under a fifth of that because this luxury apartment belonged to the council. Amazing what strings you could pull when your uncle was Johnny Too.

Steven watched the office muppets steaming over Blackfriar's Bridge like worker ants and shook his head. Mugs. He was never going to work for anyone but himself. What was it Paul Weller had sung? No corporations for the new wave sons .... He heard footsteps behind him and felt arms circle his belly and squeeze before the hands dropped down and grabbed at his groin, gently squeezing the tip of his cock until it started to harden.

"How's yer head?" Sally asked. Steven turned around and kissed him. "How about giving us some?" he smiled. They'd been in Leicester Square last night for the premier of *Snatch* and as Sally dropped to his knees and took Steven's cock in his mouth it was Brad Pitt they were both dreaming of. Steven took less than a minute to come.

"You going to return the favour?" Sally asked.

"I'll have to owe you one," Steven replied. "I'm seeing Johnny this morning for breakfast, remember. And I'm late, darling."

"Can I come along?"

"Don't be daft, Sal. Besides, you'd hate it. You know Johnny, he was born with a greasy spoon in his mouth. It'll be fry-ups all round, not a croissant in sight."

Steven often wondered how Johnny Too would take the revelation of his sexuality. Pyro Joe and the boys would ostracise him, he was sure, but not Johnny. Steven was convinced his bright, cunning uncle would be able to cope with a homosexual nephew. He'd probably use him to get into the gay porn market.

By sheer coincidence, Johnny was discussing celebrity "bandits" with Marco the chef as Steven arrived ten minutes later in Mario's, an Italian café just round the corner from Waterloo station.

"Ah, Steve, just the boy," Johnny said. "Marco here tells me he was reading an article that said that Jeremy Spake cunt was married. I had him down as a shirtlifter, what do you reckon?"

"I wouldn't know, John. He's camp but who in their right mind would fancy that, man or woman?"

"What about Dale Winton?"

"Gay!" shouted Marco. "Gay as a French horn."

Steven smiled. "I honestly don't know," he said. "Maybe he helps 'em out when they're busy."

Johnny laughed. "I don't mind 'em," he said. "Proper poofs are all right. That Lily Savage is a funny fucker. It's cunts like Peter Tatchell I can't stand."

"I make you right, Unk," said Steven.

Johnny caught his eye and winked. Does he know? Steven thought. Should I let on? No, sod it, change the subject.

"Any chance of a boiled egg, Marco?"

"Sure, boy. You want soldiers to dip?"

"And there we are back with Dale Winton," Steven replied.

All three men laughed. Johnny Too drained his cuppa. "So what was *Snatch* like?" he asked.

"Great direction," Steven said.

"But?"

"Cardboard characters, lightweight plot, and Brad Pitt's Oi-rish accent is a joke. But it was fun, y'know?"

"So not exactly *Goodfellas*?"

"Not in the same ballpark. Not even close."

"And Mike Reid, what's he like in it?"

"Like Frank Butcher with added swearing. I kept expecting to see Peggy snapping at his ankles."

Johnny laughed. "Will you fuckin' turn it in," he said, in a reasonable Reid rasp. "I bet his ears look a fucking treat on the big screen, the fucking size of 'em on telly."

"They was like satellite dishes," Steven affirmed.

—

"Yeah? It's a wonder he never got done for receiving then. Have you seen how thick they are? You know when you're a kid and yer mum says 'Keep playing up and I'll give you a thick ear'? he must have been a proper little fucker to end up with lugs like that."

Both men laughed. Steven liked being around Johnny Too. He was class. Steven wouldn't have a word said against Joey by anyone, but he could never relax with his brutish uncle the way he could with Johnny. It was all down to brains at the end of the day. Joey was staunch but thick as shit. John was sussed and sorted, real street smart. He was asking Steven about cybercrime and e-commerce as early as 1997. Granted the Bakers had never seriously progressed the idea – a bit of dope from the Dam and the legit e-florists was as far as they'd gone. But the fact that Johnny was on to the Net so early had impressed Steven. Now he had to convince Johnny to give him a bit of seed money to play around with on his latest project, a gruesome video game called Mobster which gave the player the opportunity to wipe out rival gangsters and emerge as New York's criminal kingpin. Johnny listened intently and at the end of Steven's spiel he said just two words: "How much?"

Even Steven was surprised. He had anticipated having to reel off figures for sales of *Front* magazine and videos of *Lock Stock*. But Johnny didn't need telling about plastic gangster chic. It pissed him off to see middle-class boys like Guy Ritchie coining it in, although he didn't mind the likes of Dave

Courtney working a flanker. Steven's idea made perfect business sense.

"Five grand would do," Steven said hesitantly. "Just to get the graphics sorted out and that."

"No problem, drop by the Ned this afternoon. Cash OK?"

"Christ, yeah. Thanks, Uncle John."

"Ain't nothing to do with thanks," John said, getting to his feet. "It's a fucking investment, innit?" He kissed Steven's head, tossed a £20 note at Marco and started walking.

"See ya," he shouted.

"God bless you, Johnny Too," said Marco. "You come back soon, OK."

Moments earlier, a little under two miles away, Harry Tyler had sauntered into a bijou café just a cosh's throw from the Ned where Slobberin' Ron Sullivan was tucking into a fry-up breakfast. The meal should have been advertised as a cardiac arrest special: three eggs, chips, fried bread, spaghetti hoops, bacon and two sausages.

"What?" joked Harry. "No black pudding?"

"No," Ron smiled, "me guts were a bit iffy this morning so I thought I'd give it a miss. Must have been a bad cockle I ate last night."

"Nuffin to do with the eighteen pints, of course!"

The two men laughed. On the surface this meeting was accidental. In fact, Harry had planned it to ascertain if Dougie The Dog's peculiar behaviour had harmed the operation in any way.

"What was all that about last night, then?" Harry asked.

"Forget about it," said Ron through a mouthful of sausage. "I was like that after me first purple heart. The bloke's a prick, but he's family so we suffer him."

Harry nodded silently. He was transfixed by the older man's eating habits. Slobberin' Ron was digging into his breakfast with the relentless efficiency of a JCB. Drops of sweat were forming on his temples as he shovelled the remains of his fry-up into his salivating gob. The waitress, who looked like the missing link between Pauline Fowler and something recognisably human, appeared at the table.

"What can I get you, gorgeous?" she asked Harry.

"I ain't got no appetite this morning, darling," he replied. "Just give us a coffee."

"He takes his coffee like he takes his women," Slobberin' Ron leered.

"Yeah, one big-titted coffee, please, love," Harry smiled. "Nah, I'll take it strong and black, ta. Unless you can run to caffeine in a syringe."

The waitress looked at him blankly and turned away. Ron took a huge slurp out of his tea. "No," he went on. "Don't worry about Dougie, mate. The way I hear it he's not right in the head. Way I 'ear it, he was knocking off this dirty sort from down Peckham way and Dougie keeps banging on about wanting to try it up the aris. Anyway the way I 'ear it, one day she has enough of it. She gets him spread-eagled on the bed, all tied up to the bed post with belts an' things, then she whacks a dildo on, KY Jelly and wallop, she gives 'IM one!"

"No," said Harry, struggling to keep a straight face.

"Yeah! And it gets better. Apparently he's liked it and wants it every fucking night. Well, I'm not saying he's a closet, but well, makes you think, dunnit? Mind if I smoke?" he asked.

"I never mind if people smoke, Ron," said Harry. "Especially when they're good company. I only mind when people tell people they can't smoke, especially in them bars up town. OK, there's some places where the smoker should exercise discretion, like, maybe a cancer ward or at the business end of a petrol tanker. But a fucking pub? Grow up."

"A man after me own heart," Ron said. "Dougie won't give you any more grief, H. I'll have a word with Johnny."

"No, don't," said Harry. "I appreciate it, but don't make it bigger than it is, mate. I'm not around tonight. I'm fucking off to Amsterdam to see a man about some horses. By the time I get back he'll have found some other poor bastard to persecute."

"Amsterdam?"

"Yeah, so me phone's off till tomorrow night. All right?"

"Don't do anything I wouldn't do with all them dirty birds."

"That don't rule much out then," Harry smiled. He downed his coffee and bunged two quid on the table.

"Not taking Lesley, then?"

"Nah, don't wanna spoil her."

"You're sweet on her, though."

"She is a double lovely girl, Ron."

"I know, mate, but take care. You're south of the river now, H, and round here even Cupid carries a cosh."

"I'll bear that in mind, mate."

"OK, H. See ya."

"Yeah, laters."

Harry waited until he was back in the car before he allowed himself the sigh of relief. He wasn't going to Amsterdam at all. That was just a cover story to give himself a nice night with Kara and Courtney Rose. Before that he would drive to Brentwood to make his notes and be debriefed. But first he would nip back to the flat and give Elaine a quick portion. It would have been rude not to.

Johnny Too strolled down to Waterloo embankment, lit a cigar and stared at the Thames. He did his most creative thinking by water. Uppermost on his mind was the challenge of going legit. He hadn't told Joey yet, but his plan was to channel the whole Baker operation into straight businesses by the end of 2002. They would still be taking their cut from the drug trade, but not directly. Johnny's dream was to turn the Firm into a small-scale version of the Mafia with nothing to connect the top dogs with the street-slime. His decision was partly selfish, partly pragmatic. Crime in London was changing yet again. The Yardies were upping the stakes. And although he had no problem with his black counterparts, their violence and expansion was certain to have consequences for the Bakers. The police were turning a blind eye to black crime for political reasons, but there would come a point when the Yardies would provoke a clampdown.

Besides, who wanted to spend the rest of their life looking over their shoulder? If pressed, Johnny Too would hold his hands up and admit he was a man of violence. He had never backed down from a ruck in his life, never forgiven a slight, real or imagined. But his success had given him a taste for the good life. There was a world beyond SE1 and he wanted in. Money gave you the key, far more than reputation alone ever could, and clean money made him invincible. But how to get it? The Bakers were making fortunes from drugs. In Johnny's own words they were "making more money than a whore with two cunts". He and Joey's matching holiday villas in Marbella had been financed entirely from cocaine and ecstasy profits. The flow was so sweet it was a hard fix to kick. Granted their pubs were thriving, but much of the trade was drug related. The e-florists was nicely in profit, but it wasn't turning over enough to sustain him in the style to which he wanted to become accustomed. The mini-cab company would have been clean if he didn't use the drivers to deliver packets of Charlie. He had tried to diversify his crime base, but increasingly circumstances pushed him back to drugs and knocked-off hooch as other areas of criminal expansion were frustratingly closed off to him. The Old Bill were hammering the counterfeit video games racket, with council trading standards officers hard on their tail.

Snide clothing? That was suffering with lorry-load after lorry-load being seized as soon as it hit the street markets. The snide perfume trade had all but run aground, and mortgage fraud was being worked to death by the Africans.

Johnny had considered investing in a movie. He had even met up with the actor Ray Winstone in the Phoenix Apollo restaurant in Stratford for a thoroughly pleasant evening. Trouble was he'd missed the boat on gangster flicks, and if he had got seriously involved who would have run the rest of the Baker operation? Steven was the only one with the brains but he was still too young to be giving the orders. Johnny had to work with what he had, and what he had were the Three Stooges …

At that moment Pyro Joe and Rhino were pulling up outside Dougie The Dog's council flat. Their mission this fine Autumn morning was to drive over to the Mile End Road in East London – West Ham territory! – to negotiate a price on a large, quality parcel of snide Thomas Burberry and YSL tops. It was a test of initiative for the trio who were the firm's main physical enforcers, Johnny Too's trusted lieutenants.

Dougie groaned as he got in the Merc, a half-eaten bacon sandwich in his hand. He rubbed his groin as he slumped in the back seat.

"Fucked this bird last night," he said. "Very fucking posh she was. I think she's given me lobsters."

"Don't your missus ever get the hump with you fucking other birds?" Pyro Joe asked.

"Why should she?" Doug replied. "I'm fucking her as well."

All three men laughed. In the front seat, Rhino was reading the *Daily Star*.

"Did you see this in the paper?" he said. "Mike Fitzgerald is dead."

"How'd he die?" asked Dougie.

"Natural causes," Joey grunted.

Rhino looked puzzled. "It says here his throat was cut, and his head bludgeoned with a pick-axe handle ..."

Pyro Joe shook his head. "He crossed Harry May and Fatty Lol sorted him out," he said. "Like I say, natural causes."

"What, Lewisham Lol?" asked Doug. "Ain't he South London West Ham?"

"Yep," said Joey. "And they're not a firm to take lightly."

Dougie snorted. "'Ere, Rhine, can you stick this on?" He handed over a CD. Rhino read the cover.

"*Worldwide Tribute To The Real Oi*," he said. "What's this?"

"I bought it yesterday," said Dougie. "A load of Yank bands have done covers of old Oi! songs, Sparrer, Cockney Rejects. They've got a couple of Last Resort songs on there, Millwall Roi's band. They do 'Violence In Our Minds', right? But they get the words wrong. You've gotta hear it. Roi sings, 'We go to football matches, we always have a laugh, we always get some bovver in before the second half,' but ..."

"Bovver!" Rhino snorted.

"Yeah, well, it was 1980. Anyway, these Yanks sing we always get some Bovril in. It's fucking hilarious."

"They got any Sham on there?" asked Pyro Joe.

"'Hey Little Rich Boy'," Dougie replied.

"Not 'Hurry Up 'Arry'?" Joe said, disappointed.

"Don't think so," said Doug.

"Nope," said Rhino, studying the case.

"I fucking love that song," said Joe, who burst into song. "We're going dahn the pub ..."

"Fuck me, Joe, your voice," joked Rhino. "I'll stick the CD on, shall I?"

"Yeah," Joey laughed. "The Pakis'll love that when we turn up with a fucking 4-Skins song blaring. They'll think it's the fucking Southall riot all over again."

Madan, Johnny Too's latest contact in the world of illicit manufacturing, was a Bengali who prided himself on his cunning, but he hadn't been shrewd enough to meet Mr Baker's redneck representatives on neutral turf. Rather he had arranged the meeting at the Latief café, a veritable mecca for curry connoisseurs. Such was the quality of its menu, customers were happy to put up with Os the owner's peculiarities, the chief one being that Os, a Muslim devout to the point of fanaticism, refused to sell alcohol. South London's finest had arrived early and demanded lager.

"No beer, just food," Mohammad, the elderly waiter, explained.

"Oi," snapped Joey. "I want a fucking beer while we're waiting, capice?"

"No beer," said Mohammad, shaking his head.

"Look," reasoned Rhino. "We don't care if it's warm or piss weak. We don't care if it's shit Paki lager. What d'you call it? Cobra? Just as long as it's beer."

"No beer," Mohammad said. "No beer, just food."

"What are you, a fucking parrot?" snapped Joey.

Hearing the commotion, a young Bengali known as Oli emerged from the kitchen.

"What's the problem, gents?" he asked in pure Stepney Cockney.

"Ramsammy 'ere won't serve us a beer," said Dougie The Dog.

"We haven't got a licence, mate," said Oli pleasantly. "People just bring their own."

"Well maybe Ramsammy can pop down the offie for us," Dougie said.

"We're a bit busy, sir," Oli said calmly. "And we're about to get our lunchtime rush from the City. There is an off-licence about fifty yards down the road towards the Highway, though."

There was a malevolent flash in Pyro Joey's eyes.

"Do you realise," he said slowly, "if all you cunts went home, we'd get an extra hour of daylight in London?"

Oli bristled. This *was* his home. He'd been born 500 yards from here in the long hot summer of 1976 when British Movement neo-Nazis were prowling the streets around Brick Lane every Sunday looking for confrontation with the immigrant community. Oli weighed up the man, the size of his shoulders, the spread of his nose … this was not a fellow to agitate. Besides, the fact that one of his objectionable companions was black ruled out the possibility that he was BNP. Perhaps he was just winding him up.

"I'll tell you what, sir," Oli said brightly. "Give me five minutes and I'll pop down the offie for you myself. That suit yer?"

"Lovely, man," said Rhino who was starting to suspect that their mission was going pear-shaped before it had begun. "Very kind of you."

"Yeah," said Dougie. "Very considerate. And while I'm waiting I'll 'ave one of these."

He produced a fat, ready-rolled spliff, stuffed with finest Dutch super-skunk.

"NO!" snapped Oli. "Not here!"

Pyro Joe slammed his fist into the back of the waiter's head. It was a race between Dougie and Rhino to punch and kick him across the tables, scattering dinners, drinks and poppadoms everywhere. Then, for good measure, they gave old Mohammad a slap. As they walked towards the door, three kitchen staff emerged brandishing kitchen utensils. The last of them was knocked unconscious just as Madan arrived. Joey Baker poked the snide clothing producer in the chest and snarled, "What's the matter with these cunts? You tell them to sort the fucking beer next time. People like us expect respect."

Pyro Joe's face was contorted with hatred and excitement. He was loving every minute, thought Rhino, who suspected his boss was rapidly descending into madness. As they left the café, Dougie turned and put his right hand into the left side of his leather jacket, just under the armpit. He yanked it down to show just enough of a revolver, an ex-US Army Colt .45, to guarantee Madan wouldn't go screaming to the Filth. That was the key, to keep the thought of what might happen to the victims if the lads happened to be summoned to an ID parade.

"Ever been Jihad?" Dougie sneered. "You fucking tossers, that was for all the British tourists your people kidnap and murder in Chechnya, all right? Cunts."

Pyro Joe was in hysterics. Rhino was laughing too. "I fucking hate Pakis," the black man chuckled. "Where did you get 'Ever been Jihad' from?"

"*The 11 O'Clock Show* I fink."

Buzzing with adrenalin, The Dog dived into a nearby Asian corner shop and cleared the till at knife point, helping himself to a box of crisps on the way out.

"Sorry, pal," he smirked at the terrified shop-keeper. "Y'see my problem is I'm just too proud to beg."

They laughed at that one all the way home.

Johnny Too had heard the bad news from an irate Madan 20 minutes before his away team emerged through the Rotherhithe Tunnel. Joey could not understand his brother's rage. "Who needs the little Paki cunt anyway?" he growled. The point was, empire-builder Johnny did. Not only had the arse well and truly dropped out of the snide clothing supply route, but also the firm had just lost a new supply of respectable-looking Asian cocaine mules.

Harry Tyler rapped on the front room window of Lesley Gore's flat. It was her afternoon off, and Harry knew what to expect. He'd taken a couple of Ginseng tablets to help him keep up with the barmaid's insatiable appetite for sex. Harry had always fancied himself as a stud but he had never met a woman as demanding and inventive as Lesley. He liked the girl, probably too much. She had a good heart and she was obviously concerned about him. Before she had even ripped off his strides, Lesley was questioning Harry about the incident with Dougie.

"Be careful with Doug," she counselled. "His temper is shorter than his dick."

Lesley had already told her mum she had fallen for this rough diamond dodgy dealer who treated her well and made her laugh. On their second night in bed, she'd asked him what his favourite position was and the silly sod had looked at her straight-faced and said, "Centre forward, I think." It still made her grin even now. Lesley had no idea that the ultimate joke was on her; and that her employers would get the punch-line.

Harry was now an almost daily commuter into the South East London heartland. To the casual observer, he and Lesley had a good thing going which is why he was spending so much time away from Stratford. Obviously. In truth, Tyler's mission was long term. Against a firm like the Bakers any attempt to move quickly would smell whiffy. But his infiltration had purpose and strategy and now Harry judged it was time to move from the outer ring of the Firm towards the centre. The lovely Lesley and

—
150

Slobberin' Ron Sullivan were merely his stepping stones.

A report had appeared in Tuesday's *Sun* about a lorry hijack on the outskirts of Coventry. The cab and trailer had been found abandoned, minus the load, on farmland near Harold Hill, an East End overspill council estate area not far from Romford in Essex. The usual faces on the estate would have been looked at but, as the report said the police were appealing for information, none of them were in the frame.

The trailer had been wedged top to bottom with export whisky. Anyone doubting the veracity of the *Sun*'s story could have made enquiries that would have allayed all their suspicions. A call to the West Midlands police would have confirmed that they were indeed looking for three or four men. Romford CID were certainly aware that West Midlands detectives had travelled down making all the right noises. They even brought down their own photographer and forensic guys. If anyone had looked further the police national computer would also have revealed that the lorry and trailer were reported stolen and that the driver had been beaten about the head, tied and taped and left in a hedgerow – surely enough to satisfy anyone? It was only then that more prying would have uncovered the unexpected. Why, for example, had the driver never gone to hospital? Why were the investigating officers not local but a special squad working out of Lloyd House, the Birmingham force HQ? The stolen load was, in fact, another gift from the Church, and there was no danger of the

£15K reward ever being claimed because no one was ever going to get nicked.

Slobberin' Ron had read the article and given it some thought. Johnny Too was also aware of it and had assumed it to be the work of a bold little crew from Harlow, Essex who had been going country-wide ripping off lorries. No one knew who they were, but Johnny knew of a connection down at Canvey Island. The one thing that was certain was this crew were making bundles and the Bakers weren't on the gravy train.

Slobberin' Ron was slightly flabbergasted when Lesley Gore gave him a tug and asked if Ron could meet Harry at her flat after closing time to discuss some "private business". Ron couldn't wait, and smelling pound notes he jogged straight round.

He found Harry dressed in shorts, T-shirt and moccasin slippers, watching *EastEnders*.

"You've got yer feet under the table with Lesley," Ron smirked. "You want a chat?"

"Yeah. I'll turn this shit off first. I couldn't bear to see Frank humping Fat Pat again."

Harry switched off the TV and poured Slobberin' Ron a large brandy.

"Ron, I know you're sweet," he said. "Here's the situation. I've got a parcel of export gold watch, forty foot of it. It's gotta be placed cos the Filth are doing the rounds on the slaughters. The fella who would have had it has shit out cos there's a red-hot scream on it and he won't play. Can you help?"

"Where's it from?"

"Up North."

"That lot in the Currant Bun?"

"Could be."

"You've got a 15-large price on your head, me old son."

"Only to any cancerous bastard that puts it up."

"How quick's it got to go?"

"Yesterday."

"What price are you looking for?"

"I ain't in a position to turn down a fair offer. The geezers who went up front have fucked off to Marbella till it calms down. They've hit too much recently, chasing the big 'un."

"Yeah, it's always greed that fucks ya. Let me go talk to Johnny Too … "

That's your first cock-up, thought Harry. Never show your cards, never reveal who is going to finance anything. He grinned inwardly and went to the broom closet by the front door. Slobberin' Ron could see twelve or thirteen cases under a bed sheet. Harry pulled out one case and covered up the rest.

"Do you want to take one of these as a sampler?"

"What's that come to, H?"

"Fuck off. Nix, it's for Larkin."

Ron tucked the case under his arm and left. Half an hour later Lesley was back indoors.

"Ron gave me the evening off," she said. "He said for us to go back about closing time. I'm starving. Have you eaten?"

"No, darling. In fact me belly thinks me throat's been cut. Fancy a Ruby?"

It was 10.33 pm when they arrived back at the Ned, stinking of madras and Cobra. The pub was strangely quiet. Johnny and Joey were up at the bar with Dougie and Rhino. Slobberin' Ron was behind the jump. In the corner near the stage were a couple of unfamiliar faces and that was it.

Harry said, "Ron," and nodded hello to the others.

"What'll it be, Harry?" Ron asked.

"Fosters and a G&T and whatever anyone else wants, please, mate."

Johnny Too sat on his customary stool with his back to the happy couple. The other three men were standing in a semi circle around him all in sight of Harry.

"Johnny, would you like a drink with Mr Tyler?" asked Slobberin'.

Johnny Too didn't swivel round. He just pushed forward his near-empty bowl glass and said "Yeah, stick a fucking large Scotch in that."

The others laughed, Ron grinned and nodded. They all got the joke but Dougie was staring straight at Harry and let a knowing smile crease his face. Harry knew the look. He also knew not to make eye contact with violent scum like Dougie The Dog. He averted his gaze and said, "How much, Ron?"

Ron shook his head. "No, mate," he said. "It's sorted."

Johnny Too rose and began to bark orders. "LES! Get behind the jump, sort out the glasses, luv. Ron, go and sort the books."

Lesley drained her gin and disappeared into the kitchen with Ron. Johnny Too got up from his stool and without saying a word strolled off into the gents.

As the door shut behind him, Dougie the Dog stepped up close to Harry. So close the detective could smell the chilli sauce from his last kebab on his breath.

"So who are you then, Harry?" he said softly.

"Sorry?" Harry replied.

"Don't be fucking sorry. I said, who are yer?"

"Just a geezer making a living."

"So why don't you fuck off down to Forest Gate or wherever and do yer business that end?"

Harry took a step back. Had he misjudged things? This was starting to look messy. Pyro Joe loomed up beside him. "No-one knows you up here," he growled.

"Look, mate," said Harry. "I'm only trying to do a bit of business. I don't want ag."

"So you're shagging Lesley, then?" That was The Dog.

"Could be. I wasn't planning on marrying it, though."

"See it's a fact that all them cunts over the other side of the river are fucking wrong 'uns," Doug went on.

Harry's back went up. "How's that, then?" he said.

"West Ham mugs. They're all shitters and runners and fucking grasses."

Harry bit into his bottom lip and mustered his self-control. "Mate," he said finally. "I ain't here to talk politics, all right. I don't want trouble. I'm just here to deal."

"Well, you can fuck off, SHITTER!" Dougie exploded. The "shitter" was slurred.

Pissed again, thought Harry. Probably had half a gram up his bugle tonight. Was this down to Les? Unlikely. This animal was too thick, too self-absorbed, to care. Maybe it was just mindless hatred of anyone who wasn't from the manor coupled with a large pinch of jealousy that this outsider was pushing straight up the ladder. Everyone on the Baker crew was kith and kin, either directly or by historical friendship. It was the secret of their success. Dads knew dads, mums had been to school with sisters. Family had done bird with family, from borstals to the Scrubs. Faced by an outsider, all the defences were up. All the metaphorical guns were loaded and aimed. Harry knew the one great certainty was that no one thought he was Old Bill. It had never even been suggested. But where did he go from here? He couldn't bottle it. Once Harry Tyler walked out the door he would never walk back in. He couldn't afford to lose face. He could have taken Dougie no problem and would have loved to, the dickless resentful psychopath had the sort of face that was crying out to be filled in. But Dougie, Joey and Rhino ... Maybe it was worth taking a kicking if he could lay Dougie out first. By the looks of it the operation was fucked ...

The Dog shook his head and started to speak again. "We don't know who you are," he repeated. "You come round my manor, spending like Harry fucking Splattercash, like you're Billy Big Potatoes ..."

Harry could almost taste the tension in the air. Dougie reached into the pocket of his leather jacket that was slung haphazardly across the bar. Harry watched for the tell-tale glint of a steel blade. He could hardly believe his eyes when his twisted tormentor pulled out a fat, but plainly dead, black rat instead.

"Recently found brown bread in Ron's cellar," Dougie said, grinning excitedly. Pyro Joe smirked. He'd seen The Dog do this trick with dead mice and birds, even a handful of wriggling maggots.

"Now open wide," Dougie instructed, "cos you are gonna chew on this beauty."

Harry stepped back. "Fuck off, Doug," he said simply.

Joey growled.

"You don't understand," said Dougie, stepping forward. "You ain't going nowhere till you've had a nice few mouthfuls of cold rodent supper. Think of it not so much as an initiation test as a gift from yer old mate Dougie The Dog."

Harry stepped towards the bar and picked up an empty bottle of Becks.

"Now, now, Harry," said Doug. "Don't play rough."

"That's enough." It was Johnny Too. "Dougie, leave it alone. Harry, come and sit over here."

The Dog meekly obeyed his master's voice. The threat was over as quickly as it had begun. Harry wondered if it had been the reverse swindle of the Old Bill's good-cop, bad-cop routine. And if so, had he passed whatever test it was? He picked up his pint and moved to where Johnny Baker was now sitting. To his right, sitting quietly but watching everything, were the two unknown faces. He had a strange feeling about them. He couldn't put his finger on it, but they just didn't add up. Harry knew he didn't know the men. He had as much faith in his total-recall memory as he did in his chameleon-like ability to get into character and stay in it. So who were the two guys? He felt them looking him up and down. He wasn't comfortable about them but he didn't feel threatened. As he sat opposite Johnny Too, he put his suspicions on the back burner and got down to business.

"Ron's spoken to you, Johnny?"

"Yeah, it's the parcel from up Brum way."

"Yeah."

"How quick can it go?"

"Now. It's alight down that end."

"How much you looking for?"

"Two quid a bottle."

"How many cases?"

"A trailer full. It's all on the floor at the moment, and I ain't got the wheels to move it. Well, not in one hit."

"Where's it now?"

"In a slaughter near Epping Forest."

"Sold! Ron's got your mobile number?"

"Yeah."

"I'll get it off him. Rhino and Doug can sort it tomorrow. Got any problems with that?"

Harry hesitated. "Who's weighing me out?"

"When it's got, I'll leave the readies behind the jump with Ron."

Harry looked Johnny Too in the eye. "Has Dougie got a problem with me?"

"Only if I say so."

The parcel went, the money arrived and not a single bottle surfaced for two months; then every pub was awash with cheap Scotch, every Asian off-licence from Bermondsey to Peckham and from New Cross to Kennington was doing the right customers good discounts on whisky, but no honest citizen ever walked into the local nick and mentioned that the liquor was being moved at £6 a bottle.

When Harry Tyler collected his cash from Slobberin' Ron the tapes were rolling and Ron let slip a curious thing, something Harry replayed several times. Ron said simply, "They're happy with you now, now you've been vetted." It only made sense when Harry next spoke to DI Suckling – Harry's car had been checked out by a couple of CID officers from an office not a million miles from the Ned Kelly. Bingo. That's who the two faces in the bar had been. It amused Harry to learn that his name had also been run through the police computer. The inquisitive eyes had seen what they had wanted to see – one conviction three years earlier at Havering magistrates' court for possession of one gram of a class A drug, fined £175 plus costs. The address on file was now the site of a new ASDA supermarket, while Harry's wheels showed the address of what appeared to be an empty council flat in Beckton, east London. So, Johnny Too had clearly invested a few quid in research. He obviously saw the potential of this new trade route.

A couple of days after the whisky trade Harry

took a call on the mobile.

"It's Ron Sullivan," said the voice. "Are you down your manor?"

"Just up the road, can be later. Why?"

"Me and Rhino will be down that way about twoish, meet us for a beer?"

"What is it now? Eleven? Can you make it half-three, I've got something on."

"Yeah, round your place?"

"No, go to my local. It's only ten minutes from me. It's called the Trojan, just past the one-way system at Manor Park, opposite a big Nissan dealership on the right and a Shell garage. If you reach the Ford dealership on the right you've gone past it."

Harry grinned as he ended the call. The flies were coming to the spider. He punched a number into his mobile and got busy.

At 3.15 pm, Johnny Too, Pyro Joe and Dougie The Dog strolled into the Trojan, a roomy free house full of customers. Johnny noted how cheap the Scotch was. As the three men reached the bar, the whole pub went quiet. "Welcome to Tombstone," said Johnny under his breath. Dougie shifted from foot to foot. He looked decidedly ill at ease. A crew of six men, all lumps, glared at them from one corner. The three hounds playing darts stopped to look them over, their interest duplicated by the mob around the snooker table. Two black men further up the bar muttered to one another in a hostile manner. Their close-cropped heads, sharp clothes and mobile phones said drug dealers to those in the know.

Pyro Joe felt compelled to stare back at the first

six.

"Not in here, Joe," said Johnny softly but with authority. "What are you having?"

Cyril the landlord gave them a half smile and said, "Looks like rain."

"It always does over this side," grumbled Dougie.

"It's not that bad," said Cyril.

"Fucking is," the Dog replied eloquently.

"Has Harry been in?" asked Johnny Too.

"Harry?" Cyril countered. "Harry who?"

"Harry, Harry Tyler," said John. "You know Harry."

"Harry Tyler?"

"Yeah, we're mates. He told us to meet him here."

One of the watching six, a mountain of a man dressed like the Motorhead roadie time forgot, manky long hair, beard, jeans stuck on with old grease and an Anti-Nowhere League t-shirt that was white fifteen years before, ambled up to them. Johnny clocked his massive tattooed arms. The guy looked strong enough to lift a family saloon above his head and change a tyre with his spare hand.

"Who you looking for, mate?" he growled.

"Harry Tyler," said Johnny. "Know him?"

"And who wants him?"

"We fucking do," snapped Dougie.

Johnny squeezed The Dog's bicep to shut him up. "I do," he said. "He asked us to meet him here."

"He's a mate, is he?"

Johnny nodded.

"Three pints here, Cyril," said the big man,

nodding at the South London trio. "Give him a ring on his moby, mate. It should be on."

He re-joined his drinking buddies.

"Do you do food, mate?" Dougie The Dog asked Cyril.

Just then the public bar door swung open and in bounced Harry, big smile on his face and looking good.

"Johnny, Joe, Doug ... I was expecting Rhino and Ron. Good to see ya. What y'having?"

"Come on, H," said Cyril. "Keeping these fellas waiting. He's always late, he'll be late for his own funeral he will."

"Yeah," Harry replied. "I won't be late for yours, though, you old bastard."

The man mountain walked over, and smiled displaying a mouth full of broken teeth.

"All right, H?" he said.

"Geezer!" Harry smiled. "How's it hanging? Johnny, this is Pete, Pete, Johnny."

The entire atmosphere in the pub had changed with Harry Tyler's arrival. The place started buzzing again. This was good times. Johnny noticed how much calmer and self-assured Harry seemed on his own turf.

"Oi, Cyril," Harry yelled. "Where's Carol?"

"She'll be down in a mo, H. She's on the phone. I think it's superglued to her earhole."

"Cyril's other half," Harry said to Johnny. "Nicely put together. Late forties but well turned out. The sort you might have gone over the side for ten years ago but not that beautiful that you wouldn't have gone home after a shag."

At that moment, the landlady came down the stairs and into the bar. As soon as she saw Harry it was hugs, kisses and banter all round. Insults flew, none intended to hurt, and jokes were told. Within the space of an hour, some 30 people had drifted in and out of the bar and Harry Tyler was clearly the man. If people didn't come up and shake his hand, they nodded and smiled. Within what seemed like minutes, Carol had rustled up a spread of sandwiches and chicken legs on the house. What better to tempt fast-drinking punters with fat wallets to linger longer?

"Don't get this in the Ned," said Dougie as he bit into two sandwiches at once.

"I'll stick a score behind the bar tonight and get Ron to lay it on, you greedy sod," said Johnny. "You mind you don't get claret and blue poisoning."

Dougie scowled but didn't stop eating.

Harry pulled Johnny Too aside. "What brings you down this end, John?" he asked.

"We were out for a drive, that's all."

Harry raised an "Oh-yeah?" eyebrow. This was no accidental meeting. This was the look-see, and Harry felt honoured that the top man had come to check him out for himself. Johnny Too hadn't missed a trick. He had clocked the clandestine chat H had been engaged in with the two dealers. He had noted the large wedge of notes subtly transfer from Harry to the taller black man and how they had got up, shaken hands and left smiling. Yeah, there was now no vestige of doubt in Johnny Baker's mind. Harry

Tyler was proper.

"You still here, H?" Carol joked.

"Yes, darling. And I've heard all about you buying yerself crotchless drawers." He paused to draw in the maximum audience. "It's not for sex," he said. "It's just to get a better grip on the broomstick."

This got a roar of approval from every man in earshot.

"Bastard!" said Carol, smiling. "I'll get you back."

The crack sparked off an orgy of joke-telling, the funniest and sickest gag of the day coming, surprisingly, from Pyro Joe who claimed it was a true story from his time fighting as a mercenary in Croatia.

"Fella I was with, Dagenham Dave, slipped out on a recce and came back three hours later claiming he'd had the best sex of his life in a dug-out not a hundred yards away. He said he'd come across this Serbian girl and that he'd fucked her every which way, on top, underneath, side to side and up the arse. I asked him if he'd got a gobble. 'No,' he said, 'no gobble.' 'Why not?' I said. 'I couldn't,' he replied. 'She didn't have a head.'"

"That is sick," said Carol. But the blokes were on the floor.

"Was Joe in Croatia, Johnny?" asked Harry.

"Was he fuck."

"Listen, mate, I've got to go and service Lesley. Any chance of a lift back when you go, only I'm well over the limit."

"Not a problem. Now OK?"

"Sweet."

The four men drove off towards Mile End, dropping down to the Commercial Road for the Rother-hithe Tunnel. Dougie was driving, dreaming of sweeter smells south of the river. He was so wrapped up in his own thoughts that he didn't have a clue about the police motorcycle behind him until the blue lights came on.

Easy Rider poked his head through the window of Doug's Sierra and recoiled at his brandy breath. "You were over the limit, sir, but I have reason to believe you have been drinking. Blow in this, sir."

Johnny Too was the only reason The Dog didn't go for it, that and the two patrol cars that pulled up five yards behind.

"I've fucking forgotten more about the law than you'll ever know," Dougie ranted. "Do you know who I am?"

"Not yet, sir, but I soon will."

The two police cars disgorged their passengers. The Baker brothers and Harry Tyler gave the slow-moving rubber-neckers plenty of freebie entertainment as they had their pockets turned out at the back of the Ford. All three gave false names and addresses, then, leaving the hapless Dougie to the mercy of the uniforms, they strolled off to catch a mini-cab. None of them doubted that out of sight, free from Johnny's restraining influence, the Dog would show his teeth. Dougie now had one more reason to hate East London, that and the three-year ban he was about to pick up and ignore.

The fun-loving criminals got back to the Ned where Slobberin' Ron, already aware of the Dog's misfortune, offered little conversation. Harry downed a pint almost in reverence, as if poor old Doug had died, then with a huge smile, he announced, "I'm off for a shag."

Lesley looked great. "You look good enough to eat," Harry told her.

"Fanny first," Lesley replied, dropping her drawers and lifting her skirt. Even Harry was surprised by this speedy turn of events, but he wasted no time getting stuck in, tracing the alphabet letter by letter on her clitoris with his tongue. He had just reached K the second time around when the longing got too much and he started unbuckling his trousers.

"No, not here," Lesley said. "Let's go somewhere else. Let's go to Southwark Park, or a lay-by, or a field. I fancy a bit of fresh air."

"A fucking field? Where am I going to find a field in Rotherhithe?"

"I know a place, down by the docks."

"And there was me thinking you were a virgin ..."

Barmaids like Lesley Gore were two a penny in South London, but when it came to shagging she was top dollar. She was in to everything, uniforms, fantasy games, bondage – Les had this thing about being tied up and blindfolded. They had schoolgirl night, nurses night, Nazi night. Then there were the times she dressed as a nun, tied Harry to the bed and walked around him swinging one of those metal balls reeking of incense. Underneath the habit,

Lesley wore a black basque, black stockings and suspenders. In her hands she carried a fat tallow candle and baby oil. Harry would be on the bed with a stonker, watching Lesley entertain Colin the candle … Happy days. No wonder that whenever he did manage to get home to Kara Harry was content to sit in a garden chair with his feet up reading the *Sun*.

The day after Dougie was breathalysed, the Baker firm had even worse news. Young Steven Richards, the bright computer-literate nephew, was under arrest at Bexleyheath police station in Kent. Steven had been nicked at a public toilet in nearby Erith where he'd been caught giving a stranger a blow-job. The gents in question had been under surveillance, and Steven was one of 36 men to get lifted in the three-day operation. To Pyro Joe, his arrest was clearly a fit-up: this was the Filth extracting revenge on them for their screw-up when they'd raided the Ned.

According to the Police Inspector's version of events, Steven had been caught two-up in the cubicle with another man, both had their trousers and underpants down. One officer had seen them over the top, a second cop had looked under the door and corroborated everything. The fellow on the receiving end was Samuel Taylor, a secondary school teacher from Crayford, who was keen to let the whole thing blow away as quickly as possible. The two men had not met previous to their gross encounter.

Johnny Too was lying in bed with Geraldine

when he heard the news. Steven's father, Trevor Richards, rang. He was beside himself with rage. Trevor had done enough bird to know about "boy-girls", he could even understand it, but the thought of his bright beloved son at it with some dirty nonce school teacher was too much to bear. Trevor was inconsolable. All Johnny Too could do was promise to put Maurice Bondman on the case asap. With Maurice in control, the family could already hear the "Not Guilty" verdict, but Steven walking away from the charge couldn't begin to take the sour taste out of the Bakers' mouths.

Johnny Too lay back in bed, hands behind his head, gazing at the ceiling. Geraldine hugged him.

"Fucking iron," Johnny said. "How can Steve be an iron? He's got it all, the looks, the clothes, the money. Birds love him."

"John, it's different these days," said Geraldine. "If he's gay, he's gay. He's got to be who he's got to be. Talk to him. Don't blow up. I know Trevor is upset. I know you're upset, but talk to him."

"Trev is going ballistic."

"He's bound to, but he'll see sense. Steven is still his son. He's still your nephew. He's still the same bright boy he was this morning. Nothing has changed."

The more they talked, the more Johnny saw the pieces coming together. Salih, yeah, Sally; the way Steve never had a steady girl … yes, of course. It hurt Johnny's masculine pride and his family pride, but Geraldine was right. The writing had been on the wall.

Johnny got up and wandered into the shower on auto-pilot. He towelled himself down, dressed, kissed Geri goodbye and then walked to his car as if he were in a trance. By the time he reached the Ned, the clan had started to gather. Pyro Joe and Dougie The Dog were in the mood to firebomb Bexleyheath nick, but Johnny talked them round. His choice of words was not opportune. "Geri says", "Geri thinks", "Geri knows ..." Pyro Joe was not the brightest of men, but he knew that family business should stay family and eventually he snapped.

"What the fuck's it got to do with her?" he roared at Johnny. "She's not fucking family. Your brain is in yer fucking dick where she's concerned."

And that was it. The brothers were going at each other like rampant stags. How long had it been since this had happened? Five years? Eight years? Ten? When they were teenagers they were clashing all the time, but onlookers were genuinely shocked to see the two South London crime lords at each other's throats. Anyone who wasn't in the Baker inner circle discreetly left the pub as close family and confidantes pulled the two raging fools apart. Rhino parked his 16-stone body between them and stopped the scrapping. But Joey was still seething. The TART had come between the brothers and nothing and no one should ever do that.

Word of the bloody brother bust-up soon spread amongst the womenfolk, and Joey's wife, Barbara, the mother of his lunatic kids, felt it her duty to stick the poison in to Johnny's wife, Sandra. Sibling jealousy was probably only 80 per cent of her motivation. Dark clouds were gathering behind Johnny Too's back, but he was too pumped with vision and confidence to see them.

Peter Miller was one of the last to hear about Johnny and Joey's fall-out. If truth be known, he was having enough trouble coping with being relegated from Harry Tyler's premier league of pals. Even a dumb drunk like Miller realised that his former best mate with the cash-dispensing wallet was no longer sending the light ales across with the frequency to which he had become accustomed. Now H was trading with Slobberin' Ron and the Brothers, Peter was starting to feel hurt. How was he to know that his usefulness had ended the day Harry had done his first bit of business in the Ned?

Keen – make that double keen – to redress the status quo, Miller had made it his business to find something, anything, to grab Harry's attention. He had heard of a couple of nice tools being touted by Roger Davies, a drummer and a weasel of a man, who had given Her Majesty almost as much pleasure as HRH Stavros. So now Miller and Davies sat in Harry Tyler's video car and Davies, on Miller's recommendation, let his greedy mouth run away with him. He wanted £800 for a revolver and an automatic handgun with twenty lugs of ammo. Harry got on his mobile and had a two-minute conversation with an unnamed buyer: "Are you still in the market for a couple of those things? Yeah, with lugs, yeah." And so Roger Davies became yet another yesterday man, taped, photographed, housed and waiting in line for a nicking … and two more pieces were off the street. Lovely job.

There was a danger Harry might get snowed under, buying every parcel up for grabs in the Ned. He was aware of it, and started to exercise discretion. The small fry were worth rounding up to a degree but nothing could be allowed to let him lose sight of the big target. And as days passed, it was easier for the Bushwhacker to knock back minor trades, although none of the lowlife jerks realised he was actually doing them a favour. Naturally all of Harry's "No, not interesteds" filtered back to Johnny Too, demonstrating that the East Londoner wasn't a greedy player.

Johnny Too liked Harry. His attitude was sound, he had a terrific sense of humour and an admirably free-wheeling love life. Clearly no woman could tie Tyler down. Johnny saw the way Harry would tell Lesley Gore to back off when he needed space, and had to be somewhere to trade. He also realised that half the time H disappeared he was obviously off shagging over Stratford way. Hey, everybody had to have a mystery. Where would he be without Geraldine?

Harry wasn't one to talk about relationships and emotional shit, but he'd had Johnny Too in hysterics with his reports about his and Lesley's sexual activities. The best story had to be the time Les was giving H a gobble in a private road on a huge building site in Wapping. He was just reaching his vinegar when a huge Irish security guard had come lumbering towards them shaking his fist. Harry alerted Lesley who stopped what she was doing and flung the car into reverse. Unfortunately, H was too far gone and as Les sped off, her brand new Schott top was splattered with Harry's semen – or Harry's Harry, his Harry Monk – as Johnny called it when he passed the story on with relish and embellishments to the hounds at his favourite poker game. In Johnny's version Harry had also been tied to the steering wheel with a skipping rope, leaving Lesley, dressed in full St Trinian's kit, to lean over him to change gear and get all that hot fish yoghurt in her hair. "And I bet she pulled a fair old pint and all," Johnny would laugh. They were very much alike, him and Harry, Johnny decided. Both loved to tell a story, both were born to be at it, and both were natural comical bastards. Two peas in a knocked-off pod.

When DCI Susan Long ordered Harry to have a few days back home, he was actually disappointed. But it had to be done. Because of the round-the-clock surveillance, research, exhibits, telephone taps and covert equipment, the backload of work was piling up and Long needed breathing space.

Harry went home for five days' leave in a good frame of mind. He had told Lesley he had to go back to the Dam to sort out a bit of business, and wouldn't be answering the mobile. But as soon as he got home, everything went pear-shaped. He hated being there, the atmosphere was claustrophobic. Time itself seemed to slow, as if the tick of the clock had been replaced by a dull, distant thud. He felt trapped. He resented being forced back to this half-life that was his real world. Unable to get the operation off his mind, Harry barely spoke to Kara at all that first day. His wife put two and two together and made 69. He was having an affair, she knew it, and she screamed accusation after accusation at him: you FUCKING BASTARD! Harry fielded her rage with lie after lie – he'd been in Paris, he couldn't get to a phone ... he ducked, he dived. But after the first hour it no longer mattered if she believed him or not. He stormed off to his local, enjoyed a lock-in, rolled home about 2.30 am and kipped on the couch.

The next day, the atmosphere was fraught. Kara tried to make amends, but her heart wasn't in it. Deep down she knew Harry wasn't over the side, but somehow that made it worse. If her only competition was his job, she knew she had already lost. Some people worked to live. With Harry it was the other way round. Nothing mattered more than the job. On day three they made love. The session was brief, mechanical almost. They did it because they thought they better had or else ... or else what? Kara didn't want to lose her husband, on the contrary she wanted to rediscover him, but Harry would have to find himself first. And Harry? When he came he was seeing Lesley Gore's face.

The night before he went back to his undercover work, he made her the same old promise: "After this job, I'll go back to being a copper." Kara knew it meant as much as the times he'd told her, "After last night I'll never drink again."

Back on the job, Harry felt liberated. It was almost as though he meant something in this other life that he had ceased to mean at home. Harry felt himself watching Pyro Joe, and hating him more each day. He resented the man – not for being Johnny's brother, how daft would that be? But for being a bully and for being thick. If Johnny Too was a brighter Grant Mitchell, Pyro Joe was a beefier Mr Bean, holding him back. Maybe Joe was the reason Johnny turned bad. Maybe Johnny Too could be saved. It was 11.15 am when Harry Tyler sauntered back into the Ned. Johnny Too sat at the deserted bar chatting with Joe and Slobberin' Ron. When he saw Harry he shot off his stool and greeted him like a prodigal son.

"Wanna a beer, H?" asked Ron.

"Bit early, innit?"

"Early for a pint?" said Johnny.

"No," Harry replied. "For fucking silly questions."

All four men laughed out loud.

"Nice one," said Ron.

"Fancy a livener," Johnny Too asked his brother. Pyro Joe nodded. John emptied half a gram of cocaine out on the serving hatch and chopped it finely with an American Express gold card – he felt it tasted better chopped with a gold card, the same way that some blokes prefer their beer in a straight glass rather than a jug.

Johnny rolled up a five pound note and snorted three fat lines. Joe took another three.

"Best way to start the day," the big man chuckled.

"You want some, H?" asked Johnny Too.

"No, ta, mate. I knocked it on the head eighteen months ago. I kept it in the fridge and at night it used to call out to me."

"What did it say?"

"It used to say: 'If you eat me all up tonight, you won't have to buy any more ever again. I'll be your last bit.'"

"And was it?"

"Was it fuck. Then one day I just got sick of it, sick of the whole idea of it. I took what I had left, only about half a gram, and just flushed it down the khazi. And I ain't used it since. I've moved a fair bit since, though."

"Still get it?"

"No. In the market for a lump, though."

"How much?"

"Half a key."

"What about down your way?"

"It's all Club Class shit. No, in truth, John, I'm looking to open up the market. The last run from over the water got burned."

Johnny lowered his voice. "How's £15 gib on the half key sound?"

"If it's good percentage gear the price is OK."

"Can you stick five grand up front, the other ten COD?"

"I'll sort it," said Harry.

"Start with the half," said Johnny, "and if the trade builds we'll speak about an increase."

Harry's face was poker straight, but inside he was

doing somersaults. He couldn't wait to report back. This could be it! His taskmasters agreed. £15,000 in cash was going to be allowed to run, and a no-arrest strategy was worked out whereby Harry would hand over the 15 grand and walk away with the gear. Of course, they were all going to get lifted later, but this was the little fish to catch a shark approach.

Two days after that conversation in the Ned, Harry Tyler was in possession of £15,000 in used notes, all twenties and tens, all serial numbers having been recorded. He drove to the Ned with the money in a carrier bag concealed under the spare tyre in his boot. When he strode into the bar, Johnny Too was in light conversation with Slobberin' Ron Sullivan.

"John," Harry said. "Have you got two minutes to have a look at the motor?"

"Sure."

Once outside, Harry continued, "John, that other thing we spoke about, I've got the wedge together. Can it happen?"

"Where's the wedge?"

"In the motor."

Unseen and unheard, the cameras were rolling and so was the hidden tape recorder.

"I can't get my hands on half a kilo for a day," said Johnny.

"Well take the 15 and give me a shout."

"Don't you want a sample?"

"For what you say it washes up good, that's all I need."

"H, you're too trusting. How you ever gonna be a rich man?"

"I don't trust many people, John, but I trust you. There's a thousand people I don't, but you won't knock me."

"Why?"

"Cos if you do, I won't tell you no more jokes."

Johnny laughed. "No, mate, you hold on to the wedge until I'm holding."

"John, if I take that away I'll stick it on a dog."

"You sure?"

"Yeah. I know you won't knock me."

The two men shook hands. "Did you see that about Reggie Kray coming out," said Harry. "They say he's dying."

"Gotta be a scam, ain't it?" Johnny replied. "He comes out with one week to live, I bet he's on the Costa for Christmas dinner. I bet the doc took a bung, he's pulling a moody."

"You going to the funeral if it ain't?"

"What, with all the plastics? No, mate. We never knew that lot anyway. Different generation. Me dad had no time for 'em. Too high profile. That's why the Filth had to take 'em out. They'll never get us, H. We ain't got no boyfriends in the aristocracy."

"Yeah," agreed Harry. "You're too smart, John."

They walked to the boot of Harry's car, the rolled-over bag went straight under Johnny Too's armpit and was hidden by his black leather jacket. The movement was as swift as a cruise ship magician concealing a playing card, but not too swift for the camera in the boot to miss.

"Go and have a pint," Johnny said. "I'll be back in a while."

The gangster strolled off towards the neighbour-
ing council estate, then turned back towards Harry
and asked for his car keys. Harry separated them
from his flat keys and threw them over. No more was
said.

A little under an hour later, Johnny Too strolled
into the Ned, slung an arm around Harry who was
sitting at the bar and slid the keys back to him along
the bar.

"Your spare tyre's sorted out, H," he said. "You'll
probably want to shoot off home."

Harry rose and shook his hand. Both men smiled.

As Harry drove off he was tempted to pull over
and check the boot, but he knew better. Instead he
kept on driving, checking constantly in his mirror to
make sure he wasn't being tailed. This was either the
real thing or a major test. He did several roundabouts
three or four times, joined A-roads at one junction
and left them at the next. When Harry was satisfied
he wasn't being followed, he put a call in direct to
Susan Long.

"Can't stop, luv," he said. "I've got the shopping.
I'll be home in ten minutes."

Even he thought he was being over-cautious, but
it had occurred to him that in the hour he had spent
waiting in the Ned, Johnny Too could have stuck a
tape in his car. In the event, he hadn't, but you never
knew.

After forty minutes on the road, Harry turned
into the back yard of a safe house. The doors closed
quickly behind him. DI Suckling was there, and
Harry handed him the keys.

"Baker told me it's in the boot," he said.

"It probably is," Suckling replied. "The snapper at the OP has got some good smudges of Mickey Fenn unlocking your boot and sticking something in there. But neither of the Bakers went within a hundred yards of it."

Mickey Fenn? Seventeen-year-old Mickey? Harry was impressed. "The little shit," he said. "I've got Johnny on tape offering the Charlie up and taking my car keys off me."

They waited as the scenes of crime officer wearing gloves opened the boot. A photographer snapped away. Under the tyre cover was a taped ball-shaped object. More photos. The officer raised it, bagged it and sent it straight off for finger-printing. Before the day was done, they would all know that the parcel contained a half-kilo of 84% pure cocaine, but there wasn't a single dab on it. Not that it mattered. Johnny Too was now nickable.

Harry put in a quick call to Baker, all taped. "John, thanks for helping me out with that puncture. You fancy a knife and fork tomorrow? I'm taking Lesley out to one of them Yankee-style restaurants where the steaks come by the square yard."

"Yeah, blinding. I'll get hold of Geraldine and pick you up round Lesley's at eight."

"Sweet."

"Tell her to get some Pouilly Fuisse in. I'm pig sick of Strongbow."

"She'd have me up against the wall with arrows through me hands."

"Well, you know, Harry, whatever gets you

through the night ..."

If Johnny Too seemed unusually bright, even by his own formidable standards, it was with good reason. The Crown Prosecution Service (often dubbed the Criminal Protection Squad) had begun to drop assault charges from the bungled police raid on the Ned, while young Steven had recovered from what John had dubbed his "spot of botty bother" and was in serious talks with two major software companies about his Mobster game. None of which explained why he rang Harry's phone at the flat at 7.00 am the next morning and asked him to pick up a parcel from Geraldine's home address. Johnny was insistent that the job was double urgent and no-one else was to know about it. The call was all recorded. Harry and the back-up team were curious and excited. What would the parcel be? More drugs, guns, counterfeits? Whatever, it had to be another nail in the coffin of the Baker empire.

At precisely 11.30 am, Harry rang Geraldine's door-bell. She answered the door wearing a towel and apparently nothing else. Fuck, thought Harry, does she know how horny she looks? He noticed a tell-tale white powder mark by her left nostril and knocked his finger against his own nose to give her a clue. "Oh, ta," she said, wiping her nose with the back of her hand. "Come in, Harry, I've got something for you." Harry made himself comfortable in the large, white, leather armchair in her living room. It looked like something out of *OK* magazine. The CD in the corner was playing "Unforgivable Sinner" by Lene Marlin.

"Drink, Harry?"

"No, ta."

"Go on, just a quick one. I could do with some company."

Was she deliberately talking in double entendres?

"OK, small brandy."

Geraldine poured a large Hennessey from a crystal decanter, handed it over and perched on the arm of the chair Harry was sitting in, running her fingers gently over the erect nipples that were making their presence felt through the towel.

"Harry, do you think my boobs are too small."

"Not for me to say," he said stiffly. "If John's happy with 'em, and you're happy, where's the problem?"

She grabbed his free hand and pushed it against her left breast.

"But what do you think?"

Harry pulled his hand back. "I don't think anything. Where's the parcel I've got to take to John?"

"What's wrong, Harry, don't you fancy me?"

"I don't even see you as a woman, Geri. I see Johnny as a mate. I also value my cobblers. Now, I don't know what game you're playing but I do know it'll get people hurt."

He got up and set the brandy down. "No offence, Geraldine. But you're a mate's girl, so please leave it alone. Where's the parcel?"

She got up in a pretend sulk and then giggled.

"Well, if you're sure," she said. "But if you change your mind you know where to find me."

She picked up a lightly taped square card box, no longer than a TV remote and about as deep as two stuck together. It weighed well under a kilo. Harry was puzzled but he took the parcel straight to the Ned. Every time he stopped at traffic lights he looked it over. There was no way he could open it without breaking the tape, and it would be taking a big chance to try and reseal it so he left it as it was. As soon as he walked into the pub, Slobberin' Ron sent him upstairs. Harry found Johnny Too sitting alone at the kitchen table.

"Trouble, John?"

Baker's face was stern. "Have you opened it?"

"Leave it out, John, it ain't my business."

"Why didn't you open it?"

"Because I know what happens to nosey bastards."

"Open it."

He handed Harry a knife. Harry cut the tape and opened the lid. A toy Jack-in-the-box shot out covering him in flour.

Johnny Baker almost wet himself laughing. Harry, who had nearly tripped over his own legs getting out of the way, glared at him.

"What the fuck is going on, John?"

Baker was still in fits of laughter. "Geraldine's tits are too small, ain't they?"

The penny dropped. He had been tested again. Harry affected the air of having the hump, then as Johnny Too rocked with laughter, Harry turned the box upside down and emptied what was left of the flour into his right hand. Johnny Too realised what was coming and shot out of the kitchen and down the stairs towards the bar, laughing all the way. Harry was right behind him and as he reached the bar door he slapped the flour all over the gangster's hair. The two of them burst into the bar, knocking Lesley and Ron backwards, then collapsed on the floor giggling like kids.

"What the fu … ?" said Lesley.

Harry rubbed what was left of the flour into his own crotch.

"Don't worry, Les," he said solemnly. "It's self-raising."

And the two men, the villain and the undercover cop, were lost in laughter and lager for the whole afternoon. They never did make the steakhouse.

The day after Steven's arrest, two angry men made their way to a public toilet near Plumstead Common. One waited in a cubicle while the other loitered by the urinals. They didn't have to wait long. A gay man, a Marxist Sociology lecturer from the University of Greenwich, wandered in and made the assumptions he was supposed to. His clumsy pass was repaid with a savage right hook. As he struggled to get up again, another bigger man appeared from nowhere and joined in the vicious flurry of kicks and punches.

"My kid could have been taking a leak in here," screamed Dougie The Dog.

"You shitter!" snarled Pyro Joe as he stomped on the man's head.

"You're dog shit," yelled The Dog as he delivered the blow that knocked him senseless.

Panting, Doug looked across at Joey, smiled, unzipped his flies and started to urinate on the man's shoes.

"Why piss on his feet?" asked Joe. "What's wrong with his face?"

As Dougie redirected his stream, Pyro Joe unzipped his trousers and joined in.

"It's a shame he missed this," said The Dog.

"Why?"

"It's probably one of his fucking fantasies."

CHAPTER SEVEN

MILLWALL AWAY

The nicking of young Steven Richards gnawed away at Joey Baker's mind like hungry termites in a timber yard feeding frenzy. To Pyro Joe and the equally belligerent Dougie The Dog, this indignity was a major affront to the Bakers' reputation. OK, Steve may have been caught bang to rights playing YMCA on the pink piccolo – the SICK BASTARD! – but he was still FAMILY. They had to show their support and face down any detractors, real or imagined; and that meant being there at Bexleyheath magistrates court for Steven's appearance and remand. What Steven felt about their company was immaterial.

So Joey and Doug sat bored outside court number one in the foyer, watching Steven chat to Matt Mohan, one of Bondman's junior solicitors. The cold austerity of the building and the suffocating presence of various agents of the law going about their business did little to improve their mood.

"What a fucking thing to get nicked for," moaned Joe for the hundreth time that month.

"Un-fuckin'-believable," agreed Doug.

"Receiving stolen goods is one thing, but swollen goods? What's all that about?"

Dougie sniggered then became deadly serious. "We oughta go torch that pervert teacher's drum," he said.

Joey nodded and cracked his knuckles. "If that clock went any slower it'd be going backwards," he said.

"Fancy a tea out of the machine?"

"Yeah, three sugars."

A fatal car crash on the A2 near the Dartford river crossing interchange had caused chaos for motorists coming in to London from Kent. The magistrate and the chief clerk were among those delayed. Ironically, a week from now the opposite problem – too little traffic – would be equally disruptive as the petrol blockade by hauliers and farmers kept cars off the road. In anticipation, Johnny Too had just taken delivery of 25,000 litres of agricultural red diesel, which was illegal on British roads but perfectly efficient and, as it happened, a nice little earner.

Joey was so bored he picked a copy of the *Guardian* out of the bin and flicked through it. How could people read this shit, he wondered. Even the cartoon was dull. A sudden commotion yanked his eyes away from the paper's snidey gossip column. It was Dougie The Dog kicking the tea machine. Joey laughed, chucked the paper back in the bin where it belonged, and strolled over.

"What's up, mate?" he asked.

"Fucking thing," said Doug. "Taste this. I pressed tea and it's given me Oxtail soup."

Joey sipped it and pulled a face. "It's too salty for Oxtail. You sure you didn't press Bovril."

"It don't even do fucking Bovril," Doug exploded.

"Guys, please!" It was Steven.

"Come on, Doug," said Joe. "Let's go get a beer. Gi's a bell if anything starts happening, Steve."

"Yeah, no problem."

Still shaking with frustration Dougie The Dog and Pyro Joe made straight for a sports bar just off Bexleyheath Broadway. They got there thirteen minutes after a mob of British National Party bootboys who stood around the bar like a clenched fist. By coincidence, the neo-Nazis were there for the court, too. One of their heroic number had courageously chucked a bucket of human excrement into the worst of the four curryhouses in Sidcup High Street. Several locals opined that the crap could only have improved the menu, but the cops weren't as forgiving. The chucker, David O'Dell, an IT recruitment consultant from Erith, was popular with his comrades for his cruel sense of humour. The previous year O'Dell had seen a group of Asians collecting for Bangladesh Flood Relief outside Somerfield and had contributed a bucket of water flung from a moving car.

The BNP contingent were all in their early 20s, dressed to a man in football shirts – two West Ham, five Chelsea. Dougie The Dog walked straight up alongside them. "I thought you Chelsea cunts hated these West Ham wankers," he said, adding as an after-thought, "Two pints of lager, and three packets of crisps, love. Do you do hot grub at all?"

The barmaid stood motionless as the six-foot-six gorilla in the Chelsea top turned and snarled, "What did you say, you little prick?"

Dougie looked straight at the barmaid. "Make that Fosters, darling. There's a good girl, and cheese and onion crisps."

"Are you deaf as well as fick?" Chelsea snapped. "What did you fucking say?"

All seven men moved into a semi-circle around The Dog. Pyro Joe reached over for a heavy glass ashtray and slammed it hard against the giant Chelsea supporter's head. The big man went like a bought-off boxer on a Don King bill.

"He said, what fucking team do you tossers really support?" Joe explained helpfully.

Doug slammed his fist into the nearest West Ham face. His mate spun and delivered a perfect round house karate kick that knocked The Dog off his feet. As he fell, three BNP boots went in. Pyro Joe grabbed a heavy bar stool and spun it round like it was made of plywood, smashing into all of them. Coughing up blood, Dougie struggled to his feet, grabbed an empty Budweiser bottle and smashed it over David O'Dell's head. Claret spurted all over his Dennis Wise shirt. The BNP had four men down. The remaining three backed off as Joey kept the bar stool swinging.

"When them cunts come round, tell 'em they met Millwall," grinned Dougie.

They left the pub colliding with a teenager in a Charlton shirt who was chatting into his mobile phone. Joe grabbed the mobile and smashed it into the kid's face.

"There y'go," smirked Dougie. "It's true what they say, using a mobile is bad for your health."

"MILL – WALL!" Joey chanted. "MILLLLLWAL-LLLLL!"

Laughing, they jogged up the road towards an old white van that Doug had borrowed from his painter and decorator dad for the day.

"White Van Man says messing with Millwall is too risky," Dougie joked.

Pyro Joe laughed too. "I fucking needed that," he said.

"Me, too."

"Where did those wankers get to? Shitters! They didn't even come out the boozer."

Doug opened the van and they got in. "Here, Joe," he said. "Remember that time in Bulgaria when we were drinking in that bar full of secret police and you went in and picked up those two stools with the tarts sitting on them and held them above yer head?"

Joey nodded.

"What did you say again, Joe? How did it go?"

Pyro smiled. "We're English, how d'ya wanna be?" he recalled.

"They bought us drinks all fucking night!"

Pyro Joe suddenly looked serious. "Wonder how Steve got on," he said.

"Dunno, I'll ring John, see if he's heard."

The mobile had just connected when the van was

swamped by a dozen uniformed cops. Two of the BNP boys were already on their way to hospital with fractured heads and broken bones.

Steven Richards was remanded on bail and left the court. He arrived home several hours ahead of Pyro Joe and The Dog. No charges ever arose from their sports bar fracas, because no-one would ever pick them out from an ID parade, but for some reason Johnny Too didn't find news of their brutal antics as amusing as they did. The Baker brothers had another almighty row and Johnny stormed off home where Sandra was still percolating with fury over Geraldine. As her brains were never the equal of her beauty, Sandra saw John's arrival as another opportunity to give her husband a bit of verbal GBH; even the uncharacteristic slam of the front door didn't warn her off.

At first Johnny Baker tried to keep calm and reasonable. Lying through his teeth, he assured her that he had finished with Geraldine, that she had meant nothing to him anyway, he was just using her for sex – the usual old fanny. But Sandra kept on like a dog with a bone until Johnny snapped and everything came out in the wash – she didn't satisfy him sexually any more, she drank too much, she was holding him back ... what was wrong with Chislehurst for fuck's sake? Why not improve yourself?

"I bet *she'd* like fuckin' Chislehurst," Sandra screamed.

"Who?"

"Your fuckin' WHORE!"

"Don't call her that."

"Why? She's a fucking old whore. A slag. A slapper, a fucking prostitute."

That was it. Crack! Johnny Too slapped her hard, then hated himself for it. Sandra broke down in tears. He turned round and walked, slamming the door and driving straight back to the Ned.

Johnny slept in the office that night. He thought of going to Geri's but wasn't sure he could afford a divorce right now, not with Chislehurst going through.

The next morning he summoned Harry Tyler to the Ned for a chat. The conversation threw him entirely.

"Sit down, Harry," said Johnny Too. "Beer?"

"Bit early, mate."

"Yeah. Look, H, I'll get straight to the point. I've heard you spend a bit of time across the water in Holland."

"Yeah," Harry said slowly. "Just to the Dam really, bit of social, window shopping for a shag, the odd puff, y'know."

"I've got some business in Amsterdam this weekend and I need a bit of cover."

"OK, no problem, John. Tell the old lady you're doing some biz with me over the East End and stopping out."

"No, no, not like that. I've had a right up-and-downer with Sandra, but that'll blow over. No, my problem is Joey and Doug are like magnets for shit at the moment and they need to calm down. They're attracting attention and I don't need it. I've got some boys coming up from Malaga who want a meet in Amsterdam and I need someone who knows what's what to watch my back out there."

"Right, John. I'm there, I'm your man. I appreciate being asked."

Johnny lit a fat cigar and inhaled deeply. "You might wanna invest as well. I've got a fuck-off parcel of Charlie on the way up. It's the bullet, know what I mean?"

"How much are we looking at?"

"How much finance can you put up?"

"John, I ain't in your division. You're Premier and I only just got promoted into the first. At tops I can move 5K at the right price. That's tops. But I can't finance it till it's here. Mate, you're sweet for the offer but I ain't got that sort of dough around me."

Johnny leaned forward and lowered his voice. "Look, H, there's a lot riding on this. A few faces have sunk their houses into financing it. One fuck-up and a lot of questions are gonna be asked. When I say it's the big one, I mean 'kin' HUGE. It's fucking Man United and Microsoft. It's *serious*. It's gonna sort out all my worries and then some."

"I'll put me cards on the table, John. I ain't a patsy and I ain't a wrong 'un. If there's a deal for me, I'm there. I can slaughter a good parcel to trusted people, me to them, one to one for ya, but I ain't telling no one to get their dough ready up front cos a mountain of snow is on the way. Once it's here I can move bundles COD to sweet geezers but me, personally, I just ain't got the wedge."

"Right, I get the picture, mate, and it's digitally enhanced. It's not a problem. The main thing is you're on for Amsterdam. I need someone I can trust. I'll get us booked on a flight for Friday coming back Monday. What's a good hotel?"

"The Jolly Carlton off Dam Square works for me. What time scale are we working to for the parcel, or shouldn't I ask?"

"If all goes well, my old son, we'll have a result in two weeks. It's already on its way. I've just got to sort a few loose ends out."

"And you're sure you want to meet in Amsterdam?"

"There's a reason, H. Nothing to fret about."

"You're the boss."

"That's right, pussy cat. And I'm SMOKING."

Harry Tyler left the Ned as quickly as possible. He was screaming inside. He was IN! He was on the firm. Then the doubts came screaming in. Why wasn't Baker using someone else, an old-established soldier? That didn't quite gel, and yet the vibe with him and Johnny was good. Harry felt cautiously optimistic. His immediate priority was to get authority to travel overseas. Then surveillance at Gatwick and on the aircraft had to be sorted, Dutch co-operation confirmed and surveillance from Schiphol Airport until they came back to Blighty. Harry's head was buzzing. He had to discover the cocaine's point of entry into the UK, how it was coming, where it was going, who would receive it, would the Baker clan have hands on, who were the other major players involved in financing it ...

Harry was on autopilot for the remainder of the day. He drove back to East London first, just in case he was being tailed, took the last lager out of the fridge – a can of Heineken export, all the way from Holland, an omen? – then made his coded calls on his mobile. Within the hour he was winging his way to Southend for a top-level conflab. He was given authority to travel, and assured full back-up. It was agreed that if anything urgent arose he was to leave a message in a sealed envelope in the wall-safe in his room, which the locals would pick up while he was out of the hotel with Johnny Too. Harry left his superiors feeling tired but elated. The future of the Baker firm was now in the hands of the national police élite.

The early morning call at 4.30 am proved unnecessary. Harry had slept fitfully and had been watching the clock since 3.13 am. He showered, shaved and left the flat, pausing momentarily outside Elaine's place, imagining he'd caught a whiff of her L'Eau D'Issey and fantasising briefly about rekindling fading passions. It was a beautiful but chilly Friday morning. *En route* to Gatwick, Harry made a quick call, a simple coded message and was assured that not only was everything in hand but also, even as he sped along the M25 towards the M23, that he was "under control". Harry marvelled at how shit-hot the surveillance on him was. He would often look for "ghosts" but seldom detected any. He glimpsed in his rear view mirror. A blue Vauxhall saloon was holding its distance behind him. Harry knew instinctively that this was his escort. He knew it until the moment it sped past him with a woman driving and kids who stared blankly at him, all asleep with eyes wide open.

At 7.30 am, Harry nestled the motor into the long-term NCP car park, missing the connecting bus by seconds. He was maybe five minutes late when he reached the British Airways check-in desk, but it wasn't that making him feel flustered. Johnny Too was where he said he would be and looking sharp, dressed head to toe in the finest designer clobber the black market could provide. No, what threw Harry out of his stride was the sight of Geraldine and Lesley standing next to Baker, Armani-ed up to high heaven clutching passports and tickets in their hands.

"Surprise, surprise," Johnny Too sang like some demented Cilla, a banana smile wedged across his face. "The unexpected waits with open thighs …"

He high-fived Harry boisterously. "Knew you'd appreciate my little twist," he said. "What better cover, eh?"

"Yeah, nice, yeah, great," Harry said, as enthusiastically as he could. "We're all in the same hotel I hope?"

"Are you taking the piss?" Johnny replied. "Of fucking course. You like their gear? New outfits courtesy your old pal Johnny Too. Got 'em from the Armani And Navy surplus store."

"Ouch, John. That fucking pun hurt."

Baker roared. "Who loves ya, baby?" he bellowed. "Harry, we have got one fuck of a weekend ahead of us."

Harry smiled and gave Lesley a kiss. He checked in then motioned to Johnny that it was time to visit the gents. Inside, Harry's mask of agreeability crumbled.

"John, what the fuck is going on?" he moaned. "I thought we were going to do business."

"Two birds with one stone, H." Johnny Too shrugged. "I've had a blow-up with the missus so I needed to get away to be with Geri, and while you and me can handle the biz the girls can shop till they drop. Geri knows the score, she can blow all the dough as long as she blows me afterwards."

"Mate, you might have clued me. I could have had two bits of skirt meeting us at the other end."

Johnny laughed as he sprinkled the urinal. "Well, I never mind sharing," he grinned. "Chill out, Harry, just enjoy the weekend. It's gonna be special. We'll get the work over quick. We've got a meet tomorrow morning at ten near the station."

Harry smiled weakly. Having the two women about might make slipping away for urgent updates tougher, but he'd manage if he had to.

On the plane he sat next to Johnny Too. They chatted about football briefly, both agreed that Charlton Athletic would stay up this time, and then more passionately about neglected rock bands that mattered. Johnny suggested The Ruts, The Skids and the UK Subs; Harry came up with Rose Tattoo and the Drop Kick Murphys. Both rated Cock Sparrer, the Stone Roses and The Business.

"What about The Grams," asked Geraldine.

"When was they about?" said Johnny Too.

"Oh, recent," Geri grinned. "You just don't read the right books."

She took a copy of the Kevin Sampson novel *Powder* out of her hand luggage. "The best book about the rock business since *Platinum Logic*," she said.

"That's fucking cheating," Harry complained.

"Since when did you know about the rock business?" asked Johnny.

"I was raised on it," said Geri. "My brother used to roadie for The Blood."

"Good band," Johnny and Harry said as one. Johnny added: "I was there at the old Marquee when they chain-sawed a blow-up doll stuffed full of butcher's offal."

"Sweet," said Geri sarcastically.

"Here, have you seen this?" piped up Lesley, who was reading the *Sun*. "Police in Texas have arrested a suspect who had £6,000 in cash hidden in his buttocks, it says here, from dealing in marijuana."

"They sure it weren't crack?" roared Johnny Too.

"Talk about dirty money," laughed Geraldine.

"Maybe it's a new way of laundering," suggested Johnny.

"Yeah," said Harry. "But here's where it gets painful. It was all in fucking quarters."

Johnny was in hysterics. Then Geraldine noticed an article in her *Daily Mail* about the latest IRA terrorist to be let out of the Maze and claim "compensation".

"This is mad, John, isn't it?" she said.

"It's sick," Johnny Too scowled. "It really is the old joke, Kill a Brit and win a fucking Metro."

"It makes you die," Harry added angrily. "Break a speed limit and you're Public Enemy Number One. Bomb Canary Wharf and not only will HM Government let you walk, they'll fucking sub you for your trouble. These politicians are completely out of touch."

"It's like these paedophiles," said Lesley. "the *News Of The World* was right. They should be named and shamed."

"It'd be different if Tony Blair found one re-housed in Downing Street," said Geri.

"It doesn't happen like that, though, does it?" Harry said. "They stick 'em on council estates, let the working class suffer. Same with asylum seekers."

"Why should the politicians care?" added Geri. "They don't live in our world. They live in a world where Lord Irvine can spend £1,528 of public money on two heated hand towels."

Harry smiled. Geraldine was right, of course, but he found her middle-class indignation funny for some reason he couldn't fathom. Not to mention a turn-on.

"Anyway, fuck all that," said Johnny Too. "Who wants a shot out of Uncle John's hip flask? It's Knob Creek sipping whiskey, 100 per cent proof."

"Me," said Lesley.

"And me," Geri shouted greedily.

—

"Who sang 'Uncle John's Band'?" asked Harry.

"Grateful Dead," answered Johnny Too. "Next question …"

The flight was over as soon as it had begun. As the four strolled towards the airport exit, a young, hippy type tugged Harry's arm.

"Where's the Customs, man?" he asked.

"There ain't any, son. They don't pull you going in."

"So we're in Holland, then?" the kid said.

"Yeah."

"No Customs?"

"No."

The scruffy teenager reached down the front of his trousers and into his underpants. He pulled out a spliff and sparked up. "Fucking lovely," he said, and walked off giggling.

Harry smiled. "Coals to Newcastle," he said.

"Muppet," snorted Johnny Too. "Where do we get the sherbet?"

"No, we don't need a cab, mate," said Harry. "We'll walk down that way and get a funny old double-decker train to Central Station. When we get to the other end it's a straight walk down through Dam Square. It takes longer by cab.

Amsterdam Central Station was crawling with long-haired beggars. "Fucking hippy shithead," snarled Johnny Too as he shoved one sad case out of his path. "Go take a bath in the canal. How far's this fucking hotel, H? Let's get a cab for fucksake."

"Hold up, mate," said Harry. "Just over the road there you've got the best herring stand in Holland."

"What, roll-mops?" moaned Lesley. "I don't like roll-mops."

"No, it's fresh with onion on top," Harry said. "Trust me, darling, it's good scoff."

They had to stop at the herring stand to ensure that the surveillance team were with them.

The Jolly Carlton is next to the Bloemarket, a collection of market stalls selling the most beautiful and fragrant flowers in Holland.

"They're fabulous," enthused Lesley.

"If the Dutch know how to do one thing well, it's growing plants," said Harry. "And not just the kind that make you happy."

They checked in and went off to inspect the spacious rooms, which were quite splendid for the price. In the Tyler camp, Lesley bent over to undo her travel case. Harry admired her perfect pins and decided to make the most of the situation. He grabbed her waist and threw her on the bed. They kissed and he slipped his hand up inside her miniskirt. Lesley reached down and grabbed it. "Not today, H, I can't, the painters are in. I'll be OK tomorrow."

"I don't mind getting me red wings."

"You filthy sod."

"Well, get me dick out and give it a jostle or something, darling, I've had a lob on all the way up here."

"Well, really, Mr Tyler," said Lesley in her best *Gone With The Wind* accent. "I do believe you're a-wooing me."

She unzipped his flies, released his eager member and fellated him silently – well, she was a good girl and her mum had brought her up never to speak with her mouth full. For his part, Harry envisaged the petite Italian brunette, a Karen Baggoley look-alike, he had fucked not five minutes from this hotel the last time he was in Amsterdam. He came in 90 seconds.

"Cor, you really needed that," said Lesley after she'd swallowed his semen.

"Yeah, ta, doll."

She tried to kiss him.

"Fuck off, you dirty cow," he said, holding her at arm's length. "I don't wanna taste me own spunk, do I? Brush yer teeth and let's go for a beer."

"Hold up, Harry. I'm going to have a shower and unpack. You go down and have a pint with Johnny."

"They don't have pints over here."

"Well, you know what I mean."

Harry sat alone at the hotel bar as the bar steward warmed up a large bowl glass for his brandy in a small metal box heater. He was just finishing his second when Lesley and Geraldine finally joined him. The vapour from the fumes had made Harry feel quite high. Maybe he imagined seeing Geri give Lesley an over-long squeeze as they parted to sit down.

"Johnny won't be long, he's ringing his mum from the room," smiled Geri as Harry got a round in.

Johnny Too turned up 20 minutes later and gave Harry a covert thumbs up, and ordered more drinks. Johnny put an arm round Harry and said softly, "The girls are going shopping tomorrow. You and me can go and have a beer."

Then he reached over to a bowl on a nearby table, scooped up a handful of Japanese crackers and crammed them into his mouth.

"We eating, then?" Johnny said loudly. "I'm famished."

For the rest of Friday they did the tourist thing: beer, more beer, the red light district for a snigger, the sex museum, a meal, and a live sex show, followed by a smokey session in the Bulldog Café which sells the finest puff in Europe. Johnny Too loved the café's logo, a snarling cartoon bulldog's head in a circle, and bought four XL sweatshirts there and then. From here they strolled slowly along the canals, looking at the stars, and on down past the "skinny bridge", the couples splitting apart to kiss and cuddle "just like normal people", Johnny observed the next day.

Harry and Lesley fell into bed at 2.57 am according to the clock in the room. When he awoke at 8 am he could remember fondling her breasts but nothing more. Dressing quickly, Harry left Lesley a note and wandered down for breakfast. A hung-over Johnny Too wasn't long behind.

"Bad head, mate?" smiled Harry.

"That fucking dope was too heavy."

"That explains it. I knew it couldn't be the beer, the brandy or the red wine. You having breakfast?"

"Fuck no, just coffee. Black and sweet."

Harry poured him a cup and said, "What's happening, then?"

"We've got a meet at one o'clock outside the front of the sea museum. I've got the address."

"It's OK, I know it. I'll steer the girls in the right direction for the shops. The Hooftstraat area should do 'em."

"I've bunged them a few hundred each to get something nice to wear."

"Cheers, Johnny."

"When I meet this bird, just hang around and keep dog-eye for me. She's gonna give me some times and places. I've got to go somewhere on me Tod first to pick up a hold-all. Just keep an eye on me with that till I hand it over to her."

"Yeah, no problem."

"It's just running expenses. The rest is sorted. I'll meet you back here at eleven."

"Cool, I'll go up and have a shave and whatever."

"Yeah, and give her a whatever for me, too." Johnny Too threw back the coffee. "I've already told Geri I'll see her here with Les at about seven tonight."

"Fine."

Baker got up and said, "Laters, then." He left the hotel. Harry couldn't help but notice the villain didn't seem half as cocky here as he did in South London. He watched an elegantly dressed woman leave the hotel behind Baker. She was smart but not showy, not the sort of woman you'd notice in a crowd. He was confident she was surveillance, but who knew? Harry finished eating, left a few gilders tip and went back to his room. As he got there, Geri was coming out.

"Morning, Harry," she said with a huge grin. "Just checking what time we're going shopping." As she drew level with him she gave him a kiss on the cheek. "Has Johnny gone out?"

Harry felt her right breast nestle against his arm. "Yeah," he said. "I'm meeting him here later. You want me to show you two where to go shopping?"

"No, that's OK. Us girls have got a nose for shops. Don't worry about us. We won't be back until our little purses are vacuums."

"That's what I was worried about."

Geri laughed and slinked away, letting her right hand brush his leg. Harry swore she wasn't like this with anyone else. Was it another Baker test? He let himself in.

"Is that you, Geri?" Lesley called from the shower.

"Nah, me. She's gone back to her room."

Lesley stepped out dripping wet. She wrapped a towel around her hair but wasn't in any hurry to cover up her magnificent body.

"I thought you'd gone out with Johnny."

"No, I'm meeting him later, hon," said Harry letting his eyes feast on her nakedness.

"Well we better make up for lost time then."

As they made love the thought of Lesley and Geri at it instead played around Harry's mind. Could they be having a little thing going on? He'd have paid good money to watch if they did …

The girls left within the hour. Harry bought a *Daily Mail* at reception. It was 11.20 am, so he strolled round to the bar and had a small beer. He glanced through the paper. There was never much in it on a Saturday; he only bought it in the week for Keith Waterhouse. Bored, he glanced around the bar. There was a smartly dressed woman of about fifty standing at the far left end chatting away to the bar steward in Dutch, or was it German? The barman laughed politely and Harry looked away. There was a young couple sitting to one side, holding hands, who failed to hold his interest. Once again Harry had failed to spot the surveillance team.

Moments later, Johnny Too appeared carrying a black Head hold-all in his left hand. The gangster looked strangely unsettled.

"Get us a beer, H," he ordered.

"You OK?"

"Yeah, no problem."

Johnny Baker sat down, wedging the hold-all firmly between his ankles.

Harry nodded at the bag. "Any trouble?" he asked.

"Nah, mate. Once I'm out of this, the engine's oiled."

"Looks heavy."

"Well freighted, know what I mean?"

The trade-mark Baker brashness had dissolved, he clearly wanted the hold-all away from him.

"Cake O?" asked Harry.

"Fucking wedged corner to corner, top to fucking bottom."

"How soon do we ..."

"Five minutes, maybe ten. There's enough shekels in there to buy every pussy in the red light district tonight."

"If they're the same old hounds as last night, you could probably get 'em three times over."

Johnny Too laughed, but it was forced. Harry had never seen Baker look stressed before, but he hoped beyond hope he would see him even more worried, and soon.

"So, the sea museum, then," he said. "Have you got a cab booked?"

"Nope," said Johnny. "I changed the meet, she's coming here."

Curious, thought Harry. Did Baker suspect something was up? Can't do. If he did, they wouldn't be sitting there now. Johnny leaned towards him.

"I had to put a call in when I collected the wedge," he said softly. "I told them to change the meeting place, said I wasn't happy with their choice. It's no problem, she's already here."

Johnny Too's eyes darted to two women at the bar. The smartly dressed fiftysomething, whom Harry had eyeballed earlier, had now been joined by another slightly shorter woman with darker hair. Johnny gave the smaller woman a nod.

"Just follow us into the lift, H," he instructed. "Keep your eyes about you in case I get rolled."

As the women walked across the hotel lobby, Harry noticed that the darker one was carrying a large, barrel-type red leather hold-all. They waited by the lift, Johnny stood a foot behind them, with Harry two feet behind him. As the lift doors opened a huge black man stepped out. Harry tensed himself but he walked straight past them.

"Thank fuck he didn't want to know," he whispered.

"Don't worry," said Johnny Too. "I've got the equaliser kit with me."

He made the sign of a gun with his left hand.

"What?"

The women walked into the lift. Harry held Johnny back.

"You must be mad carrying that over here, John."

"What am I, a pilchard? I had it delivered. It's been pugged up in the room and it goes before we check out. Now come on, it's rude to keep ladies waiting."

The taller woman was holding the door. When the men entered she pressed the top floor button. The doors closed and the short woman took a blonde wig from her hold-all and pulled it on. Then she put on a pair of glasses and turned her jacket inside out. Harry looked down and spotted a second Head bag, identical to Johnny's, inside her hold-all. She pulled it out and exchanged it for Baker's one. Not a word had been said. As if on cue, the lift arrived at the top and the doors opened. The woman in the wig stepped out with her red leather bag. An Asian man waited for the others to exit, but the remaining woman spoke to him in Dutch. He nodded, said something back to her and stepped in. Harry guessed that she had simply told him they had got the wrong floor. She pressed the third floor button and ground.

The Asian man got out at floor three. The doors

began to close. The woman looked at Johnny Too and spoke in English for the first time.

"It's a shame I have a plane to catch," she said. "I could sure fuck you two tonight."

Baker laughed. "Just make sure my gear arrives next Friday or I'll be fucking you with a baseball bat on Saturday."

The woman allowed a crease of a smile to cross her lips.

"You English are such charmers. My associates will not disappoint you, Mr Baker."

The lift reached the ground and she stepped out first, saying, "You boys have a nice day," in a forced American accent. With that she made straight for the main entrance and was gone.

"Fuck me, John," said Harry. "Red skies over Moscow or what? What was all that about? I feel like I'm in a Bond film or something."

"Then let's hope we meet Pussy Galore. Come on, H, I'll buy you a beer."

Harry followed Johnny Too back to the bar.

"Two beers, me old Dutch," said Johnny who was noticeably happier. "I'll get these, H, I'll just have a lash. Tell him to put 'em on room 317."

"Were those ladies with you?" asked the bar steward. "She has left her lighter and cigarettes."

"Yeah," said Harry. "I'll give 'em to her later."

As the barman turned to pour the beers, Harry wrapped up the lighter and cigarettes in a serviette and slipped them into his jacket pocket for DNA testing and finger-printing. Johnny returned and motioned for Harry to join him in an alcove. Harry brought over the beers as Johnny rummaged through his new Head bag. He pulled out a padded Jiffy bag and read its contents silently. Harry was bursting to know what it said but knew better than to ask. Instead he sipped his beer and stared at the floor.

"Harry," John said eventually, as he replaced the bag and its contents in the hold-all, "do you know what I like about you?"

"Don't say fuck all, John, or I'll get the hump and burn your puff."

Baker's smile vanished and he jabbed his right-hand index finger at Harry.

"No jokes, H. What I fucking like about you is you're the only fucking geezer I know who didn't ask what was in the envelope."

Harry frowned back at Johnny, mirroring his seriousness.

"You know why I never asked, John?"

"Why?"

"Cos I read it all backwards in the window reflection behind you."

Baker glanced over his shoulder. The windows were about twenty feet away. Both men laughed.

"No seriously, John. It ain't my business. I don't ask questions if it ain't my business."

"H, I don't need a degree in psychology to know you're proper. I've got a good sense of judgement when it comes to people. I can tell if someone's a wrong 'un in minutes, sometimes seconds. You probably can yerself. Nah, you're top dollar, mate."

"So what does it say, then?"

"Joking aside, this time next week I am fuckin'

rich. We've got a lorry to meet filled to the roof with onions and tomatoes."

"Lovely job. Never tried snorting onions meself ..."

"Makes yer fuckin' eyes water."

"Do you need me to help out, John?"

Baker paused, then shook his head. "No," he said. "I'm sorted for the slaughter, I've got a place down Bermondsey docks, and plenty of faces on the plot, but I might need you to keep dog-eye around the manor as the lorry rolls in. Y'know, keep an eye out for the Filth."

"John, I ain't gotta say be careful," said Harry, his voice heavy with concern. "There's a ton of bird waiting if you get caught with that parcel."

Johnny Too made the sign of a handgun again. "They'll think World War III has broken out if they try and take us. Don't worry, H. I've got plenty of scouts out and a good firm to unload it. I just wanna see it's there and then I'm out of the scene, know what I mean."

Harry gave it one more push. "You want me to drive you?"

Baker shook his head. "Nah, Geri's gonna run me in, looks less iffy with a bird driving."

Harry Tyler was shocked. What kind of a man puts his woman on offer?

"Mate, you sure?" he said. "It ain't my business but ..."

Johnny Too cut him short. "H, I appreciate your concern, but she's sweet as. She's a big grown-up girl and she knows what she's getting into."

Harry knew not to say any more. So Geraldine would get nicked with the rest of them. In the immortal words of Grant Mitchell, "Oh dear, what a pity, never mind." Johnny's logic made some sort of sense and, besides, he was hardly treating Lesley like Sir Galahad.

Their business in Amsterdam was done, but they still had over six hours before they were due to meet the girls and so Johnny Baker and Harry Tyler, the gangster and the undercover cop, set off on a marathon bar crawl.

The third bar seemed the friendliest. They sat at the bar talking about football to a couple of young Dutch men. It was all very pleasant. Then Johnny Too went for a slash, and the man next to Harry put his hand on the detective's thigh and asked with a smile, "Can I come in your mouth?"

Harry may have moved faster in his life but he couldn't remember when. He collided with Johnny Too who had made the same discovery just from the posters in the gents. They didn't even stop to finish their drinks.

"You must have known," said Johnny accusingly.

"How would I know?"

"You come here all the time."

"Yeah, but I'd never been to that bar."

"So why was your mobile number written on the khazi wall?"

"It can't be ..."

"It is now!"

"Bastard."

"You must have noticed there were no women in there."

"Did you?"

"I just thought they were, y'know, football geezers ..."

By 4.00 pm, they found a bar they liked and settled.

"This is OK, H," said Johnny. "Amsterdam. I like it. I like the vibe, if not the weather."

"I never want too much sun," said Harry. "Why do I want to lie on a beach and fry for a fortnight? What am I, a fucking lizard?"

"You grumpy bastard! You've been to Spain, though?"

"Menorca, once."

"Where d'you stay?"

"Cala N'Porter."

"Nice. Jimmy Jones has got a villa there. Two I think."

"Kinnel!"

"Where did you eat?"

"La Polette, up by the caves of Zorro."

"Xorai. Pukka grub up there, a bit dearer but ..."

"But worth it."

"Ever been to St Pete's Beach in Florida, Harry? It's a little slice of paradise. I fancy getting a little waterside condo over there once Chislehurst is done and dusted."

"The working-class dream, eh, Johnny? Moving out to respectable suburbia, holidays with Mickey Mouse."

"You taking the piss?"

"No, mate, that would be my dream, too."

Johnny Too lit up a spliff. "You vote Labour, H?"

"I voted for Blair."

"Why?"

Harry shrugged. "Dunno – now," he said.

"I'll tell you why, cos your dad was Labour and your granddad and probably his dad an' all."

"Yeah, but Labour stands for the working man, equality, fraternity, a fairer society."

"Fair? What's fair? You ever see a nature documentary, Harry? You see the lion taking down the gazelle? Where is the fairness in that? That's life, H, the survival of the fittest. Do you wanna be the lion or his fucking dinner?"

Harry went to say something, but Johnny Too ploughed on. "Society is built on lies, mate," he said. "And you've just hit on the biggest. All men are equal? Where? It's bollocks. The basic truth of human life is that all men aren't equal. Tom is stronger than Dick who is cleverer than Harry. Life is about winners and losers, H, the élite and the also-rans, and if you're born at the arse end of society like we were, all that matters is, if you're hard enough and smart enough, you have to become part of the élite. Kick, claw or cheat your way in. It don't matter how. Otherwise you'll just be ground into the dust with all the other monkeys."

"So you wouldn't call yerself working class?"

"Why wouldn't I? I was born working class. I can't stand to be with middle class people; even those that work for me I only tolerate. I like working-class people. I like their company, their culture, if you like. The people in South London are much the same as they are over your side, or probably in any English city – they're good people, solid, loyal. They look after their own. They're inward-looking, too, which some people think is a weakness but I think is a strength, and they're fiercely patriotic. But basically the English working class have been hoodwinked."

"How d'you mean, John?"

"You talk to the fellas in the Ned, specially the older ones. Their idea of the world and England's place in it is entirely defined by the papers they read, and it always harks back to World War II, 55 fucking years ago. That England don't exist any more, Harry. It's been destroyed by the Arabs and the Muslims, Europe and the bogus fucking asylum seekers taking us for mugs. The way England is going, it's gonna end up the Islamic Republic of North West Europe."

Harry felt a shiver down his back. He's right, he thought. He's fucking right.

Johnny Too downed his beer. "Ratbag politicians and big businesses who don't give a fuck about England exploit their patriotism," he went on, "and they'll carry on exploiting it until they're pushing up the fucking daisies.

"So, yes, I'm working class, but that ain't the be-all and end-all. I've been poor and I've been rich and believe me rich is better. All you can do is look after yerself and yer own, Harry. Carve out your territory and defend it mercilessly. Now get a fucking round in before I get signed up for *Panorama*."

Harry ordered two beers. "I don't wanna bang on about politics," said Harry, "but I think the welfare state is the thing that really made England weak. It was a great idea in theory, to create a safety net to look after the old and the sick but it turned into a dossers' paradise. We've turned nature on its head so much we're in a situation where ..." He paused, searching for the correct quote. "It's like 'when all men are paid for existing and no man need pay for his sins'."

"Kipling," said Johnny.

"Yeah," Harry replied, surprised. "I didn't know you were a reader, Johnny."

"Now you insult me."

"No, it's just I could see you soaking up Tarantino, but not Nick Hornby."

"Talk daft," Johnny spluttered. "I wouldn't have that cunt in the house. Did you ever read any Nick Hornby, Harry? This is supposed to be men's writing – go to football, eat a fucking curry. Not exactly Hemingway, is it? Tom Wolfe is the only living novelist I'd give the time of day to. But Kipling was the boyo. In his time, men were men and Britain meant something. They had an Empire to believe in."

"So what do you think of villains who write autobiographies, these kill-and-tell books?"

"Anyone who writes a book like that is a grass," Johnny Too proclaimed. "Unless they're working a flanker and mugging the publishers like Courtney. So don't get any fucking ideas."

"I'll turn the tape recorder off, then," Harry grinned.

On they talked and drank until Harry realised it was 7.15 pm. They scrambled into a cab and arrived at the meeting place at 7.28 pm. The girls didn't let on they had only been there five minutes themselves.

"Leave us standing on the corner for half an hour," moaned Lesley. "It's fucking 'taters and we've had blokes coming up thinking we're on the game."

"Don't say you turned them down," said Johnny Too. "You could have made a few bob, paid me back for my generosity."

"Pig," said Lesley.

"She's right, John," Harry deadpanned. "Be fair, they wouldn't have made a penny. They'd have had to pay the fellas."

"Oi!" said Geraldine with mock indignation.

Johnny Too laughed. "What can we do to make it up to you?" he asked. "I know." He reached into his jacket pocket and produced a fistful of cigars. "Fancy a ten-inch Cuban?" he asked.

"I'd rather have an eight-inch Cockney," said Geri grabbing his crotch.

"OK, you lovebirds," said Lesley. "Any chance we could eat first?"

"I know just the place," said Harry. "A little Argentinian steakhouse five minutes down the road from the Bulldog, they do the best steaks in Holland."

"Argies?" said Lesley with disgust.

"The war's a long time over," said Johnny Too.

"And you can always go down like the *Belgrano* later," laughed Harry.

"Here, we went in a gay bar," said Johnny.

"Yeah," said Harry. "John dropped his wallet in there and kicked it all the way back to the hotel."

They ate, then drank, smoked a little weed and

then drank some more. It ended up just Harry and Johnny drinking brandies in the hotel bar at 1.30 am. Johnny gave an impassioned speech about cannabis and cocaine, and again Harry Tyler found himself following the logic of his argument which was basically anyone who wants to take drugs can get them so why waste millions of tax payers' money trying to impress people who don't take them? People who don't even understand that a bit of ganja is ten times better for them than a bottle of malt, y'know?

"More and more of the population have tried drugs," he said. "Millions smoke dope, fucking doctors recommend it. But leaving that aside what we're talking about here is a nanny state trying to regulate supply and demand.

"I'm a capitalist operating in a Prohibition. People like Ann Widdecombe are living in the fucking dark ages. I'm not forcing anyone to snort, H. I'm just supplying them that want, grown-up people with minds of their own."

"But it ain't like going to the offie for a can of Stella, mate," said Harry. "You hurt people."

"Only fuckers who take liberties, H. You've gotta show out, you gotta be respected or you lose it all."

He was starting to lose it, Harry thought. He heard the slur in the gangster's words. Half an hour later, Johnny Too had his arm around the detective's shoulders, drawing him closer. "Thing is, H, if next weekend goes to plan I am going to be fireproof," he said. "I'll be able to move away from the dirty stuff and take my family with me."

"Joey included?"

Johnny shook his head. "He's become my anchor," he said. "You unnerstan', Harry, you unnerstan'."

When Harry Tyler got into bed just after 2.15 am, he couldn't sleep. For the first time in his police career he was having doubts about the justness of his cause. Maybe Johnny Too was right, maybe he was just a modern-day buccaneer, an alternative entre-preneur following market forces in defiance of arcane laws. Why was dope banned, anyway? What harm did Charlie do? Johnny wasn't exactly kidnap-ping schoolkids and stringing them out on smack. Pyro Joe was clearly holding his smarter brother back. If Harry took Joey and Dougie down, maybe Johnny could blossom into the next Branson.

Against all his instincts and his training, Harry Tyler had started genuinely to like this funny, dangerously articulate man. Johnny Too was one of life's cavaliers bucking roundhead laws, he decided. He was a red-blooded, devil-may-care Englishman denied greatness by the circumstances of his birth, and the baggage around him. A tooled-up Toby Belch to Harry's Falstaff. Well, maybe it was time for Falstaff to hammer out a Faustian deal …

That night he dreamt that he, Lesley, Geri and Johnny Too were drinking champagne with dolphins on a beach in Cala N'Porter, inexplicably re-located to Florida. They were lying on sunbeds and when Harry looked at them more closely, they were made of dollar bills.

Sunday went much the same as Saturday – sex, booze, sightseeing and clubbing. On Monday morning they cabbed it back to Schiphol Airport.

Harry felt physically and mentally drained. Keeping pace with Johnny Too was like trying to train with Arsenal. He closed his eyes on the plane and didn't wake up till touchdown. It was Baker's idea to round the trip off with "one last drink" at the Ned. Geri couldn't be seen there, of course, so Johnny's driver, Tony Boniface, drove her home after dropping Johnny off. It was just unlucky that he mentioned it in passing to his wife who was straight on the phone to Sandra Baker. Harry and Lesley pulled up at the Ned ten minutes after Johnny and 15 minutes before his wife who burst in shouting and swearing about "the SLUT".

There was hardly anyone in the pub: Johnny, Harry, Lesley, Slobberin' Ron and young Mickey Fenn. They watched open-mouthed as Sandra pulled Johnny's own .38 Beretta on him.

"You fucking bastard!" she screamed. "Why are you still fucking that slag?"

Johnny Too snapped. He ran straight at her, tore the gun from her hand and knocked her to the floor.

"You wanna play fucking gangsters?" he roared. "I'll show you how to be a gangster."

"NO, JOHN!" Harry shouted. Too late. Johnny Too squeezed the trigger. The Beretta jammed. Harry grabbed Johnny's arms. Slobberin' Ron took the gun off him and fired it at the ceiling. The second round went off perfectly. Johnny Too fell to his knees and sobbed, pulling Sandra into his arms. Both were crying.

Ron turned and said, "Nobody saw a thing, right?"

Everyone nodded. That was understood. Harry

made his excuses and left. He drove the car for about a mile, then pulled over and butted the steering wheel with his head. How could he have started to believe Johnny Too was OK? The guy was a fucking psychopath. He punched his leg in frustration, then started up the car and drove to a phone box in Shoreditch to call his overlords. It was 6.37 pm. They wanted a meeting at Southend police station at 10.30 pm. Harry was weary but he knew time was against them. He drove to his flat, showered and changed, then checked his messages. There was nothing that couldn't wait. Peter Miller had called several times. His first messages were short, the final three were longer every time – a clear indication of his sobriety. The short calls were when he was sober, they got longer as the evening wore on. Apparently, Miller felt Harry needed to know that while they were away Pyro Joe had got charlied up and gone looking for some minor irritant who had failed to pay the few hundred he owed the firm. According to Miller, Joey had hung the poor wretch over the second-floor balcony of his Deptford council flat and the idiot's shoe had come off causing him to fall and break his legs.

Miller was laughing all the way through the message. Harry was incensed. What kind of sick bastard could find a man falling two floors remotely funny? He shook his head. Bet the silly git wears lace-ups from now on, he thought.

Harry got to Southend early. He spent 20 minutes making sure he didn't have a tail on him. As arranged, a covert van pulled up next to him then reversed into a side alley. Harry pulled the hood of his sweatshirt over his head and walked back to the van. The back door opened and he was in and gone.

He was driven to a small police station about a mile from Southend city centre. To Harry, it looked like a traffic warden base. The meeting with top brass lasted into the early hours. It was agreed to place additional technical surveillance equipment on Geraldine. Her car interior would be wired for sound, and tracking devices fitted. The buzz in the room was hyper. One hundred kilos of cocaine was on the way – enough to put the Bakers away for a very long time. As tired as he was, Harry was boosted by the energy of the others. His role in the coming maelstrom was to stick to the Baker brothers like shit on their shoes.

After the meeting, Harry took a coffee with DCI Susan Long.

"So how are you, Harry?" she asked pleasantly.

"Fuck me," he said. "Woops, sorry, ma'am. Do you know you're the first person to ask me that in months? Yeah, y'know, fine. Glad it's getting to the end."

Long smiled. She dunked her shortbread biscuit into the murky depths of a Colchester United mug and whispered, "Did you know Geraldine and Lesley were fucking one another?"

Harry choked his coffee back into his mug and laughed. "No," he said. "But I had an idea."

"Yes, while you and Baker were drinking in a bar, the fourth of the day I think, the two sisters were doing it for themselves in Baker's room."

"Was the room wired for sound only, or do I get to watch the video?"

There was a twinkle in Susan Long's brown eyes.

"Keep your mind on the job, get a good result and I'll arrange a private showing after."

Harry nodded. "I presume the CPS won't get a copy when it comes to disclosure?"

"No, I've got the only copy in England under lock and key."

Harry didn't bother to ask if his room had been "camera-ed up". He just took it for granted that it was.

"You, err, you seem quite close to Lesley," Long said.

"Just taking a DNA sample, ma'am," Harry replied.

"Without a swab, that's clever."

"Had to make do with what I had to hand."

"Well," his boss said with a straight face. "Just as long as the innocent aren't being fingered."

Harry got up to leave.

"Oh, Harry," she called.

"Yes, ma'am?"

"Nice size truncheon."

Harry raised an eyebrow. Was she coming on to him? He pushed his luck. "I'll look forward to you de-briefing me, ma'am," he said with a smile, then turned and left.

Harry was grinning all the way back to Stratford. As soon as he opened his flat door he realised he hadn't phoned Kara. Bollocks. He'd do it in the morning. Bound to have time in the morning. Besides it was odds-on that Elaine would be pleased to see him.

CHAPTER EIGHT

ARMAGEDDON

It was early afternoon, Tuesday. Harry Tyler lay in bed with his eyes closed and his mind racing. He had a million and one things to do, but he stayed there under the warmth of his duvet all the same. Harry felt as if the life force had been drained out of him. His thoughts wandered to his wife and what he was going to have to do to sort his life out, for him and for her. Reality loomed, looking as dark and foreboding as an ocean storm, but before the tidal wave of depression could drag him under, Harry made a conscious decision to think about something – anything – else.

Geraldine and Lesley were the first image that sprung to mind, and he held it there. He pictured the two women in bed, kissing, touching, stroking, strumming, with him in between them, like a Harry sandwich, standing and delivering on demand. He was in the middle of taking Geraldine from behind as her flickering tongue lapped at Lesley's clitoris, the Venus butterfly and the penis scuttle-ride in perfect synchronisation. It took five rings on Harry's mobile to drag him back to reality. The voice on the phone belonged to Johnny Too.

"Harry, you about?"

"John, I'm still abed."

"Anyone I know?"

"Just the Dagenham Girl Pipers. Nah, I'm on me Tod, mate. I slept bad last night, gutache."

"Listen, I've just come back from the doctors. It's bad news."

"What?"

"The big 'C'."

"Not ..."

"Yeah, dyslexia."

"Bastards."

"Listen, we're going Up The Creek tonight to see a couple of comedians. You wanna come?"

"Who's on?"

"Terry Alderton."

"Cool. Who's going?"

"Me, you, Geri, Les, few others. No idiots. Just a night out."

"What time?"

"Get to the Ned for seven."

"Why don't I meet you over there, eight, eight-thirty? Greenwich is just through the pipe from me."

"Whatever, but bring a few bob in case we get the taste for it and hit a club after."

Harry hadn't really fancied a session, but he knew he had to hang on to Johnny Too's shirt tails as much as possible now. Groaning, he swung his legs out of bed, shaved, showered and then admired his body in the mirror. Love handles aside, he still looked fit. Didn't he? There may have been a bit of a beer belly, but his upper torso was nicely toned. He thought about tidying up but couldn't be arsed. Leaving the flat quietly, he glanced back along the balcony walkway. No sign of Elaine. This job couldn't end quickly enough now. He looked at the graffiti-blitzed walls by the lift, which stank of urine. How the fuck could people live like this?

Harry drove off and made straight for the Trojan. It was strangely empty. The barman, Liam McGarry, greeted Harry with a smile. He was half-heartedly drying a pint glass while reading Mike Ward's TV column in the *Daily Star*.

"Busy then," said Harry.

"Rushed off me feet. Did you see *EastEnders* last night, Harry?"

"No, mate."

"That fucking Mo Slater. She has to be the worst actress I've ever seen."

"Ain't seen her."

"It's like she's reading the words off a board."

"I wish my social life was as full as yours, Lee."

They both laughed. Harry handed Liam a sealed envelope. "Give that to me uncle, will yah?" he said.

The barman smiled and placed the envelope under the bar.

"How's it going?" he asked.

"Getting there."

"You want a beer?"

Harry shook his head. "Nah, I'm at it tonight over Deptford. Who's been about, anyone?"

"Just your lot and a firm from down south, other

than that, not a lot on. Everyone's tucked up and as busy as hell. You OK?"

Harry nodded. "You know," he said. They shook hands and Harry left. He had just reached the car when his mobile rang.

"Harry, it's John. Where are yer?"

"Down the Trojan."

"Hang on there, we'll come over."

"Problem?"

"No, no. Just need a chat about the other thing. We'll be about an hour."

Harry dashed back into the pub and started making calls from the office phone. Johnny Too arrived nearly ninety minutes later, with Pyro Joe and Greg Saunders. Harry was surprised to see the latter. Saunders had never really figured as part of The Firm. He was just the Ned's Charlie dealer.

Harry was sitting at a table at the far end of the pub, playing poker with a huge bald black man known as Bear and two scruffy 30-year-olds who looked like travellers.

The bar, so empty an hour ago you half expected to see prairie tumbleweed blowing across it, was now teeming with drinkers, black, white, Asian. It was like the fucking UN, mused Johnny Too.

Harry acknowledged Johnny's arrival. "Give us two minutes to lose this hand and I'll be with you," he said.

The Bakers ordered beer. Liam nodded to Harry. "On your account, H?"

"Yeah," Harry replied. "On account I never pay it."

Smiling, the Bakers moved to the opposite end of the bar and chatted amongst themselves until raucous laughter erupted from Harry's table. The Bear had accidentally knocked a full pint over one of the pikeys. The game had been breaking up anyway, with the other traveller pocketing the score or so of pound coins when the pint went over. The soaked pikey stood up.

"The state of me," he roared. "Now oi'll have to go and put some more fickin' rags on."

Bear was on his feet too. "Sorry, Michael," he said. "I'd pay for them to go through the dry cleaners but it's only the caked-on shite that's holding them together."

The three men left. Bridie, the young, flat-chested Irish barmaid fired the parting broadside. "It's OK, boys, I'll clear up your mess. Just leave it to good old Bridie," she moaned.

Harry Tyler crossed the pub and shook hands warmly with Johnny Too before nodding at Pyro Joe and Greg Saunders.

"Everything OK, John?" he asked.

Johnny Too nodded. "Yeah, yeah. Just mooching, killing time."

Harry raised an eyebrow. "What's on your mind?"

Baker smiled. "I need to lay something down for a couple of days, can you help?"

"What is it?"

"A few tools."

"What, you want 'em pugged up for a while?"

"Yeah, and delivered somewhere Thursday night."

—

231

"How many?"

Pyro Joe leaned forward. "A bag full of shooters and lugs," he growled.

"Where are they now?"

"Outside in Greg's boot."

"Give me five."

Harry nodded at Liam, then they both went to the far end of the bar. After a minute or so of whispering, Liam handed Harry a set of keys and walked off to the gents. Harry strolled back to the Bakers.

"Yeah," he said. "Let's do it."

Saunders got up and led Harry to his Mondeo saloon. A woman and her infant daughter were sitting in the back. The rear of the car had a stick-on cab aerial. Saunders took a navy blue holdall from the boot, handing it to Harry. It was weighty and had a small, locked padlock across the zip.

"I'll be off then," Saunders said, and got into the driver's seat.

Harry went straight back into the Trojan, going behind the bar, through the staff doors and upstairs. About five minutes had passed. After two, Pyro Joe had wandered into the gents. Liam was busy in trap one, admiring his gorgeous pouting Starbird while smoking a menthol cigarette with his free hand. Joey went through the motions of urinating, then zipped himself up and returned to the bar.

"He's having a Tom Tit, John," he said.

"Who?"

"The barman."

"Whatever."

Bridie piped up from the bar. "Do you boys want another drink?" she asked.

"Yes, please, same again, ta," said Johnny.

"And shall oi get the other fella, yer man, shall oi pour him another, or has he gone?"

"Nah, he's gone," Johnny replied. "Where's Cyril and Carol today then?"

"They're at an LOV meeting. They'll be back tonight."

"I take it in Carol's case LOV stands for Lots Of Volume."

"Will you be telling her that yerself?"

Harry Tyler bounded back. "Sorted," he said.

"Thanks, H," said Johnny Too. "We need 'em back Thursday night."

"You just say where and when."

Pyro Joe got up to play the fruit machine.

"You fancy seeing this Alderton fella tonight, then?" asked Johnny.

"I do as it goes," Harry replied. "He was shite on *Red Alert* but he's funny as fuck normally."

"He's getting hold of that Dee Ivens, isn't he?"

"Yeah. Lucky fucker."

Joey returned, grumpy and out of change. "Those things are safe here, are they?" he grumbled.

"Yeah," said Harry. "Belt and braces."

"Right," said Johnny Too. "We're heading back to God's own country. You coming, H, or laters?"

"I'll see you there, mate. Got some business this end to sort out."

In the event, Harry Tyler reached the Up The

Creek comedy club five minutes before Johnny Baker arrived with Geraldine and Lesley. He was waiting outside with bad news.

"Alderton's pulled out, bad throat," he said.

"You're kidding," Johnny groaned.

"So who is on the bill instead?" asked Geraldine.

"Ian Stone, unfunny cunt off *The 11 O'clock Show* and this new bloke called Eric."

"Eric what?" asked Geraldine.

"Dunno. Just Eric it says here."

"Don't fancy the sound of that," said Lesley.

"Fuck," said Johnny Too.

"Fret not, best mates," said Harry cheerfully. "Your uncle H has learnt of the presence of the great Micky Pugh performing in half an hour at the Montrose Social Club in Sidcup. Ten minutes away."

"Micky Pugh? He sounds a bit end of the pier," moaned Geraldine.

"No, he's a legend – and he's fucking funny," said Johnny Too. "I saw him at the Circus Tavern last year. Harry, you are a fucking genius."

He pulled Harry close and planted a kiss on the top of his head.

"Oi, I'm getting worried about you two," protested Lesley.

"What's sauce for the goose ..." Johnny Too replied, winking. Geraldine smiled, Lesley blushed.

"What about the others?" she asked.

"Fuck 'em!" said John. "We can't wait. Let's go see the Pugh-meister."

"Me car's around the corner," volunteered Harry.

Johnny clasped him around the shoulders.

"Harry Tyler," he said. "Truly, you are a man amongst men. So, Alderton's got a sore throat, has he? Too much noshing Dee Ivens I reckon."

"Johnny," said Geri in mock disgust. "That's all you ever think of."

"I know," he replied. "That's why you love me."

At Johnny Too's special request, Micky Pugh did his legendary two drunks routine and joined them at the bar afterwards.

"Classic, Mick," smiled Johnny. "You fancy coming to Kempton Park with me and the boys tomorrow? We're having a bit of a Ned beano."

"Can I bring Willie Thompson?" asked Micky.

"Yeah, he's another funny fucker. No problem. Meet us at the Ned at 11am."

Harry left Sidcup at about 1 am, leaving Johnny, Micky Pugh and Geraldine propping up the bar of a friendly local, one of the hundreds known to the drinking man's comic.

"You staying tonight, Harry?" Lesley asked.

"For a while. I've got business to sort out before the races."

She reached over and massaged his neck.

"You look a bit tense, Harry, shall I give you a proper massage at mine?"

"That would be fucking wonderful."

"Then we can act out a fantasy for you," she said. "Can you think of a good one?"

She was obviously tipsy and had been to see her uncle Charlie during the evening, but Harry didn't think she'd be up for phoning a friend for a quick fifty-fifty. The thought of her and Geri hard at it made his dick as erect as a Grenadier Guard on parade.

"I'm sure something will come up by the time we get there," he said.

"Oh, it'll be up before then," she said, squeezing his cock through his trousers.

At 1.35 am Harry was lying naked, face down on Lesley's bed. She slipped off her Kanga panties, straddled him and began to rub sweetly scented body oil into his back.

"You thought of anything yet, Harry?" she said.

He rolled over so his body was in between Lesley's legs. She rubbed her lower body back and forth on his erection.

"Yeah, you got a vibrator or something?"

Lesley rolled over and took a slim six-inch dildo out of a drawer.

"What do you want me to do with it?" she asked coyly.

"Make out I'm not here and play with yourself," he ordered.

Lesley coated the dildo with KY Jelly and lay back on the bed. She grasped her own breasts and writhed for a while before running the tip of the dildo around her vaginal lips. Harry played with her nipples and watched her until he could wait no more.

"Go on all fours," he commanded.

Lesley obeyed. He poured oil on her back and massaged it firmly as she slipped the dildo into herself.

"Leave that and rub KY Jelly on my cock," he said.

"I don't think you'll need it."

"Just do it."

Slightly stunned by his insistence, Lesley did what she was told. Harry increased the pressure on her back.

"That is soooo nice," she said.

He reached down and felt her fanny. It was dripping wet. He stopped rubbing and teased her with his helmet.

"Don't, Harry." She gasped. "Give me it all. Fuck me, Harry. Fuck me hard."

Instead, Harry pulled back and slipped his lubricated erection up Lesley's backside.

She gasped. "Harry, no!"

"It's what I want," he grunted.

God, she was tight. She was also clearly uncomfortable, but that just made it feel better. He came quickly.

"That hurt, you bastard!" she said accusingly.

"Sorry."

"You don't sound it." She was sobbing now.

"I didn't mean to hurt you."

"You should have asked, Harry. I'd never done it like that."

"I know. Sorry."

"I thought you were different."

He held her tight, feigning concern, but in the dark he was smiling.

A distant church bell was mechanically chiming out 4 am as Harry drove back to East London. So, they're not all mosques over here, yet, he thought. He got to within a mile of the flat and then veered off his regular route at speed. Even now he had to be 100 per cent surveillance aware. Harry found a phone box and updated his superiors about the day's events, joking that his watchers would need "a nice few quid" for Kempton Park later that day. It was 6 am before he was in bed, and at 10.15 am he was back on the road en route for the Ned, having knocked back a bottle of gold Purdey's as a breakfast livener.

About a dozen of the Ned regulars were heading to Kempton Park in a hire van driven by Dolly Burns, a blousy gangster's widow with a mouth fouler than Chubby Brown in a temper. Harry Tyler joined the Bakers and Dougie The Dog in the Merc, which was chauffeured by Tony Boniface. Within minutes Pyro Joe was chopping out lines of cocaine on a hand-mirror and snorting them with a cut straw from McDonald's. Harry feigned sleep as Joey nudged him for a line.

"Joe, am I a-fucking-kip or what?" he moaned.

"Ooooooo!" the rest of the car responded to a man.

Harry turned the other cheek and let rip with a suspension-rattling fart.

"Fuck me, H, you'll blow an ounce on the carpet," laughed Johnny Too.

"You dirty bastard, that fucking stinks," complained The Dog.

"I think a rat's died up your arse," roared Pyro Joe.

"I'll open a window," said Tony Boniface.

"NO!" hollered the Bakers as one.

"Not with £200 worth of Charlie on the mirrors," muttered Johnny.

Everyone laughed. Harry yawned. "That's that poxy bitter from Sidcup," he said.

When they arrived at Kempton Park, Johnny Too asked Harry to stay in the car when the others got out.

"Tony and Greg are gonna come over on Thursday and collect that shopping, is that OK?"

"You want me to deliver or them to come east?"

"They'll come to you."

"What time?"

"After *EastEnders*."

"After fucking *EastEnders*?" Harry laughed.

"Yeah, Tony's a soap nutter. You can't get him out the flat until *EastEnders* has finished."

"Hope he don't get too upset about Ian Beale, Lesley tells me he's going down the pan like a dodgy curry."

"Mug!"

"If Tone would rather watch it down the Trojan, I'll stick some jellied eels on for him. Get a fucking pearlie behind the bar."

"Nah, I'm serious, H. If the flat was alight he'd burn before he switched off. Got pictures of fucking Melanie cut out in a scrapbook."

"That is sad, John. But no problem, mate. I'll be in the bar waiting."

"I'll put 2K on bail to you next week so you can go to work, same price as the last."

"Yeah, anything else need doing?"

"No, mate, we're sorted for security and, as it happens, I ain't taking Geri now. Can you run her around for a bit of shopping uptown just to take her mind off business?"

Harry felt offended. He wasn't a fucking gopher, but then he had been told that the incoming parcel was under control and he was glad Geraldine wasn't on the plot just in case it got messy. Doubtless she would still be wiped up on a conspiracy charge but that's life. You lie with dogs, you get fleas. It crossed his mind that the Bakers might still not fully trust him, after all he wasn't family ...

"Johnny, no worries," he said finally. "I'll take Geri and Les up West, Kings Road or Knightsbridge, y'know."

"Cheers, H, I ain't rowing you out but I can't use you this time."

"John, I was never in, just bear me in mind if you need emergency back-up."

Johnny Too nodded. "Catch up with the others, mate, I need ten with Joey. We'll be along shortly."

As Harry got out, Pyro Joe got in. Tony Boniface was enjoying a small cigar.

"I hear you're an *EastEnders* fan, Tone," he said.

"Love it, mate."

"I had fucking nightmares thinking of Pat and Frank at it."

"Yeah, not a pleasant image, is it?"

"You know what the technical term for having sex with Fat Pat is?"

"No, what?"

"Going the whole hog."

Boniface laughed. "You wicked fucker."

Harry glanced back. The Bakers were deep in conversation, blissfully unaware that the Mercedes had more bugs in it than a dosser's vest.

Harry had managed to successfully blow £150 of tax-payers' money until the last race of the day. His decision to stick £50 to win on 12/1 East End Delight, in honour of Tony, was met with hoots of derision from the Ned Kelly faithful. The mood changed when it romped home three lengths clear of the 9/2 and the 3/1. Harry scooped £650 in readies, earning him a nicotine snog from a clearly half-cut Dolly Burns, and Johnny Too broke out the champagne.

Back at the Ned, the first two rounds were on Harry as the tale of East End Delight's glorious victory was re-told and magnified. It was Johnny Too who rained on his parade.

"H, you understand about Friday, don'tcha?"

"John, it's fuck all to do with me. I appreciate the two other things on bail, though, geezer, but I ain't got a problem. Just remember, any shit and I'm on the mobile."

"Cheers, mate. Geri knows about the parcel and she's getting tuned up. Just keep her mind off things. I'm going on the missing tomorrow, early doors, and I'll give her a bell Friday night, OK?"

"Sweet. When will you be about?"

"Not till Sunday night or Monday morning, but I'll bell you Friday night."

"You sure you don't want me to run the other things up tomorrow?"

"Nah, you're a good man, H. I'll send the other two down about nine-ish."

Johnny Too was swaying on his feet. He was so filled up with beer his epiglottis had probably drowned, thought Harry. Joey and The Dog were getting boisterous so Harry called a cab and went home. He knew he'd had too much to drink because he made the driver stop for a kebab. He had two theories about kebabs. One was that if working-class men stopped drinking, every kebab shop in Britain would go belly up. The second was that the bigger the chilli sauce stain on the wrapping paper the next morning, the more pissed you had been the night before.

There was a stain the size of a cabbage on his.

Thursday morning found Harry at Maidstone police HQ in Kent for an 11 am briefing with more than 100 crime squad officers. He had just sat through a 90-minute meeting in the senior officers' canteen where battle plans were laid down over tea and digestive biscuits. His superiors already knew that the delivery was due for about 2 pm at a warehouse off Plough Way, Rotherhithe. The coming articulated lorry was already under complete control. It was known to have an unspecified amount of cocaine on board. The good guys were buzzing.

After the briefing, Harry thought about ringing Kara. He wanted to, but he couldn't face the questions. It would only be a couple of days now and he'd be on his way home. Lesley popped into his mind and went just as quickly.

If all went to plan, Harry would be back here in Maidstone on Friday watching the results of the arrests going up on the whiteboard. The weekend would see every poor sod who had done deals with him being wiped up in a huge operation that would have South London talking for years to come.

He went to find a toilet and passed a glass walkway that overlooked the car park. Dozens of blue boiler-suited firearms officers were disembarking from armoured land rovers. A few of the vehicles had battering rams welded to the fronts. Harry stopped and looked out at the smiling faces. He admired how professional these dedicated men and women were, how ruthless and cold they could be when it was called for. These people faced down the sickest and most merciless scum loose on the streets, guttersnipes who would execute the innocent for under a grand. The excrement they dealt with abided by none of society's rules or laws. How could the yellow liberal press be so fond of defending them and so quick to attack the good guys? A shot cop meant nothing to them, but if a police officer let loose a round or two in the name of justice, before the villain's sorry arse had hit the floor the PCA – Prosecute Coppers Association – would be racing eagerly to the scene to seize the weapon and suspend the officer. A "fair" investigation would follow and would possibly result in the hero peacekeeper gripping the rail at Number One dock at the Old Bailey.

Why did they bother? Harry didn't know, but the fact that they did made them special. Like him, they were prepared, probably wrongly, to put the job before their families, before anything. Possibly even their lives.

That evening Harry sat in the Trojan watching the clock. *EastEnders* had long since finished. Liam was behind the bar shooting the breeze about Sony's Playstation II with a young Chinese guy. Four black men sat across from Harry playing poker. A crop-haired white guy in a West Ham top was standing alone at the bar drinking bottles of Foster's Ice with his Staffordshire terrier at his feet. Harry picked up a discarded *Evening Standard* and started flicking through it, looking for the Gary Larson *Far Side* cartoon. It was 8.43 pm when Tony Boniface finally walked in, looking so nervous he might as well have had "Guilty" stencilled across his forehead.

Harry stood up. "Beer, Tone?" he asked.

Boniface shook his head. He smiled unconvincingly and sat at Harry's table.

"You all right, mate?" asked Harry. "You look sick."

"I always get a bad gut running the things about, mate. I hate 'em."

"You on your own?"

"Nah, the bird's in the motor and I've got another car running with me for cover."

"Take it easy, mate."

"Got the bag?"

"Yeah, outside in me boot. Under the headless corpse."

"You what?"

Harry laughed.

"You CUNT," Tony said fiercely, adding, "That ain't funny, H."

"So why are you grinning?"

They left together. Boniface's moll sat in the driver's seat of a red Vauxhall Astra. Harry glanced further to the left and saw the unmistakable bulk of Pyro Joe in the passenger sear of a Suzuki 4WD jeep. He didn't look long enough to ID the driver. Moving quickly he retrieved the hold-all and crossed the road to the Vauxhall. Boniface held the boot open and slammed it shut as soon as Harry had dropped the bag into it. Flustered, he then went to get in the driving seat, then seemed stuck as he decided whether to go round the front or the back of the vehicle. He finally settled on the back.

"Good luck, Tone," Harry called as he crossed back to the pub. He didn't look at the Suzuki again. He heard the two vehicles pull away behind him, not at speed, but too fast for the area.

"Fucking amateur," he muttered.

Back in the bar, Harry phoned Geri. She couldn't have been friendlier.

"Hi, gorgeous, what time are you picking us up tomorrow?" she asked.

"I'm only the driver, luv. You tell me."

"Lesley's coming over to keep me company and have a little drink. Why not join us, then we can work out what we're doing?"

"I'll call you back in five."

"Don't be long, sweetie."

Harry put the phone back and thought it through. If he was down the Ned, there might be some intelligence to be picked up. But then again, Johnny Too was off the plot and an evening with Geri and Les might be good wanking material if nothing else. He would never see either of them again after tomorrow. Any evidence he might be required to give in court would be behind a screen. So, purely in the interests of justice, Harry rang back and said he'd be right over.

Harry parked his car eight streets away and walked the rest of the way, which gave Lesley the time to arrive. Geraldine greeted him at the front door wearing a figure-hugging red dress held up over her shoulders by two slender straps. She handed Harry a champagne cocktail. Lesley was on the settee dressed in the shortest miniskirt and a flimsy white blouse which made no attempt to disguise the black bra underneath. Harry kissed her and sat opposite, noting the brilliant white panties under the skirt.

Geri stood behind Harry's chair and rubbed his shoulders. "Thanks for coming to protect us," she purred. Both women giggled. She walked over to a glass-top table and unfolded a paper wrap of cocaine, which she chopped into several lines, then dabbed her finger into the remaining pile and rubbed it into her gums. Lesley rolled up a £5 note and they took turn snorting two lines apiece.

"Help yourself, Harry," Geri invited.

"Later," he said. "Perhaps later." He watched Lesley rub cocaine across her teeth. "So Johnny's not about tonight?" he added.

"No, he's not back until after the weekend," said Geri, brushing Lesley's hair with her hand. "You know how it is."

Harry got up and topped up his glass with champagne. The new Sade CD was playing softly and sensuously in the background. He sat back down. "So where am I taking you two tomorrow?" he said.

Geraldine sat on the arm of his chair.

"Harry, relax," she said. "Don't worry about tomorrow yet." She stroked his hair, and caressed his neck. Geri looked across at Lesley who smiled and nodded. Geri kissed his forehead and got up. The women started to dance to a slow, smoochy number. Harry sipped his drink and felt his cock stir. Geri put her hands on Lesley's hips and kissed her gently on the lips. Lesley gyrated in time to the music and plunged her tongue into Geri's mouth. Harry was mesmerised, his cock now fully erect. Geri eased back and danced away from Lesley, moving back towards Harry. She took a mouthful of Buck's Fizz from a fluted champagne glass, her lower body swaying gently to the music.

Suddenly Geri reached down and rubbed Harry's hardness. Her eyes were closed and the sheen of her metallic red lipstick glistened in the light of a standing lamp behind her. Harry gripped her leg and thrust his pelvis forward. Lesley stopped dancing and joined them, kneeling between his open legs and running her hands up to his groin. It felt so good.

Geri started to unzip his trousers. Suddenly alarm bells started to go off in Harry's head. They were so up for it, it hurt, but what if Johnny were to call Geri tonight or tomorrow morning? What if she blabbed? Everything could still go pear-shaped. He reached down and pushed the women's hands away.

"Sorry, girls. This ain't right. I can't do this to Johnny."

"He'll never know," said Geri.

"No, he's a mate. It ain't right. I'm going home." He got up. "I'll pick you up at eleven-thirty, OK, Geri? Shall I get you from home first, Les?"

"No, no, darling," said Geri. "She's staying."

"Fine. See you at half-eleven then."

Harry drank his drink and walked over to open the door. He glanced back to wave but the women were too busy kissing to notice him. He watched Geri slip the straps off her shoulders before walking out. Strap up! His erection was so hard it was almost painful. Harry pulled out his mobile and dialled Elaine's number. No way was he going to waste it. The packing could wait till tomorrow.

By 6.30 am. Johnny Too had finished his run across Streatham Common. He hadn't slept well, but that wasn't unusual the night before big business. It was a cold, misty morning but that just served to heighten Johnny's senses. This was going to be good. He jogged back to a safe house in Streatham Vale and let himself in to the large Victorian semi. Pyro Joe and Dougie The Dog were getting stuck into a fry-up.

Three automatic handguns lay on the kitchen table in the living room. Rhino, dressed top to toe in black, was putting a sawn-off pump-action shotgun, with a looped rope through the stock, over his shoulder. He had a .38 revolver in an underarm shoulder holster under his left armpit. Four two-way radios and several mobile phones were on the small coffee table. Johnny Too trusted Rhino with his life. He knew he'd take a slug for him, he was a proper soldier.

John Boy Saunders sat beside him reading yesterday's *Sun*. Johnny waved hi and went through to the kitchen.

"Any word, Joe?"

"The ferry ain't even in Dover yet, John. Ease up, have some bacon and eggs."

Rhino and John Boy joined them

"Where's the party tonight, then?" asked Rhino.

"Over Essex way," said John. "Little pub in Aveley, safe as houses."

Doug grabbed John Boy's paper. "It's fucking yesterday's," he moaned.

"The shops ain't open yet."

"What's in it?" asked Rhino.

"Stuff about French cows having mad cow disease."

"Ha-ha-ha," laughed Johnny Too. "La BSE nouveau."

"Fucking serves them cunts right," said Pyro Joe. "Burning our beef."

"Oh, look," said Doug. "It's Bjork's birthday today."

"Shouldn't that be her b-jirthday?" joked Rhino.

"What's her kid called?" asked John Boy.

"Dunno," said Doug. "Moon Unit?"

"No, you prat, that's Zappa's kid," said Johnny Too.

"Dougie, stop scratching your cock," barked Joey.

"Can't, I've got Hermes."

"You mean herpes," Joey said.

"No, I'm a carrier."

"That's it, fuck you," Joey snapped. "I'm gonna watch *Big Breakfast*."

"Good call, Joe," said Johnny Too. "Let's have a good butcher's at Denise's tits."

Joey turned on the TV, which came on with GMTV's Lorraine Kelly instead.

"Fuck me, the Paisley Pig!" yelled Rhino. "Turn that over!"

"Yeah," said Dougie. "I wouldn't fuck her with yours, Rhine. Her vibrator has to wear a blindfold."

Pyro jabbed at the remote. Nothing happened.

"The battery's gone," he grumbled.

"Get that beast off the screen," shouted John.

Dougie The Dog stepped forward and shot the TV set.

"Dougie!" snapped Joe.

"You fucking wanker," Johnny Too said simply.

"You're becoming a liability, Doug," Joe growled.

The Dog shrugged. "Chill out, fellas," he said. "I'll put Mike Osman on the radio."

"Clear up this fucking mess first," fumed Pyro Joe.

"Shoot anything else and I'll shoot you," said John.

Even Dougie realised he was serious.

Bang on 8 am, a white Ford transit pulled up outside, driven by young Mickey Fenn. The van had been stolen three months before and had been plated to a straight transit sitting on a car lot, owned by a Baker associate down in Croydon. Mickey, also wearing all-black clothes with black leather gloves, rang the doorbell once. Doug let him in and they bashed clenched right fists. For Mickey Fenn this was it, the day he became one of The Firm, the day he became a man.

Johnny Too was going through his ritual of wrapping surgical tape around his fingertips before pulling on his gloves. Johnny nodded a welcome to Mickey. "Kitted up, son?" he asked.

Fenn patted his left chest area. "Yeah, the 9 mil."

Johnny nodded and said "Let's go."

The van went straight to the Plough Way warehouse. Shutters up, van in, shutters down. The warehouse was empty. It had been hired on a false company account six-month lease and could easily accommodate an artic. On the far side of the warehouse were two cars, a series 5 BMW and a Volvo Estate. Both vehicles had been bought for cash at an auction "up North" eight months before and were now registered to separate addresses in Kent that were no longer used as mailing addresses. A pile of newly made-up cardboard boxes sat at the rear wall.

The Baker mob left the transit. To the side of them was an orange-coloured fork-lift truck. Rhino started it up and drove it over to the two cars and parked it.

9.30 am, bingo! One of the mobiles rang. Johnny Too answered it. "Yes … No … Yes. … OK."

The others stood in expectant silence. Johnny hung up and punched the air. "YES!" he exclaimed. "It's there! It's cleared the docks."

A cheer went up.

"How long?" asked Joey.

"Here at two o'clock," said Johnny. "Ring the others."

A few miles away, Harry Tyler was showering. He had been woken earlier than he'd have liked by a phone call from Geraldine. There had been a change of plans, she'd said. It was Lesley's mum's birthday so she was going to treat her to lunch in South Ken and could Harry pick them up earlier for shopping and wait to take them back later in the afternoon? Why not?

Pyro Joe made two calls and said the same sentence both times: "It's me, we're going to the races on Saturday." End of conversation. These calls triggered six others to sweep the entire area for half a mile around the warehouse. Only two roads approached the entry. Every car, every van, every house and shop window *en route* would be checked every 15 minutes for the next five hours. The manor was a fever of activity. The sweepers had set up their own observation posts on friendly flats on the approach. Every innocent walk or drive through from the local police was enough to start hearts pounding.

Johnny Too put two-way radios and disposable mobile phones in every vehicle, while Pyro Joe moaned continuously about being hot in his bullet-proof vest.

"You're turning into fucking Victor Meldrew," snapped Johnny.

"He's dead," said Joey.

"You better watch yer back then."

"Boys, boys," said Rhino. "C'mon. Calm down, take it easy. The waiting is killing us all, but think of what's coming."

Harry was outside Geri's at 10.30 am and the women were in their first shop by 11. It was impossible to park in Knightsbridge, so he kept on circling Harrod's until they came out ... at a quarter to one.

"Fucking hell, Les," he moaned.

"I'll make it up to you, darling."

"You will, won'tcha?" he snapped.

"Well, if she doesn't I will," said Geraldine.

"Maybe we both will," said Lesley. "If you don't run away this time."

She kissed him on the lips. He drove in silence to Sloane Square station where Lesley's mother was waiting.

"Right," said Lesley. "I'll take Mum to lunch. We won't be long, she'll have to get back to work. Where am I meeting you?"

"The Gore Hotel at three," said Harry. "How can you forget, Les? It's your own surname."

"Silly me. OK, see ya later, lover."

"Which one of us was she talking to then?" Harry asked Geraldine.

"Both of us, I think."

"So where to now, ma'am? More shops?"

"Oh I think we deserve a drink, don't you, Harry?" she said mischievously. "Let's go straight to the Gore."

In the warehouse, the Baker mob had been amusing themselves for the last two minutes watching Dougie The Dog psyching himself up by pulling aggressive faces in the reflection of the BMW window. In the end, they could hold their laughter in no more.

"You doing all right there, Doug?" roared Joey.

"He thinks he's David Beckham on the fucking cat-walk," laughed Johnny Too. "He'll be wearing a sarong next."

"Fucking leave it out, John," Doug said feebly.

"Your missus ain't posh, though, is she, Doug?" teased John.

"No," said Joe. "But I bet she takes it up the arse."

Everyone except The Dog laughed uproariously. Pyro Joe led them through an impromptu outburst of the terrace ditty "Does she take it, does she take it, does she take it up the arse?"

"Great footballer, but fucking hell they don't half squander their wedge," said Mickey Fenn.

"Squander, what d'you mean squander?" roared Johnny Too. "Just cos they got in a hundred Gucci sandbags for the floods."

"I am fucking hungry," moaned Dougie, anxious

to change the subject. "Can't we send out for some nosh?"

"You're always fucking hungry, man," said Rhino. "You'd eat a fucking horse."

"Here, Rhino," said Pyro Joe. "Remember that time you got done for threatening behaviour to a police horse at Millwall, West Ham?"

"Yeah," said Rhino. "Then Dougie took her out."

"Who?" said Doug.

"The horse. Right dirty mare, weren't she?"

"Fuck off."

"Here," said Pyro Joe. "Did I tell you about the old trunter he pulled while you was in Amsterdam?"

"Don't, Joe," pleaded Dougie.

"Yeah, some old barmaid tart in a pub down Streatham. Ugly as a bucket of arseholes she was. He was plastered of course. The next day he said she had a fanny like a bill-poster's bucket."

"What is this, pick on Dougie day?" The Dog whined.

"What else have we got to do?" Joe shrugged.

"We could send out for KFC."

"Doug," said Johnny Too. "Shut the fuck up."

In the bar of the Gore, Harry Tyler bought Geraldine a large glass of Chablis and sat down nursing a bottle of Bud Lite. She reached over and stroked the inside of his thigh.

"I liked what I felt last night," she said in a low whisper.

"I liked what I was looking at."

"So you want to see some more?"

"How much are the rooms here?"

"That's exactly what I was thinking."

At 1.30 pm a mobile rang. Johnny Too didn't let it ring twice. "Yeah," he said. "Yeah … OK." He killed the call, and punched both fists into the air. "Yes," he said. "It's twenty minutes away. It's just passed Ronnie on Blackheath, nothing up its arse."

"Fucking lovely job," said Pyro Joe.

"John, now can I get a McDonald's or something?" said Dougie. "I'm gonna pass out if I don't eat soon."

"Go on then, you silly bastard, but you'd better be fucking quick."

Dougie started towards the exit door.

"Dougie, you plank," shouted Johnny. "Leave the fucking tools."

At 1.45 pm, Harry Tyler had just come explosively inside Johnny Too's moll. Geraldine had orgasmed twice.

"So, how do I compare to Johnny?" he panted.

"The weird thing is, you feel absolutely identical," said Geraldine. "But you're a bit rougher."

She snuggled into him. "Will there be any more where that came from?"

"You try and stop me," said Harry, who was already thinking ahead. Lesley was due in 90 minutes. Maybe he would nail them both in one go after all.

At 1.57 pm, Dougie The Dog left the Yellow Submarine fish shop, three minutes from the warehouse, wolfing down chips. Three black youths approached him.

"You got some money, mon?" asked the tallest kid.

"Fuck off, cunt," snarled Doug.

"Don't dis' my brother," said a second, burlier youth, producing a switchblade knife.

"You don't understand," said Dougie. "Don't you know who I am."

"No, but I know what you am, raasclat," said the first youth. "Now hand over your fucking money, guy."

Dougie flattened him with one punch, and grabbed the second youth by his knife hand. He couldn't do anything to stop the third kid from smashing him round the head with his portable CD player. Two of the Baker sweepers chased them away but Dougie The Dog was out cold.

At 2.03 pm, a mobile phone rang out in a Rotherhithe warehouse. Johnny Too snatched it up like a lunatic. "Yes," he said. "Yes, yes, OK." He turned to the others. "It's coming up Plough Way," he shouted. "Get the shutter ready."

Two minutes later there was a distinctive rumble followed by the sound of airbrakes punching like a steam geyser outside the shutter. The lumbering giant came to a halt. All they could hear now was the engine ticking over. Johnny Too was feeling a nervous sickness in his stomach muscles. A mobile rang. "Yes," said Johnny. "Dougie's what? No, fuck him, get off the line." Another mobile rang. Johnny snatched it. "Yes, OK, yes," he said.

He turned to Pyro Joe. "It's clean, nothing up its backside. Open up."

The shutters rolled up. Johnny went out and spoke to the driver.

"Everything cool?" he asked.

The driver nodded. "Hurry up and get it off," he said.

"Back it in to the warehouse."

As the beast roared back to life, Harry Tyler's beast did likewise. He made Geraldine go on all fours and took her roughly from behind, doggy fashion. She came, he faked it, but she was so wet she couldn't tell. Harry decided he wanted to preserve some of his libido for Lesley.

As the tailgate of the artic came down and the gates swung open, Rhino had already crossed the warehouse with the fork-lift and it sat there nudging forward impatiently, begging to be loaded. Johnny Too jumped on the tailgate.

"Where's Dougie?" asked Joe.

"Fuck him, tell you later," said John. "Get up here."

The trailer was three-quarters full of tomatoes and onions. As quickly as they unloaded the pallets,

Rhino was speeding them across the warehouse for Mickey Fenn and John Boy Saunders to line them up. It took nearly an hour to unload the lot. Johnny Too called the driver over and handed him a large brown envelope. "On yer way, son," he said. The driver didn't need telling twice.

The Baker mob were now alone with their booty, box after anonymous box of the stuff.

"So which one's it in, John?" asked Pyro Joe.

"Fucked if I know. Cut 'em all open, but be careful not to break the balls."

They tore into the first two boxes frantically. Nothing. Then the third. Nothing. Joey was starting to get the hump. Then Rhino opened up the fourth.

"Yes," he said. "Fucking yes!"

The box contained ten plastic balls, each containing a kilogram of cocaine.

"Stop!" commanded Johnny Too. The men stopped and stood motionless, watching their leader. Johnny took a small penknife and cut a slit into one of the balls, exposing the virgin white content. He put a small coating on the knife tip, wiped it on the end of his tongue and then massaged it around his top gum.

"Nectar," he said finally. "That is pukka gear."

The others cheered, then turned and ripped into the remaining boxes. Onions were rolling everywhere, but the balls of Charlie kept popping up: 12 kilos, 18 kilos, 25 … As they came out, Rhino was packing them ten to a box and sealing each one with a tape gun. Joey walked the first batch up to the transit and placed them under a tarpaulin sheet. The floor of the warehouse was now awash with onions. Pyro Joe walked back, grabbed a large tomato and lobbed it at Mickey Fenn. It hit him square on the back of the head. Mickey yelped with pain.

"Fuck off, Joey," he shouted, ripping open another box, grabbing an onion in each hand and hurling them back. Another eight kilos fell out of the box, but the jubilant gang were now more preoccupied with having a food fight. Mickey got in a good shot that blackened Joey's eye. The older gangster suddenly lost his sense of humour and chased the teenager around the warehouse. The other three were in stitches. They were blissfully unaware that outside each of their spotters was being beaten to the ground at the point of an H&K machine gun.

It hadn't taken much persuasion to get Lesley Gore to join Harry's hotel party. Now she sat naked at the top of the bed, with Harry going down on her as Geri gobbled eagerly on his erection. Harry claimed this position was number 70 in the *Kama Sutra* – 69 plus one. They spent about fifteen minutes enjoying variants of this carnal chain gang before Lesley decided she wanted to be fucked. She pushed Harry on his back and mounted him, pumping up and down while Geraldine squatted behind her and massaged her breasts. When she had climaxed the girls swapped over. Geri came and then it was Harry's turn to go on top, thrusting into Lesley as Geri caressed his balls gently with her fingernails. It was almost painful when he came and he flopped exhausted on to his back, a girl either side of him. A Harry sandwich, just like in his fantasy.

Johnny Too had just managed to restore order and get his troops back to work when Rhino slipped on a large onion and fell into Pyro Joe, knocking him to the ground. John Boy, Mickey and Johnny Too collapsed in hysterics just as two armoured land rovers hit the shutters at speed and rammed straight into the warehouse. Percussion grenades exploded and the warehouse was flooded with a rush of boiler-suited, machine-gun-toting police. The goggles and gas masks that they wore added to the terror of the attack. Screams of "ARMED POLICE!" filled the air.

Rhino scrambled to his feet and drew his automatic. Johnny Too saw it and shouted "NO!" Too late. Rhino let off three shots into the invading force. Johnny threw himself backwards. He saw Joey draw his weapon as he rolled towards a box of onions. A wall of automatic gun fire exploded at them. Pyro Joe took a round straight in the forehead. Rhino's legs were cut from under him, and Mickey Fenn was hit in the arm and jaw. He lay three feet from Johnny Too, weeping. Johnny lay face down on the ground, his arms out-stretched, shouting, "Don't shoot! Don't shoot!" He watched as his last soldier, John Boy Saunders made a dash for the BMW, his gun in his hand. He was cut down in an instant, turning and letting off three rounds as he fell. As John Boy hit the deck, his stomach muscles gave out and he discharged a brown stinking mess down his legs. It was all over in seconds.

A cloud of silver grey smoke hung inside the depot. The floor was awash with blood, onions and tomato. All Johnny Too could hear was Mickey crying and Rhino's groans of agony. He tried to look round and felt something solid smash into the side of his face. Plastic cuffs bit into his hands. Suddenly it seemed to all go quiet. The scene froze, everything seemed to be going in slow motion. Johnny heard voices but they seemed distant and drawn out. "This one's gone, sir, three need medics. This one's shot, he's shot. That one's shot and he's shit himself."

Johnny Too raised his head slowly. He could see the boiler-suited commandos everywhere. A pair of boots were right in front of him, polished to perfection. The man stood motionless, machine gun across his front, staring at Johnny. Baker looked back at him hard. The bastard wasn't shaking. He wasn't even out of breath. He just glared back at Johnny. The gangster looked to his left. His brother lay motionless. Was he …? Johnny knew enough not to ask. He wouldn't even let these motherfuckers know it was his brother lying there.

Two cops hauled Johnny Too to his feet. The flash of cameras hit him in the eyes. His gloved hands were filmed. His guns were filmed. His gloves were pulled off and his taped fingers were filmed too. Johnny surveyed the scene. It was carnage. He looked straight at the nearest gunman.

"Who's in charge?" he snarled.

The cop didn't reply. Two plainclothes officers

wearing police baseball caps approached him. The taller one started speaking: "Johnny Baker, I am arresting you ..."

Johnny Too spat straight in his face. "Fuck you, you piece of shit," he snarled. "Get AIDS and fucking die. Your fucking grass is gonna bake in an oven."

"What grass would that be, then?"

"The one I'm gonna torture."

"Not for twenty years, pal. Take him out."

Two detectives moved forward and pushed Baker into the daylight.

At 4.10 pm Harry's mobile rang. It was a message from on high, letting him know the job was done. He turned to the still writhing women and said urgently, "Johnny needs me. Sorry, girls, can you make your own way home?"

"Sure," Lesley panted.

"Is everything OK?" asked Geraldine anxiously.

"It will be soon," he smiled.

"How long is the room booked for?" asked Lesley.

"Until six."

"Lovely," purred Geri, cuddling Lesley closer.

When the two women finally checked out and went to reception to pay for extra room service and phone calls, they were surprised to be asked to settle the entire bill.

"Harry must have been in a real hurry," said Geri as she passed her gold Amex card to the receptionist.

"Yeah, don't worry," said Lesley. "He'll settle up."

The front page of the *Evening Standard* on sale outside the hotel told a different story. "SHOOT OUT IN SOUTH LONDON" screamed the headline. "Police raid villains, one dead."

Geraldine snatched a copy from the three-toothed vendor. She felt faint. A surge of anguish rose up from the pit of her stomach. Her legs began to feel numb and give way.

"No," she said. "No, not Johnny."

Lesley grabbed her to stop her falling, then the tears flooded out.

"Oh, Lesley," she sobbed. "What am I going to do?"

The barmaid sped-read the text. The dead man wasn't named, the injured weren't named, but the location of the shoot-out made it clear that this couldn't have been anything other than Johnny Too's big job.

Geraldine clasped Lesley tightly. "Is it John?" she asked.

"It doesn't say, honey. It'll be OK. Give me your mobile."

Lesley rang the Ned. No answer. Then she rang Harry Tyler and went straight through to the mobile message service. Finally she rang Sandra Baker. The phone was answered by a soft, cultured voice. Lesley hadn't spent all her life among duckers and divers not to realise who was at the other end of the phone.

"Hello, this is BT," she said calmly. "Is the subscriber at home, please?"

"No, not at the moment. Can I help?"

"When would be a convenient time to call back?

We have a number of discount schemes he may be interested in."

"Try calling tomorrow. Goodbye."

The line went dead. "Old Bill," Lesley said simply. "Come on, we'll get a taxi back to yours. Hopefully Harry will ring and let us know the SP. Chin up, Geri. Johnny's too sussed to let the Filth fuck him."

Harry Tyler never did ring, but gradually the full story filtered through – everyone had been nicked. Lesley reassured herself that Harry must have been scooped up as well. They spent a lot of hours waiting fruitlessly by the phone that night.

At 5.30 am a dozen front doors in South London were smashed in, so hard, the cops joked, that they must have hit the back doors. No-one could have realised the tidal wave of police retaliation would be this enormous. Everyone who had ever sold Harry Tyler counterfeit currency, guns, drugs and virgin cheque books found themselves sitting in the cells of six south east London police stations. The raids continued throughout the day. The Lions wouldn't be roaring quite so loud at the New Den this Saturday.

Maurice Bondman gave Johnny Too the bad news in his one-to-one, private, client-solicitor chat at Walworth police station. Bondman was so paranoid about the consultation room being bugged that he wrote it down: "Harry Tyler is the grass."

The words hit Johnny Too like a punch in the face. He shook his head violently in disbelief.

"Fuck off, Mo, you're well wide of the mark," he said.

Bondman broke his pencil trying to scribble a reply and reached for his pen.

"Just tell me, you prat," snapped Johnny.

"It's true," the solicitor replied in a whisper. "I don't know the full facts yet, Johnny, but a number of your associates whom we represent were arrested this morning for supplying your dear friend ..."

He paused to point his stubby finger at Harry's name ...

"Him, with various illegal items."

"Who?"

"Johnny, it would be easier for me to tell you who hasn't been detained this morning."

Bondman pulled out an A4 sheet of paper from the inside pocket of his pinstripe suit jacket and passed it to Johnny Too. It showed seven names next to seven serious offences.

The gangster read the list twice, then, shaking with rage, he screwed the paper up like the Queen strangling a brace of fatally wounded pheasants.

"That fucking piece of shit is DEAD," he roared. Johnny shouted so loud that two uniformed custody suite officers came racing in. Maurice Bondman dismissed them with a wave of his hand.

"Privileged conversation, chaps," he said.

Johnny Too regained his composure. "Is there anyone who's not been nicked?" he asked.

"The police are still looking for Douglas Richards."

"Right," said Johnny. "You've got ..." His voice

trailed off as he realised they could be bugged. "Give us yer pen."

Johnny Too wrote Harry's name, his home address and the address of the Trojan pub in Stratford in Bondman's notebook. He thought for a moment, then wrote in capital letters: "KILL THE CUNT AND BLOW UP EVERY FUCKER IN THE BOOZER." The colour drained from Bondman's face as he read it.

"Johnny, I can't have any part of this."

Johnny Baker grabbed him by his tie, pulling him towards him and almost choking him in the process.

"Listen, you piece of shit, you do as you're told, you crooked little bastard, or your name goes on the list, too, capice? That message goes to Dougie, right. As far as I'm concerned that's a done deal. End of conversation."

Maurice Bondman looked at his client. He was going to protest, but Johnny Too's eyes radiated such menace he didn't dare.

Tower Bridge magistrates court had rarely seen such commotion. The accused were lined up this Monday morning like a queue for a garage in petrol crisis week. One by one, the Baker firm were wheeled in and sent down in custody. No bail was granted. Johnny Too was the last one in. The crowd in the public gallery drew a breath. But Baker was determined to play the part. He was cocky, arrogant, angry.

He waved theatrically to the crowd like Royalty. "Keep yer chin up, John," shouted one old Cockney.

"Silence in court, or you'll be removed," snapped the clerk. "The prisoner may sit."

Johnny Too sat down and turned to the public gallery. It was packed, mostly with tearful women dressed suitably in black out of respect for brother Joe. Johnny looked hard at Lesley Gore nestled in the throng just to the left of Sandra. He blew a kiss at his wife then turned and snarled at Lesley, shaking his head three times. The barmaid fully understood. She was anticipating a good hiding just for letting Harry shag her.

The court arena was awash with CID, shitters. One on one they were nothing, Johnny thought. But that was academic now. He turned to face the clerk.

The hearing was a foregone conclusion. The Crown Prosecutor virtually sleepwalked through the formalities. Slowly, he informed the court that three men were under armed police guard in hospital, one man was dead, and that a significant quantity of Class A drugs had been recovered. Some passion came into the QC's voice as he explained why Baker should be denied his liberty.

As Johnny Too was led away in custody he blew a kiss to Sandra. It was all the trigger the crowd needed.

"What about the murdering coppers?" shouted Joey Baker's mother-in-law. "Why ain't they up there?"

The public gallery erupted with vocal support for her and Johnny Too. Officers rushed to quell the disturbance and push the spectators out in the street. Uniformed police in full riot gear toured the area in carriers for the next four hours, but there was no further disorder.

At 8 pm, a silver-grey Rover saloon drew up outside Harry Tyler's flat in Stratford. The driver, wearing a flat cap and red-tinted glasses, sat motionless as the rear doors opened and his passengers spilled out. He followed them up the stairs and watched them kick in Harry's door. The flat was empty. The driver took off his cap and glasses and pushed past his silent, Kosovan enforcers. As he walked from room to room he drew a silver revolver. One of the Kosovans called out from what used to be Harry's bedroom. The far wall was covered in graffiti: "Why is Johnny Baker like Millwall FC? They're both going down." Under-neath it was a crude drawing of crossed hammers. The bewildered Kosovans looked on with eyebrows raised as Dougie The Dog started to kick and punch the wall.

At 8.45 pm Lesley Gore was eating take-away chips when the bell rang. She should have known better than to answer her door. Dougie The Dog knocked her straight to the floor then pulled her screaming into the living room where he punched her repeat-edly until she was unconscious, ripped off her knick-ers, greased his cock with spit and brutally raped her while his men searched the flat for Harry Tyler.

"Anyone else wanna go on this SLAG?" he said to his hired East European help. Two of the four took

The Dog up on his offer. Doug watched them disinterestedly as he helped himself to the chips. When they had finished, Doug kicked Lesley hard, breaking two of her ribs. "You fucking whore," he screamed at her unconscious body. "Know what you're worth? Two bob." He flung a ten pence piece at her face and stomped out, with the Kosovans in hot pursuit.

At 9.37 pm the Rover was back in East London, outside the Trojan. Dougie looked at the pub in disbelief. The sign was gone, the windows had been boarded up and the front door was covered with a padlocked metal grille. The upstairs windows had been whitewashed and a "For Sale" sign was bolted to the upper wall.

The Dog got out of the car and crossed to the building. He pulled at the grille, but it wouldn't budge. As he looked up and pondered, Dougie felt a warm wetness spreading down his left trouser leg. He looked down at the small black mongrel relieving himself against the wall. "Fucking thing," he snarled, booting the dog which yelped and ran off. Doug looked at his leg and shook his head. There was no point petrol bombing the place now. He turned to stroll around the outer perimeter and saw an elderly, crippled man hobbling along supported by a pine-coloured walking stick.

"'Scuse me, mate," said Doug. "Do you know when this pub closed? I was supposed to meet a friend here a couple of weeks ago, but I couldn't make it."

"Search me, guv'nor," the old man replied.

"Couple of days ago, I think. I only went in it once and was told to clear off. No one drank there, just a load of film people."

"Film people?"

"That's who they said they was. The old boozer closed about a year ago, and they reckon some film company had it. We never see no stars going in there, though. We all got told to eff off when it opened up again."

"So where are the people who drank in there?"

"They weren't from round here, mate. Couldn't say where they was from. There was blacks and all sorts getting in there. Drug dealers if you ask me. They even changed the name. It was the Coach an' 'Orses before. They called it the Trojan. What kind of stupid name is that for a pub? Don't even know what it was short for. Trojan Horse I suppose. Oh, well, there's a good pub round the corner, the William IV if you're thirsty."

Doug said nothing. He just stared at the pub. Trojan Horse? TROJAN HORSE! The enormity of the deception hit him like a jackhammer. The Baker firm had been sucked in and blown out like bubbles. Dougie fell forward and stuck his hand against the wall to steady himself.

On Wednesday, Johnny Too asked to see Maurice Bondman. The solicitor found his client in an unusually pensive mood.

"Level with me, Mo," said Johnny. "How is it looking? Be honest."

"If I'm honest, it's not looking good. But then, with luck and mercy and your wonderful personality in the dock, maybe you'll get away with ten years, God willing."

"You know how to make God laugh, Maurice?" Johnny Too said softly.

"No, how?"

"Tell him you've got plans."

Thursday morning was beautiful. Even inside Florida's Stanford Airport terminal, the young family could feel the heat of the sun and the waiting humidity. The Customs Officer checked the UK passport and entry forms and handed them back to the pretty woman with her babe in arms, and her tired but happy stubble-faced husband.

"Thank you, Mr and Mrs Dean," he said with a smile. "Enjoy your stay in the USA."

"Thank you," said Kara Tyler, grinning at Harry. "I think we will."

EPILOGUE

John Baker was sentenced to 15 years as a category A, high-risk prisoner. The judge recommended he should serve the full term. He became a born-again Christian and wrote the occasional think-piece for *Punch* and the *Guardian* about the injustices of the penal system.

Joseph Baker was buried with all the gangland trappings. Dodgy Dave Courtney organised the security. The following Sunday, the *People* told how Courtney and his fellow hardmen snorted cocaine from Joe's coffin lid the night before the funeral. It was handy publicity for his first film, *Hell to Pay*.

Douglas Richards evaded the police for three months before he was spotted eating a pancake roll on New Cross station by the six British National Party bootboys he and Pyro Joe had battered in Bexleyheath. The beating they gave him was so severe it was nine months before he could walk again, by which time he was serving ten years in Belmarsh Prison.

Geraldine Bielfeld married a 53-year-old divorced music business executive whom she met at The Met Bar. They share a million-pound house and a £500-a-week cocaine habit in Weybridge, Surrey, where they host sex parties for swingers.

Lesley Gore recovered from the assault and left the area, but not before she and her younger brother Darren had broken in to Dougie The Dog's house and stolen goods to the value of £3,500. They now run a successful British restaurant called Nobby's Nosh in Benidorm, Spain.

Maurice Bondman, inspired by Judith Keppel's £1 million win, went on ITV's *Who Wants To Be A Millionaire*. He had reached the £500 question – name Jack Sugden's recently deceased wife on *Emmerdale*: was it a) Sarah b) Sara c) Tara d) Bernie – when he suffered a fatal heart attack. "Fllarghhraghhh" was his final answer.

Harry Tyler, real name Harry Dean, quit undercover work at wife Kara's request and transferred to the Essex Regional Crime Squad. She gave birth to a son in July 2001. They divorced 13 months later.

Stephen Richards made £3 million from selling the rights to his Mobster computer game and another £5 million from the movie spin-off. He and boyfriend Sally share a detached house in Chislehurst, Kent, and holiday homes in Nice, in the south of France, and St Petersberg in Florida.

GLOSSARY OF SLANG TERMS

Aris	Arse (Aristotle=bottle, bottle and glass=arse)
Banged up	Imprisoned
Blade-runner	Someone transporting stolen goods
Blag	Rob (originally a pay-roll or money delivery in public place
Blagger	Robber
The boob	Prison
Boost	To hot-wire a car
Boracic	Skint (boracic lint=skint)
Bottle out	To lose one's nerve
Bullseye	£50
Bung	A bribe
Charlie	Cocaine (also Chas, sherbet, marching powder)
China	Mate (china plate=mate)
Chiv	A knife
Cockle	£10 (cock and hen=ten)
Collar felt	To be arrested ('he had his collar felt')
The Currant	The *Sun* (currant bun=sun)
Dabs	Finger prints
Dipper	Pickpocket
Dog	Telephone (dog and bone=phone)
Drink	A bribe – ranging from a drink to a nice drink to a handsome drink

Drumming	House-breaking
Earner	Easy money
Filth	The police (also Old Bill, Plod, cozzers, rozzers)
Firm	A gang
Fit up	To give or plant false evidence
In the frame	To be prime suspect
Frankie	A cut-throat razor (Frankie Fraser=razor)
Friend of ours	One of us (A friend of mine means he seems OK but hasn't been fully referenced)
Gaff	A house (see also drum)
Give a pull	To impart words of advice
Grass	Informer
Gypsy's	A Piss (gypsy's kiss=piss)
Hank Marvin	Starving
Iron	Gay man (iron hoof=poof)
On your jack	Alone (Jack Jones=alone)
Jacks	£5 (Jack's alive=five)
Jacksie	Arse
K	£1,000
Khazi	Toilet
Kosher	The real thing
Long firm	A business set up and allowed to run over a fairly lengthy period with the sole intention of defrauding creditors
Mark yer cards	To give advice
Monkey	£500
Moody	Fake
Mug	A stupid person (also muppet, ice cream)

Mulla	To beat up
Mutton	Deaf (Mutt and Jeff=deaf)
Nonce	Child sex offender
Parcel	A consignment of stolen goods
Peter	A safe
Pony	£25
Pony	Crap (pony and trap=crap)
Porkies	Lies (porky pies=lies)
Puff	Cannabis
Ruby	Curry (Ruby Murray=curry)
Salmon	Erection (salmon and prawn=horn; also lob-on)
Score	£20
Shebert	A cab (sherbert dab=cab)
Slag	A person with no principles
Slaughter	A safe place to dispose of stolen goods (also slaughter house)
Sov	£1 (from sovereign)
SP	Information (starting prices)
Spiel	Patter
Squirt	Ammonia in a bottle
Stewards	Investigation (from steward's enquiry)
Stretch	One year in prison
Syrup	Wig (syrup of figs=wigs)
Taters	Cold (taters in the mould=cold)
Tea leaf	Thief
Tiddlies	Chinese people (tiddly wink=chink)
Tin-tack	Sack
Tom	Jewellery (tomfoolery=jewellery)
Whistle	Suit (whistle and flute=suit)
Wipe his mouth	To put up with the situation
Wrong 'un	Bad or untrustworthy person